P

The *Love,*

"A captivating world of g.

— Melissa Foster, *NYT* & *USA Today* Bestselling Author

"Jan Moran is the new queen of the epic romance."
— Rebecca Forster, *USA Today* Bestselling Author

"Jan rivals Danielle Steel at her romantic best."
— Allegra Jordan, author of *The End of Innocence.*

The *Winemakers* (St. Martin's Griffin)

"Beautifully layered and utterly compelling." — Jane Porter, *New York Times* & *USA Today* Bestselling Author

"Readers will devour this page-turner as the mystery and passions spin out." – *The Library Journal*

"Moran weaves knowledge of wine and winemaking into this intense family drama." – *Booklist*

"Spellbound by the thread of deception."
– *The Mercury News*

Scent of *Triumph* (St. Martin's Griffin)

"A gripping story of poignant love. Perfumes are so beautifully described."
— Gill Paul, Author of *The Secret Wife*

"A sweeping saga of one woman's journey through WWII. A heartbreaking, evocative read!"
— Anita Hughes, Author of *Lake Como*

"A dedicated look into world of fashion; recommended."
— *Midwest Book Review*

RUNWAY

A Love, California Novel

Book Number 3

by

Jan Moran

SUNNY PALMS
PRESS

Library of Congress Cataloging-in-Publication Data
Moran, Jan.
/ by Jan Moran
ISBN 978-1-942073-11-6 (softcover)
ISBN 978-1-942073-13-0 (epub ebooks)

Disclaimer: In this book we have relied on information provided by third parties
and have performed reasonable verification of facts. We assume no responsibility
or liability for the accuracy of information contained in this book. No
representations or warranties, expressed or implied, as to the accuracy or
completeness of this book or its contents are made. The information in this
book is intended for entertainment purposes only, and the characters are entirely
fictional. Every effort has been made to locate the copyright holders of materials
used in this book. Should there be any errors or omissions, we shall be pleased
to make acknowledgements in future editions.

Printed in the U.S.A.
Cover design by Silver Starlight Designs
Cover images copyright 123RF

For Inquiries Contact:
Sunny Palms Press
9663 Santa Monica Blvd, STE 1158, Beverly Hills, CA, USA
www.sunnypalmspress.com, www.JanMoran.com

Books by Jan Moran

Contemporary Fiction
The Love, California Series
Flawless

Beauty Mark

Runway

Essence

Style

Sparkle

20th Century Historical Fiction
The Winemakers: A Novel of Wine and Secrets

Scent of Triumph: A Novel of Perfume and Passion

Life is a Cabernet: A Companion Wine Novella to The Winemakers

Nonfiction
Vintage Perfumes

Browse her entire collection at www.JanMoran.com.

Get a free read when you join Jan's VIP list.

1

Malibu, California

CAMERA FLASHES EXPLODED on the red carpet just ten feet from Fianna. She blinked against brilliant blue-white auras blurring her vision, straining to see the media's reaction. Amid the lights and the flicking whir of digital cameras, a slender young actress swirled and posed in Fianna's platinum evening dress, the silk rippling around her legs. *Snap, snap, snap.* Spearheaded by a top entertainment attorney and his wife, an A-list talent agent who probably out-earned him, The Pink Ball to benefit The Women in Pink cancer foundation was one of the most well attended charity functions. *Snap, snap.*

Fianna breathed a sigh of relief. Her evening design shone to perfection now, but an hour ago, she'd been taking in the side seams for the Best Supporting Actress Oscar nominee, who was so nervous she hadn't eaten much in days and had lost weight.

Fianna leaned toward Penelope. "I'll never know how Giselle keeps her composure through such intense media scrutiny. But she seems to come alive under pressure." Fianna hoped she could do the same tonight.

"It's the adrenaline rush. She's doing great." Penelope touched Fianna's arm in support. "And so are you. Glad you could fill in at the last minute."

"Thanks again for pitching me." Fianna watched as Giselle swirled and posed once more, dazzling the media that lined the entrance to the grand tented affair on the grounds of a private estate in Malibu, where the ocean lapped just outside the power couple's home. They'd bought the house next door for double digit millions and demolished it, just so they'd have privacy and room to entertain.

"We have about two hours…cocktails, introductions, dinner, closing speech, and then we're on." Penelope raised a dark, high arched brow, a striking contrast to her spiky pink cut, dyed especially for the event. With her high cheekbones and expressive eyes, she carried it off with aplomb, lending elegance to the avant-garde color. "Nervous?"

Fianna realized she was chewing on a freshly manicured nail. "You know I am." She shoved her hands into the sleek black knit jumpsuit she'd chosen to wear backstage.

Penelope was an internationally known Danish model who walked the runways of the world's top fashion designers from New York to Paris, London to Milan. When the fashion designer who had been scheduled for the runway show had been found dead in a hotel room in Las Vegas, his family had cancelled their involvement. Penelope was one of the models cast to walk, so she'd immediately pitched Fianna as a replacement. No other designers could act as quickly as Fianna could, so she'd won the opportunity.

"I still have a lot of staging to do," Fianna said. Giselle moved on to give an interview to a television reporter, and Fianna could hear her talk about her dress, which the reporter gushed over. *So far, so good.* Connected to the elaborate main tent was another tented dressing area that had been erected for the models. The whole gilded affair had cost a fortune and looked like something from The Arabian Nights. But it was worth it; millions would be raised tonight for a good cause.

Penelope nodded toward a photographer. "I'll come with you. I have to get in makeup."

Mounting a runway show was a costly endeavor, and the fashion media was ruthless. As a relative newcomer to the fashion scene, Fianna hadn't yet planned a Fashion Week show of her collection. However, several months ago her aunt Davina had asked her to give a show in Dublin, the timing of which coincided with her cousins wedding, so Fianna already had a small collection prepared. Her friends had urged her on, calling it kismet. So she'd swung into action at her tiny Robertson Boulevard shop, which she'd opened with a loan from her aunt.

When they reached the backstage area, Fianna stepped inside. To the outsider, it looked like chaos, but Fianna was in her element. The colorful, gauzy, romantic clothes she'd designed were arranged like a rainbow on racks, shoes and accessories were neatly organized to accompany each outfit, and notes and sketches detailed each look. At a bank of mirrors, makeup artists and hair stylists were working on models, highlighting and contouring, spiking and fluffing. Lanky young women waited their turn, chatting, flipping through *Vogue*, or swaying to music piped through headphones.

Penelope pulled her shirt off over her head, and then slipped into a thin wrap. She eased her slender, well-toned frame into a director's chair.

Laughter bubbled from one corner, and Fianna frowned at a man wearing dark smoky sunglasses and high-tech earbuds seated next to a model. His long, dark blond hair was brushed from his forehead, grazing his white linen shirt in the back. He stretched out his lengthy legs and laced his fingers behind his neck. "Who's that?"

"Must be her boyfriend."

The backstage area was crowded as it was, and she didn't need some creepy guy ogling the models as they raced to change. She made her way to them. "Hi, Kaitlin. Sorry, but I have to ask your guest to leave. No backstage passes tonight, this is business." She pressed her lips together. This young model was a last minute addition after others had dropped out. Fianna had chosen her based on her model card. She made a note to be more careful in the future.

"Oh, sure," Kaitlin replied. "Niall was just leaving."

The man removed an earbud from his ear. "Your music is all wrong."

Fianna glared at him. "What?"

He waved a hand toward the rack of clothing. "It doesn't fit with your clothes."

She immediately recognized his trace Irish accent. It smacked of the city. Dublin, she'd bet. "Look Niall, I'm not changing it now. And how do you know about the music I chose?"

"I talked to the sound engineer."

Growing even more irritated, Fianna folded her arms. "Why would you do that? This is *my* show." Finding the right music had taken a long time, and it was far too late to start over.

"Sure, and I figured you've worked hard. So your show should be the best it can be." He held the earbuds to her. "I gave your engineer this music. If you like it, use it."

The nerve of this guy. "I don't have time for this. I don't know who you think you are, but I don't appreciate you going behind my back." She shot a look at Kaitlin, who was suppressing a smile.

She wouldn't hire her again.

His lips curved into a grin, further infuriating her. And he still hadn't removed his sunglasses. Why did people wear sunglasses at night? It was so pretentious. Who did he think he was, Brad Pitt? Or some wanna-be rocker? L.A. was full of those types, and she steered clear of them. All they wanted were groupies and invitations to the Playboy mansion. And what was with the ridiculous full-sleeved poet's shirt he wore?

"Come on, just listen."

"Get out now." She pointed toward the exit, her finger

wavering with anger.

He shook his head, sliding a lock of hair behind an ear. "You can't tell me you're happy with that music. Not until you hear this, anyway." He unplugged a cord from his phone and tapped the screen.

"That's it. I'm calling security." She turned to leave, but a haunting, lilting melody filled the air, and she hesitated, her feet inextricably rooted to the ground.

She lowered her eyelids. At once the music transported her to Ireland; in her mind's eye she saw rolling emerald hills and smelled the sweet scent of peat logs spiraling from country cottage chimneys. She shuddered as the mesmerizing melody increased in intensity, serenading her Celtic soul. Artistic passion awakened and bloomed within her, and she felt herself sway in rhythm to the melody.

Niall's deep voice rumbled behind her. "It's perfect, isn't it?"

Her eyes flew open. *How arrogant of him.* She whirled around, ready to kick him out. But the room had fallen quiet, and others were also transfixed by the magical score. A flash of inspiration soared through her, and she glanced at the designs she'd created. She pressed a hand to her chest, as if to stem the tide of anger washing from her. She had every right to be furious, but she'd never heard anything like this before.

"The engineer has this music?"

Niall nodded.

She lifted her chin and flipped her fiery red mane over her shoulder. "Then I'll have him use it."

"That's a grand decision." Another grin spread across his face. "If you don't mind, I'll see to it for you."

Fianna shrugged her acceptance, though she was inwardly thrilled. The music set the mood she'd envisioned. "Whose work is it?"

"Just some lad's." He rose and sauntered toward the exit. With his broad shoulders, lean waist, and shoulder length hair, he could've been a male model, or a nineteenth-century artist. The sleeves of his shirt were turned back, and dark trousers skimmed his hips.

Fianna stared after him. There was something familiar in the way he moved, though if she'd ever met him before she would have remembered. She dragged her attention away from him and twisted her thick hair into a messy bun to cool her neck against the sudden heat that surged through her. And she'd taken such pains to have her curls blown into a sleek style for the show. She clapped her hands. "Come on, everyone, back to work."

A makeup artist called out. "Who's next?"

Penelope caught Fianna's gaze. "What about your makeup, Fianna? You'll have to take a bow, too." A team of makeup artists from High Gloss, the cosmetics company for which Penelope served as a spokesperson, was cycling the models through. "You'd look great in these new colors." Penelope had helped the company create the new line that carried her name.

"Five minutes, that's all I can spare." Fianna sat next to Penelope, watching her friend's transformation in the mirror as the makeup artist went to work. Her artist touched Fianna's chin to scrutinize her face, and the woman's mouthed formed an "O" in surprise. Fianna blinked and quirked a corner of her mouth. "It's a condition called *heterochromia iridium*." She had one slate blue eye, and the other was hazelnut brown. It was always a challenge at the makeup counter.

The makeup artist twisted her mouth to one side in thought. "For your eyes I'll try purple, no, maybe green. Or cognac brown…"

Penelope winked at her in the mirror.

Fianna closed her eyes as the High Gloss artist selected her brushed and colors and went to work. A five-minute respite, that's what she needed.

Fianna stood by the entrance to the runway with her list, checking each model before she strutted onto the runway. The gorgeous young women were lined up like gazelles, some fussing with their outfits, others jiggling a leg or clicking fingernails in anticipation. Even though they were professionals, they were still young and excited.

A stylist twisted hair and sprayed tendrils, while another wielded a lipstick brush, touching up glossy lips. The magical melody flooded the night and spotlights blinked on. The time had come.

"Are you ready?" Fianna asked Penelope, her voice wavering with nerves.

"Relax, I've got this." Penelope winked, then her

expression changed as she got ready to lead off the show. "And your designs are fabulous."

Would the critics think so, too?

Looking slightly haughty with a sensual pout, Penelope took to the runway with an experienced step, prancing in rhythm with the soulful music that filled the night. The layered silk skirt she wore flowed behind her. After an expert swish and turn, applause thundered through the room.

Fianna smiled with relief. Penelope could make a Hefty bag look like a million dollars. The next model stepped up. Fianna adjusted a sleeve and sent her out.

"You're an absolute goddess, Penelope." Fianna blew a kiss to her friend as Penelope glided off the stage and hurried to change. Kaitlin was next in line.

"Dip your chin a little, Kaitlin. There, that's it." Fianna whispered, fluffing the romantic lace ruffles that flowed around a deep neckline, framing the young model's face and shoulders. She was lovely; no wonder Niall couldn't keep away from her. Fianna waited for a beat in the music. "Now go."

Glancing out, Fianna watched Kaitlin strut down the runway and pause. She had to admit, she was good.

Fianna glanced out and was pleased to see her friends at a nearby table. Verena Valent, who ran a skincare company, Scarlett Sandoval, an intellectual property attorney who specialized in fashion and beauty, and Dahlia Dubois, whose family ran one of the oldest perfume companies in the U.S. She had dressed them all, too, eager to showcase as many of her designs tonight as she could.

Kaitlin turned and applause rippled across the room again l.

"Let's keep it going, ladies." Fianna snapped her fingers above her head and turned her attention to the next model. This was all she'd ever dreamed of—a runway show of her own to introduce her designs.

One after another, Fianna sent the models out in rapid succession. And each one met with applause and approval, and until finally, she sent her evening gown selections out, with Penelope leading the way once again.

Fianna looked out. Not even her closest friends had seen these. Judging from their expressions, as well as those on the faces of fashion buyers, members of the press, and high profile charity donors, everyone loved them.

"Hurry, hurry," she said to the models. "Now, everyone out again, all together." All the girls returned to the runway for a final walk and a storm of applause.

"Bravo, bravo," she heard from the audience. Fianna drew a hand through her bright auburn mane. It was over, and she'd survived.

"Come out and take your bow," Penelope said, taking her hand and pulling her onto the runway.

Fianna paused for a moment, drinking in the sight to remember. *My first show.* A smile spread across her face as she raised her hands in acknowledgement of the audience and then applauded her models. She bowed, blew kisses, and bowed again.

Penelope took Fianna's hand again and led her offstage. "Everyone loved it," she said, and hugged Fianna as soon as they were backstage. "You did it, Fianna! How does it feel?"

"Honestly, my head is still spinning. It moved so fast."

"It sure does," Penelope said, laughing with her. "But you did a great job. You're a real pro. You were the calmest new designer I think I've ever seen. Most of them are half crazed or half blitzed."

"I was more like scared stiff," Fianna added, grinning.

"That's because you're a sane one. Genius doesn't always reside with sanity. When it does, the stage for greatness is set."

All the models hugged Fianna or kissed her cheek as they filed back, and crystal champagne flutes were quickly passed around. "Here's to an incredible show, thank you all for a fantastic job out there. You made my designs look amazing."

"That was easy enough, because they are," Kaitlin said, raising her glass. "And here's to you, Fianna."

Fianna smiled. Kaitlin's expression was genuine, and she seemed like a sweet young woman. She was probably the youngest of the group. Niall and Kaitlin were certainly an attractive couple.

Niall. Why was she still thinking of him? But she had to find him and thank him for the music. With its evocative melody, it had really helped make the show. Everything had synergy—from the models to her clothes, from the music to the lighting. If anything was out of sync, the show would suffer. Tonight, as if by magic, all the elements had coalesced, and all the stars had lined up in the celestial heavens for her.

Tonight was her night.

All Fianna needed was someone to celebrate with. She sipped her champagne, crinkling her nose at the bubbles. She loved her friends, but she wished she had someone special in her life.

Her mother often told her she had made a huge mistake leaving behind the man who loved her in Ireland. Was that true? A demanding man might get in the way of her aspirations, of the passion for her craft that many could not understand. Especially her mother. And yet, as much as she loved what she did, she missed having someone with whom she could confide her deepest thoughts and desires. She often stole glances at Verena and Lance, or Scarlett and Johnny. They seemed so happy together.

"Kaitlin, do you know where I can find Niall?" Fianna asked. "I'd like to thank him again for the music."

"He said he was joining some of his friends." Kaitlin giggled. "Look for a group of handsome guys, and you'll find him." She lowered her voice. "But I think they're all taken."

"Well, Niall is certainly taken with you." Before Kaitlin could say anything else, Fianna excused herself. She gave instructions to her assistant and the interns who were helping her organize clothes and accessories, and then decided to look for Niall.

As she pushed the door to the event space open, she wished Davina were here. Only her aunt understood how much tonight meant to her. The youngest of her mother's sisters, Davina had been like an older sister to her at first, and later, more like a surrogate mother. Davina had been one of the most popular runway models of her day before she retired.

Watching her aunt on the runway had sparked Fianna's passion for fashion design. Davina had helped her with her application to FIDM, the Fashion Institute for Design and Merchandising in Los Angeles.

Her mother had refused to condone such "nonsense," as she called her daughter's creative ambitions, saying it was much more sensible to find a man, marry, and begin a family, since that's what she would do anyway. Why run away to America to study when one had no intention of ever using that knowledge?

And then Fianna had opened her boutique on Robertson Boulevard, and her mother had stopped talking to her. So much for being proud of her daughter.

At least her sister Lizzie was getting married soon. That would alleviate some of the pressure.

Fianna paused and looked around. The crowd showed no signs of thinning out, and a singer was setting up on another stage. No doubt the party would last long into the night.

"Fianna, come join us." Verena was waving to her from the table where her friends were seated. "You should have seen it from out here. It was the best runway show I've ever seen. And the crowd loved it. Imagine, even Greta Hicks had a smile on her face."

"That's a good sign." The *Fashion News Daily* reporter was not one to conceal what she thought.

"I bet you'll have great coverage in the media. And I heard this event raised the most money ever for the Women in Pink Foundation, even topping last year." Verena had been honored the prior year at the foundation's fundraiser at the Beverly Hills Hotel.

A well-built athletic man in a tuxedo seated next to Verena leaned toward them, draping his arm around Verena. With a tender movement, he straightened the thin strap of the romantic, flowing dress in rosy pink Fianna had picked out for Verena to wear, which was perfect with her alabaster skin and fair blond hair. "Nothing could top that night," Lance said. "That's the night Verena and I met. This is our one year anniversary."

Verena laughed. "And what a year it's been." She clasped Fianna's hand. "For all of us. This is your dream, Fianna. I'm so happy we're all here tonight."

"Who's at the restaurant?" Lance and his partner, Johnny, had opened a restaurant called Bow-Tie a few months ago.

"We have an assistant manager now," Lance said. "Since it's a weeknight, it's not too crowded."

Fianna winked at him. "You mean, only a dozen or two people waiting to get in, as opposed to the line down the block on the weekends? I'm awfully glad I know you guys or I'd never set foot inside."

A dark-haired man with a red bow-tie leaned over and

pecked her on the cheek. "That's what friends are for, *mi amiga*."

"Johnny, it's so good to see you. Where's Scarlett?"

A smile lit his face as looked past her. "My lovely lady is coming this way. She stopped to talk to Greta." He held a hand out to a coppery blonde woman wearing one of Fianna's designs, a ruby red gown. She moved through the crowd with calm assurance.

"Scarlett, what did you think?"

"I think I've got a licensing deal in the works for you. That was a magnificent show." Scarlett Sandoval was an intellectual property attorney, and since she'd opened her own practice she'd promised to help Fianna secure licensing agreements for accessories such as purses and sunglasses.

"This is certainly your night, Fianna," Verena said. "The Saks west coast divisional manager for fashion just left, but she told me she's going to contact you about your line."

Fianna let out a little squeal. "And where's Dahlia? I can smell her fabulous perfume lingering here at the table."

Scarlett laughed. "I think we're all wearing one of her perfumes tonight. And Verena's skincare. Last I saw, Dahlia was going to the dance floor."

Fianna turned in her chair. The music had started again, and the dance floor was filling fast. She saw a petite, dark haired woman wearing the black evening gown she'd designed with her in mind. It was reminiscent of the classic dress in artist John Singer Sargent's portrait of Madame X. Fianna tilted her head, apprising the look. The sweetheart neckline and nipped waist was perfect on Dahlia.

Scarlett shot a look at Verena. "What do you think of her date?"

"We don't really know him," Verena said, seeming to choose her words with care.

Fianna was intrigued. "What's he like?"

Scarlett twisted her mouth to one side, and Verena threw her a *be nice* glance. "What I meant was that it's probably a little daunting meeting your date's friends all at once," Scarlett said.

"How diplomatic." Fianna grinned. "But Scarlett, that's what I love about you. You always tell it like it is."

"That's the attorney in her." Verena sighed. "Scarlett, the poor guy's not on trial tonight. You've been going after him like you're interrogating him."

"So? I look after my friends." Scarlett winked. "But I got some good information, didn't I?"

Fianna shook her head, amused. She was sure she'd hear the whole story later. "I'd love to stay with you, but I'm looking for someone, and I want to catch him before he leaves."

Johnny waggled his eyebrows. "And who's the lucky guy?"

"Just one of the model's dates. He gave me the music to use. His name is Niall."

"Niall's here?" Johnny shot a look at Lance. "I thought I recognized that music."

"Oh, you know who he is?" Fianna rose from the table,

craning her neck. She thought she caught a glimpse of him striding toward an exit.

Johnny raised his brow. "You're kidding, right?"

"I nearly threw him out for hanging around backstage. But he turned out to be really helpful. Excuse me, I think I see him." Fianna darted through the crowd after him. She felt curiously drawn to him. He was Kaitlin's boyfriend, but she had to speak to him.

She reached the exit and stepped from the red carpet onto the soft sand. She reached down and slipped off her black heels. Shoes dangling in her hand, she started for the shoreline.

At once she saw him, and her heart quickened. The moonlight illuminated his broad silhouette. He jerked his arm and threw something into the water.

Fianna was suddenly incensed. Having grown up on the island of Ireland, she was protective of the ocean. She marched toward him. What was he throwing into the sea?

2

"HEY," FIANNA CALLED out, pointing at him. "What are you doing? You can't throw trash in the ocean. What was that? It better not be a cigarette."

Niall swung toward her. The wind whipped his white shirt and moonlight lit his face. "And what are you, lassie, the shore patrol?"

"Don't *lassie* me. Littering the beach is against the law."

"Well then, you caught me. Guilty as charged." He held out a fist as if to taunt her.

She put her hands on her hips. "Open it."

With a slow grin, he unfurled his long, slender fingers to reveal a trio of smooth stones. "You mean to tell me that skipping stones is illegal in California?"

She smirked at him. "You could've told me."

"You didn't give me a chance. You attacked first."

"You're probably going to tell me it's because of my fiery red hair, that I'm a passionate woman, aren't you?"

"Actually, no."

"What then?" Fianna couldn't help herself. What was she doing? She'd come to thank the man, and instead, she'd verbally attacked him.

His eyes crinkled at the corners and he looked bemused. "If you really want to know what I think, have a walk with me."

"Aren't you waiting for Kaitlin?"

"Sure, but my sister always takes forever to get dressed."

"She's your *sister?*"

Niall lifted an eyebrow. "What did you think?"

"Well, most men who hang around backstage are just there to, well, you know what they want, what they are."

"Ah, you thought I was a modelizer." When she made a face, he added, "That's what Kaitlin calls them."

He started walking, and Fianna fell in beside him. The tide was coming in, and they walked close to the water's edge. Fianna loved the salty smell of the ocean, which was teeming with life and reminded her of home. The lights of Malibu colony glowed around them and stars sparkled overhead. As wonderful as the evening had been, Fianna was glad for a respite from the crowd in the quiet of the night.

"I want to thank you for the music. You were right, you know. It really helped make the show. It was such a lyrical, haunting song, and it helped create the magical mood I imagined."

Niall glanced at her, and a slight smile curved his lips. "We deliver the same message, but convey it in different medium."

He touched her shoulder. "I recognized that quality in your work, Fianna. Whimsical, playful, lighthearted. Like a fairy at work."

"Was that *your* music?"

"Aye."

"It's beautiful." The full sleeves of his shirt fluttered in the sea breeze. Now it made sense. The way he dressed, and spoke, and the music he created. He was an artist, just like she was. "You should try to get your music out there."

Niall skimmed a stone across a rolling wave. "You think so?" He handed her a rock.

Fianna took aim and skimmed it, dancing the pebble along a swell. "Sure. You have talent. Have you been in the states long?"

"Not long." He handed her another rock. "You have a good arm."

"Did you come with your sister?"

"Our father insisted. I'm to protect her virtue."

"What a fine brother you are." Fianna kept walking beside him, though she knew she should turn around and attend to the packing of her clothes. Her assistant, Evangeline, and the interns could handle it a little longer, she decided. Niall had a voice like golden cognac, and she found herself drawn to its warmth.

"And what are you doing while you're here?"

He leaned down to pick up more stones and handed her a few. As he did, his skin brushed against hers and she felt heat emanating from his body. "It was time for a change of scenery. I thought an ocean of distance would do me good."

"And has it?"

He skimmed a few stones, and Fianna followed his graceful motions. "Not yet."

She caught a wistful look in his eyes, which were the deep mossy green of the Irish isle. "Do you mind being here alone?" As soon as the words left her mouth, Fianna caught her lip between her teeth. He was here with his sister, but that wasn't what she meant.

"It's not my first choice," he said, seeming to choose his words with care. He turned to her and lifted a wayward lock caught in her eyelashes, gently hooking it behind her ear. She could smell the fresh scent of lavender and moss on him, the natural aromas of her homeland.

She felt her face warm and was glad it was dark.

His eyes twinkled in the moonlight. "Are you asking me if I'm seeing anyone, lass?"

"No, of course not. I meant that creative people often spend a lot of time alone, creating."

A smile tickled his lips. "That I do. I enjoy the creative process, but it can be lonely, that's true."

She curved a few more stones into the sea. Not many people understood the solitude that was a necessary part of her job. She needed time to think, to create. "What part of Ireland are you from?"

"Dublin. And you?"

"That's what I thought. I'm from the countryside. County Cork. But I spent a lot of time in New York with my aunt."

"Ah, that explains why you haven't much of an accent."

"Nor you. Why is that?"

"It was my musical training. The brogue comes back after a few pints, sure, and it does."

Fianna laughed. She could listen to him all night. As they strolled, they talked about Ireland, Kaitlin, fashion, and music.

They walked past an inlet and then came to a rocky part of the beach where they could go no farther. They sat on a rocky ledge where they lingered, talking. When they turned around, they saw the tide had come in, and seawater swirled where they had walked.

Niall peered down the shoreline, frowning. Cliffs rose behind them. They had lost the beach. "The tide came in awfully quick."

"Let's hurry back." Fianna started off, but water swirled around her shins, and she stumbled in a wave.

Niall grabbed her around the waist. "Hold on to me for balance."

They trudged through the water, and Fianna grew quiet. They'd gone too far, and they weren't watching the tide. She knew better than that, but she hadn't been thinking about the sea, only about Niall. He wasn't like any other man she'd ever met.

The sea was relentless, surging forward and growing deeper with each step they took. Fianna was having a hard time walking now, though she was thankful that Niall had a strong arm around her waist. The tent was still just a speck in the distance. It was on higher ground, and farther from the sea, but a rocky point jutted into the water between them.

"We'll either have to swim, or climb over those rocks. Think you can make it?"

Fianna peered at the rocks. It was dark, and who knew what lived in the crevices. But she couldn't think of that now. "Climbing or swimming?"

"I think we can get over those rocks, if they're not too slippery. Good thing you have on that cat suit outfit—which looks incredible, I might add. An evening gown would be quite another story. Here, take my hand."

She gripped his hand, and he led the way. The sea pounded against the rocks, sending salty spray onto their faces. Fianna shuddered as an icy wave broke against her, drenching her.

"Are you okay?" Niall yelled back to her.

Her teeth chattering, she called out, "I'm fine."

Niall clambered down the other side of the rocks and turned to her, sliding his arms around her. But as he did, he lost his footing and fell onto the rocks. Water swelled around them and seaweed tangled in their legs. He sputtered and coughed as he slipped from the surface.

"Niall!" she screamed, trying to support him. But the rocks were slimy, and she lost her footing, too. When the sea rushed out, Niall gulped for air.

"Aw, hell, I'm stuck," he said, twisting and yanking his foot.

"Let me help you." The ocean roared in their ears, and a large wave towered over them.

"It's hopeless. Get out of here," Niall yelled. "Save yourself!"

"I'm not leaving you."

"Maybe it's my time, Fianna." He caught his breath, and the wave engulfed him. Fianna rode the wave toward the rocky cliff, and then it thrust her back toward Niall.

She grabbed him by his wet shirt. "Stop it, it's *not* your time." The powerful undertow pulled them under again and she flailed about, tugging his leg.

When the tide withdrew, Niall surfaced, sputtering. "Then go and get help."

Fianna looked back at the raging ocean. A storm was brewing; the wind was driving the waves farther inland.

"Fianna, it's all right if—" Niall's voice was quieted by another wave.

Holding her breath, she dove against the wall of water, clutching Niall's torso, and then his muscular legs. She worked her way down until she found his foot, wedged in a valley of rocks. She pulled on his leg, but to no avail.

Again the sea relented, and Fianna swam to the surface. "It doesn't look good. I can't—"

"I know." Niall framed her face with his hands and kissed her on the lips. "Save yourself, lovely lass."

Fianna clung to him. "I have an idea." She picked up another stone, drew a deep breath, and groped her way back to his foot. She felt the force of the currents pulling her from him, but she latched onto his leg and began striking the stones around his foot in the dark, murky water.

She surfaced, pushing her hair from her face. "I think I can do this. Hold on, Niall."

Twice more she dove under, hammering at the rocks that held him captive. On the third try, a rock shifted, and she doubled her efforts.

Niall twisted his leg, and between their efforts, they soon freed his foot. "You did it!"

"Come on, let's go." Making sure Niall was behind her, she fought another current to reach higher ground.

The tide swept out, and Fianna scrambled along the rocks, her feet slipping as she did. She tried to catch herself, but her balance gave way. Her head smacked on a boulder near the cliff. Disoriented, she slumped into the sea, the night blackening. She gulped for breath, but instead, salt water poured into her mouth, choking her.

"Fianna!" Niall swooped down and lifted her, carrying her as the waves battered against them. "Lock your arms around my neck." She was only half conscious of his instructions.

Niall fixed her arms around him, and powered through the currents until they reached the other side of the cliffs where the beach stretched out. Niall dropped to his knees and sank into the sand with Fianna still in his arms. "Are you okay?" he pushed her hair from her face, tenderly touching the spot on her head where she'd fallen.

Fianna coughed water from her lungs. "My head...hurts...is it bleeding?"

"Only a little. Thank goodness you're okay." He crushed

her to him, rocking her in his lap until she stopped coughing.

Her gaze dropped to his ankle, which was bloodied and bruised from thrashing against the rocks to free himself. He'd lost a shoe, but they were here. *Alive.* They'd survived the wrath of the sea.

Niall's heart pounded against her, and she ran her hands across his sandy chest. His wet shirt clung to his powerful body.

In the distance behind them, the music from the party throbbed in the night. They'd nearly lost their lives, a mere quarter mile away.

Still shaking from the cold Pacific water, she pressed against him for warmth. "You saved me, you know."

He lifted her chin and stared into her eyes. "You saved me first, Fianna."

3

"WE LOOK LIKE a couple of drowned vagabonds crashing the party," Niall said as he and Fianna limped back to the tented extravaganza on Malibu beach. The music was thumping, the lights were blazing, and valet attendants were lounging near the entrance. He clasped her hand in his and was surprised at how natural it felt.

"What I wouldn't give for a hot bath right now. I'm sure I look frightful." Fianna's laughter rang like bells in the cool midnight air. Her sleek auburn hair now sprang into curls that spilled around her freckled face, which the salt water had cleansed of most of her makeup.

"Actually, you look good, like you've just been for a swim."

"Though we both nearly drowned."

"And so we'll live to welcome another fine day, we will." Fianna shivered and Niall put his arm around her. The Pacific Ocean was cold, and once the adrenaline had dissipated in their bodies, the chill had set in. They paused outside a side entrance. "I'd call my sister, but my mobile phone seems to have vanished in the sea."

Fianna pushed her hair from her forehead. "I have plenty of dry clothes and shoes here, but nothing for men, I'm afraid."

"I'm staying nearby." His eyes roved over her, and he liked what he saw. Truth be told, he hadn't really noticed her at first, but then, he hadn't paid much attention to the other half-clad models racing around backstage either. Not that he didn't appreciate a beautiful woman—Fianna was certainly lovely—but he had a gash in his heart that might never mend.

"We should go in. I have to gather the garments and take everything back to my shop." Fianna trembled again.

Niall rubbed her shoulders. "You're shivering." He wrapped his arms around her to warm her. "Let's go inside and find your friends." As they went in, he glanced over his shoulder just in time to see a man dart away. Was that a camera around his neck? He hoped not; he'd kept a low profile for years.

Most people were on the dance floor. They skirted the throng, and the few people they saw made way for the ragged pair who were barefoot, trailing sand, and dripping water.

"What a fine way to end my first runway show." Fianna nodded toward a rail thin woman in a vivid Pucci dress. "As soon as Greta Hicks sees me, it's all over."

"Who's Greta?"

"A reporter for *Fashion News Daily*."

Niall deftly guided her the opposite way. "No worries, I'll shield you." Attracting the attention of reporters was the last thing he needed. "Hey, Johnny. Wait up, buddy."

Fianna's fair arched eyebrows shot up. "You know Johnny?"

"I met him at the Polo Lounge years ago. I used to stay at the Beverly Hills Hotel a lot." Those were the early days of his career. Johnny paid special attention to the regular guests, and they'd become friends.

"He has his own restaurant now. I didn't know you'd ever been here before."

Niall grinned. *Smart lady.* Not much got past her, and he liked that. "You asked how long I'd been here, not if I'd ever been here before."

Johnny swung around, his dark hair glistening in the low lights, his tuxedo tailored to perfection. "*Dios mio,* what happened to you?"

"Yeah, look at us," Niall said. "We got caught in high tide, had to make a run for it."

"Looks like Mother Nature won that round. I heard you were here." Johnny shrugged out of his jacket and draped it over Fianna's quivering shoulders. "You've got to get out of those clothes. I'll get Scarlett." He waved across to a woman at a nearby table.

"I have plenty of clothes in the back," Fianna said, pulling Johnny's jacket around her. "But Niall needs to change."

"I'm okay. Let's take care of you first." He was practically immune to discomfort now. For years, even on the stormiest days, he'd walk the cliffs of Howth, where his castle had stood as a sentinel for centuries in Ireland.

35

Niall turned to her. "Fianna, you said your interns were packing the show. Can they take things back to your shop without you?"

She whisked a hand across her cheeks, brushing off sand. "I wish they could, but I don't think they have enough room in their cars."

Niall caught Johnny's gaze. "I'm staying nearby. Fianna and I can clean up there." He draped his arm around Fianna, and was pleased when she leaned into him. It had been a long time since he'd felt a woman do that, or even wanted a woman to. "Kaitlin has clothes you can wear, too."

"Good idea," Johnny said. "Lance and I have the SUVs we use for work. Scarlett, Verena, and Dahlia can make sure everything is collected. You guys go get cleaned up."

Scarlett stepped up behind Johnny. "What's going on here? Oh, Fianna, *what happened?*"

"We were walking on the beach and got caught in high tide."

While the two women were talking, Johnny turned to Niall with a frown of concern. "Are you going to be okay with Fianna?"

"Sure, I'll take care of her. I'll have her back in one piece in the morning. There are plenty of guest rooms at the house." His house in Malibu used to be alive with family and friends, but that was long ago, before everything in his life had been engulfed in tragedy.

Johnny shook Niall's hand and slapped his back. "It's great to see you back in town. I really mean that. You've been missed. Hope you're staying for a while."

Niall grimaced. "I came to sell the house. It was Laila's dream house, and now that she's gone..." He moistened his lips. "Too many memories there, and I'd only rattle around the rooms, even with Kaitlin there."

Johnny lowered his voice. "Scarlett and Verena were talking... Fianna doesn't know who you are, does she?"

Niall ran a hand over his damp hair. "Not a clue. I'd appreciate it if you didn't tell her."

"Then you guys should leave now before Scarlett does. Go out the back, there are paparazzi in the front. And we'll give Kaitlin a lift back."

"Thanks, Johnny. I'd like to see your new restaurant soon." It was good to see Johnny again. He'd missed his friendship. After all he'd been through, he envied the close friendships women shared. In most cultures, men were expected to bear their grief in silence. Only Kaitlin really understood how deeply he'd grieved, and still did.

Johnny tugged his tie and grinned. "It's a lot of work. Doing well, though. We're closed on Sundays, so we often invite family and friends over and test new dishes. You should join us."

"Maybe I will." Niall gripped Johnny's hand again, and moments later, he and Fianna slipped out a side entrance. This time, he didn't see anyone who looked like paparazzi. Maybe he'd been imagining things earlier.

Padding through the house with their bare, sandy feet,

Niall led Fianna across the creamy travertine floor, where moonlight spilled from clerestory windows high above. Before he and Kaitlin had arrived yesterday, he hadn't been here in three years. He glanced around, ghosts of memories passed at every turn.

He and Laila had danced across this floor, the first night they'd moved in, and then again, the last time he'd held his wife in his arms and swayed to the music he'd written for her.

Three years ago. It seemed like a lifetime ago when she'd been alive and they'd been happy. Everyone hinted that it was time to move on, to go back to work, to start living again. But how could he? He'd only gone out tonight because Kaitlin had begged him, and their father had insisted. Kaitlin often traveled by herself, but their dad still thought evil Manson followers still lurked around every corner in Los Angeles. *Bunch of fruits and nuts out there*, he'd say.

"You're awfully quiet," Fianna said.

"Lot of memories here." He stared up the curved staircase, which seemed to float against floor-to-ceiling windows that overlooked the Pacific Ocean. How many sunsets had they toasted here? He remembered his manners. "Would you like a glass of wine for your bath?"

"I'd love one."

"Red or white? Or champagne?"

"Red, thanks. Something warm."

He darted into the kitchen and grabbed a dusty bottle, a corkscrew, and two glasses. The wine cellar was still stocked with wine Laila had chosen. That would go with the house, too. He'd returned to collect some personal items—photos and mementos—but there was nothing else here he cared about. That task had taken no more than half an hour. If it weren't for Kaitlin, he'd be on a plane again.

"I think you'll like this aged Bordeaux." He stared at her, and then quickly averted his eyes. He couldn't deny that he found Fianna freshly appealing—and that alone was astonishing—but having her here in Laila's home was causing conflicting emotions.

"Are you all right?" Fianna took the glasses from him, a simple gesture that Laila might have done.

"It's not every day you nearly drown." He took her hand and started up the staircase. "I have to thank you, Fianna. There was a point when I thought it was over." He thought he'd welcome a release from this empty life, but hearing Fianna urge him on reminded him of Laila, telling him not to give up. "Guess it wasn't my day to die after all." He hummed to himself. *Not my day to die.*

He swung open a door to a guest suite. Laila had decorated it with her girlfriends and sisters in mind. "I think you'll be comfortable here." When she looked quizzical, he said, "I'm down the hall."

"Are there towels in here?"

"Oh sure." Niall opened a cabinet, relieved to find an assortment of plush towels, soaps, shampoo, and bath gel. Laila loved to pamper her guests. "I think you'll find everything you need in here. And here's a robe."

"Full service, I'm impressed."

She looked even more appealing in the soft glow of light overhead. Niall dragged his gaze away, uncorked the wine, and poured a glass. "It needs to breathe, but here's to surviving."

"To life," she said, raising her glass to his.

His eyes lingered on her lips, and he recalled the kiss they'd shared in the stormy sea when he'd thought his time had come. In that instant, he would have given his life to save Fianna. And afterward, when he'd held her in his arms on the beach. It had been a perfect moment.

"I said, *to life*." Fianna was watching him, a question in her sparkling mismatched eyes that were as unique as she was.

"Oh yes, to life," he said. And for the first time in years, he meant it. He sipped the wine, never taking his eyes off her. *What would Laila think of this?* Suddenly he felt as if Laila were looking over his shoulder watching them.

Fianna turned on the water in the tub. It gurgled from lack of use, but soon turned to a steady stream.

"If you have everything you need, I'll be off. Take your time and relax." Niall closed the door behind him.

An hour later, when Fianna entered the kitchen in a white robe, Niall stumbled from his stool in the kitchen. She looked ethereal with her glossy red hair curling around her shoulders and pink-as-a-peach skin glowing with health. Her freckled nose was adorable, but the supple curves beneath her robe were even more inviting. But there was something more about her. He knew she was highly creative, but he also sensed her strength and substance. "Have a good bath?"

She stretched. "The best. I thought I'd never wash the sand from my hair. How was yours?"

"Best ever," he said, slowly smiling. "Hungry?"

"Famished. I smell something wonderful."

"I hope you like waffles. Seems it's all I had in the house, and fortunately, I found a waffle iron to go with the mix. And maple syrup, too, though that might be too sweet with the wine." He made a face, and he liked the way her eyes lit up in response. "With or without syrup, we can eat outside. The moon is full, and the view from the deck is not to be missed."

"Wine and waffles." She laughed. "Sounds perfect." They wandered outside and sank onto a cushioned outdoor sofa.

The moon hovered above, casting a luminous glow across the ocean that stretched out before them. From their vantage point high on a Malibu cliff, they watched as perpetual waves rolled to the shoreline, where multimillion dollar homes lined the beach. "The sea sure looks harmless from a distance," Fianna said.

Her wide eyes took in the view, the house, and the property, and Niall could tell a thousand questions burned on her tongue. Or had she been jaded by Malibu, Beverly Hills, and other swank parts of Los Angeles? He knew plenty of women who sized up a man's wallet first. At heart he was a simple man, though he enjoyed the fine quality of things. Including the genuine heart of a fine woman. *Like Laila.*

Fianna could hardly believe the turn of events this

evening. Here she was, having waffles and wine on the balcony of a handsome man's Malibu mansion after nearly drowning.

"I forgot the napkins," Niall said. "Be right back."

Watching Niall pad barefoot through the open door, Fianna thanked her lucky stars. He was a fine sight to behold. After his shower, he'd changed into a worn pair of jeans and another flowing white cotton shirt.

She speared a bite of waffles. They tasted so good after what she'd been through. The evening certainly hadn't turned out the way she'd imagined. Except for the nearly drowning part, it had been a night to remember. Her designs had been well received by everyone at the important event, including the media. With any luck, she'd have coverage in *Fashion News Daily*.

She lifted her glass to her lips and felt the tension of the past few weeks easing from her shoulders. Between hurrying to complete new pieces, organizing the outfits, coordinating models, and a hundred other details, she'd hardly had time to sleep.

Let alone date.

Lyrical music floated through the air, and Fianna closed her eyes, appreciating it. It was the same music he'd given her for the show.

Niall. Who *is* this man? He was such an enigma, appearing out of nowhere, and yet he was instinctively knowledgeable about her style and what her show needed. They'd nearly perished tonight, but in that moment of vulnerability, they had connected at such a pure, honest level.

"I'm glad you like my music." He eased beside her, a clean lavender scent wafting from his damp hair.

"You wrote this?" When he nodded, she added, "And I thought you were a struggling, wanna-be musician. You sure had me fooled."

"I don't like to advertise. Music has been good to me. It's just what I do." He took her hand in his, and his magnetism drew her in.

They sat listening to the music and watching the endless tides, breathing in the night scents of jasmine and honeysuckle that tumbled in vines along the cliff top.

Fianna slid a glance toward him. Niall was different. There was a reticence about him that she hadn't seen in a man before. Most of the men she met wasted no time in making their desire for her known.

For all her independence, creativity, and free-spirited thinking, Fianna was a little shy around men she found attractive. The more she felt attracted to them, the worse it was. Besides, her creativity held her heart, and her business demanded her time. There was little time left for dating.

She asked Niall about his music. He told her he was a songwriter and played both the piano and the guitar. He wanted to know more about her business and what she planned to do, and before long they were resting comfortably against each other on a double chaise lounge, mesmerized by the rhythm of the ocean, the canopy of stars overhead, and the sound of each other's soft laughter. To Fianna, it was the perfect end to a day fraught with challenges.

When Niall drained the bottle into her glass, she clinked his glass and sipped, never taking her gaze from his soulful green eyes. *Sad eyes.* What was disturbing him?

As if reading her mind, he bent his head toward hers and said, "Tonight, despite anything else going on in our lives, we celebrate being alive. We were a breath away from death, but we were spared. For what reason, I wonder?" He brushed her forehead with his lips, and Fianna raised her face to his.

She didn't know how long she'd been lost in the warmth of his lips when he pulled away, nestling his body next to hers. He began to hum, and then sang softly to her in a rich, rugged baritone that was achingly heartfelt. Somewhere deep within she recognized the pain of loss in his voice. She'd heard this loss in the voice of her friend Verena, when her parents had been killed in an automobile accident.

That incident was what had brought Fianna to Beverly Hills when she was just eighteen years old. Her aunt Davina knew Mia Valent, Verena's grandmother, who had founded a now legendary skincare salon. When Davina had flown to Los Angeles for the funeral of Mia's son and his wife, she'd seen that Verena needed help with her younger twin sisters, Anika and Bella. And Fianna, who was soon on her way to study fashion design at the Fashion Institute of Design and Merchandising in Los Angeles, needed a place to stay and a part-time job.

It had been good for all of them. Mia had been battling cancer, and though Verena was just Fianna's age, she had stepped in to run the family business that supported all of them. Essentially, Fianna was the nanny, living in and picking up the twins from school, taking them to doctor's appointments and ballet lessons, and shopping for groceries. The Valent family became her surrogate family, and Fianna and Verena were as close as sisters.

Watching Verena learn how to run and expand the business had inspired Fianna to start her own line and rent space for a boutique when she was barely out of school. And every month, Fianna wrote a check to Davina, repaying her faith and investment in her abilities. Davina had given Fianna money to open her boutique on Robertson Boulevard, but she was retired now, and Fianna knew she was living on a fixed income.

Niall began to hum another song, and again she wondered what sadness filled his soul.

The cool ocean breeze brought a chill to the night air and Fianna curved into the warmth of Niall's body. Their brush with death tonight seemed to have pierced the veil of reserve she usually had. He continued singing, his chest rumbling. She recognized a Celtic lullaby and it filled her with nostalgia. His voice grew steadily softer.

Her eyelids grew heavy, and the events of the day caught up with her. As she drifted to sleep, the last thought on her mind was again, *who is this strange, beautiful man?*

4

FIANNA WOKE TO the sound of birdsong the next morning. Niall was curled protectively around her on the chaise, his breath warming her neck. They were high above a marine layer of fog that blanketed the coastline below.

The events of the night before rushed to her mind. The success of the runway show, the fierce tide that had nearly cost them their lives. Niall's deft handling of the evening, the waffles and wine they'd enjoyed under the stars, the sound of his voice, and the taste of his lips on hers.

Except for the raging tide, it was all she'd imagined in the recesses of her mind, where hope and wishes and dreams resided. Niall had been completely unexpected, but not unwelcome.

She shifted in his arms, and he tightened his grip on her, as he murmured in his sleep. "Mmm, Laila… missed you so much."

Fianna froze. Laila must have been the source of his sadness. *A girlfriend?* "Niall, wake up, you're dreaming. It's morning."

"Hmm?" His eyes fluttered open, and Fianna saw

disappointment flood his face. He sucked in his breath. "It's *you.*"

She managed a wan smile. "That's right. Not Laila. Sorry."

He frowned in confusion and rubbed his eyes. "I must have been dreaming."

"I'd say so." She sat up and swung her legs over the wide chaise lounge, hiding her despair. She was still wearing her robe from last night. She tugged it around her as if for protection against the torrent of feelings that rushed within her. How could she have such strong feelings for someone she'd known a few hours? "I need to change. If Kaitlin's home, I'll borrow some clothes."

"Oh, yeah. I'll check for you." Yawning, he got up and made his way through the door.

He returned in a few minutes with a blush pink cotton sundress and thong slides for her feet. "Kaitlin is still asleep, but she won't mind." He paused. "I'm in desperate need of coffee. How about you?"

"I really have to go. My car is still parked at the event site. Will you give me a lift?"

"Of course."

Niall ran a hand through his hair and stepped toward her, clearly uncomfortable with her presence. She could hardly blame him. He'd been expecting Laila, whoever that was, and he woke with her instead.

"Fianna, last night was incredible. One of the most magical nights I've had in a long, long time." He drew his hands along her shoulders.

For a moment, she was tangled in his gaze, but she averted her eyes. As she did, her attention was drawn to a large painting of Niall and a fair-haired woman mounted over the fireplace in the living room beyond them. They were on the beach, their arms entwined, their expression one of pure love. She hadn't noticed it last night because it was dark, and they'd gone through the kitchen door.

At once she knew. Laila wasn't a *girlfriend*. Niall was a married man. She pressed a finger against his full lips. "You don't have to say anything else. I understand. And nothing happened here. Nothing at all." Though that wasn't quite right, she stepped away and hurried inside with the clothes, angling her face from him so he wouldn't see her grief.

What a romantic fool she was. *This is why I don't date much,* she told herself firmly. She'd rushed after him like a silly schoolgirl, eager to thank him for his music, and look what happened. She'd nearly drowned and become involved with a married man. *I can sure pick them.*

She dressed as quickly as she could. When she left the bedroom suite, Niall was already standing by the door waiting for her, keys in his hand, sunglasses obscuring his eyes.

He tried to make conversation on the way, but Fianna had her guard up. Her answers were brief and left no openings. When they pulled alongside her car, Niall got out to open her door, but she beat him to it.

He stood with a hand on the door, sizing her up.

"Tell Kaitlin thank you for the clothes, and I'll get them back to her in a couple of days."

Niall removed his sunglasses and stared at her. "Fianna, what's wrong? You seemed so... different last night. I know we've just met, but was it something I said or did?"

She glared at him. "I saw the painting in the living room. Your wife, I suppose?"

"Ah, yes."

"Laila?"

He swallowed and nodded, seemingly at a loss for words.

"Well, then, there's nothing more to say." She opened her car door and slid inside."

"Wait, let me explain something."

Fianna started her car. "Do us both a favor. Don't." She put the car in reverse, backed out, and then headed toward the 101 highway that hugged the Malibu coastline. When she glanced in her review mirror, she saw Niall staring after her, his arms held wide, his palms still upturned as if in question.

She blinked the blur from her eyes and drove on. No doubt about it, that man would break her heart.

"Congratulations, Fianna! Did you see the *Los Angeles Times* this morning?" Verena spun a newspaper around on the table at Bow-Tie, her sapphire eyes shimmering with happiness.

Fianna gasped and sat down. She'd stopped at her apartment to bathe and change, but she hadn't had time to see a newspaper. As she read, she raked her teeth across her lower lip. Photos from the show were printed on the society page. Three in all, and of her best designs. She blew out a breath. "I'm so relieved."

Verena grinned and sipped her grapefruit juice—fresh squeezed, Fianna knew, from the grapefruit tree that still stood on the restaurant's property. Verena was dressed in black yoga wear, her pale blond hair in a messy bun, and her flawless complexion a testament to the skincare line she'd just launched. Her family's legacy skincare salon and business had been taken over by a devious investor, and Fianna was glad to see that she was making a comeback.

Verena's boyfriend, Lance, and his partner, Johnny, often opened their Beverly Hills restaurant to friends and family on Sunday afternoons. As a chef, Lance liked to try out new dishes he'd been working on, and everyone enjoyed catching up in a welcome break between their busy schedules. Johnny was in charge of guests and ambiance, though the vintage cottage that still graced a street in the commercial shopping district hadn't needed much help when they'd opened earlier in the year.

"Listen to this," Fianna said, running her finger along the newsprint, which still smelled of printing ink. "It says, 'Fianna Fitzgerald, an up-and-coming young designer, took on the monumental task of organizing a show just two weeks before The Pink Ball. But there were no frayed edges in Fitzgerald's show.'" She squealed with joy.

This made up for the disappointment Fianna felt about Niall. And wasn't that always the way her love life seemed to work out anyway? *Married.* She should have known. No wonder he'd gone backstage with his sister. Wearing dark sunglasses, he could ogle the models all he wanted.

A chair scraped beside her, and a petite dark-haired woman dressed in a sage green shift dress and strappy sandals slid in beside her. "I wanted to see you so much I practically ran from church," Dahlia said, hugging Fianna. "What a smashing debut for you." She grasped Fianna's hand, and her vivid green eyes clouded with concern. "And what a dreadful way to end the evening. Are you okay now?"

Fianna nodded. "A little bruised, but I'm fine. And I'll never forget to check for high tide again." She inhaled deeply, and the scent of gardenias filled the air. "New perfume you're wearing?"

"It's a new formula I've been working on." Dahlia shrugged with modesty. "What do you think?"

"Hmm, lovely," Fianna said, her eyes half-lidded in contemplation. At heart, they were all creators. Verena with her skincare line, and Dahlia with her perfume. "It reminds me of gardenia blossoms after a rain shower, at that moment when the sun's first rays fall on the wet leaves and blossoms."

Dahlia looked impressed. "You have a good nose."

"I still wish I had a signature perfume for my brand." She'd asked Dahlia if her family company could create a line for her, but Dahlia's grandmother Camille, who'd run the company for decades, had politely declined. "Your brand is not large enough yet, dear," Camille had told her. But Fianna wasn't giving up. She had an idea. "Dahlia, I thought Camille might like to see this review of the runway show."

Dahlia quickly read it, and then lifted her gaze to Fianna. A smile played on her lips. "Of course. I'll give it to her."

It was a long shot, Fianna knew. Just because she was friends with Dahlia, didn't mean Camille would commit funds to a new, unproven brand. She hadn't built a global portfolio of perfumes by taking unnecessary risks.

"Fianna, don't you have something else to share with us?" Verena pressed her lips together with barely concealed glee. Fianna knew what was coming next. "So tell us about last night. You stayed at Niall's house?"

"We fell asleep on a chaise lounge on the balcony. But nothing happened." Fianna realized that wasn't quite accurate. She thought of the way he'd curved his body around hers and the way he'd sang her to sleep. How quickly she'd lost a piece of her heart to a man she hardly knew.

Her heart was too easily lured, too often broken. On the other hand, her art nourished her soul, and if she allowed it to, it could consume her, day and night. Most of the time, she let it do just that.

"For a woman," her mother had told her, "you have an unnatural ambition, an unhealthy obsession with work. You've become such an *American*," she added with disdain. Her mother had meant it as an insult, but Fianna was proud of her accomplishments. She was keenly aware of the dedication and persistence required to be successful in her field.

Fianna dragged her attention back to her friends.

Verena's expression dimmed with disappointment. "Niall sure seemed taken with you. What did he say this morning?"

"He didn't need to say anything." She shook her head in disgust. "I saw a portrait of him and his wife in the living room. He's married." How could she have found herself in such a situation? She was always careful to avoid the jerks, but this one had slipped through her defenses.

Dahlia drew her finely arched brows together. "No, you're mistaken."

"He even called me by her name. *Laila.*"

Verena and Dahlia traded looks, and Dahlia went on. "Fianna, Niall *was* married. But his wife passed away three years ago."

"Are you sure?" Heat gathered around her neck, and now she felt like an idiot. She'd lashed out at him without fully understanding the situation. But then, he hadn't told her, had he? She rubbed her temples. "How do you know?"

Dahlia motioned to the newspaper. "I read the papers."

"Since when do you read the obituaries?" Fianna asked, bewildered.

"When they're on the front page of the Entertainment section."

Verena motioned to Johnny to bring more juice to the table. "It was everywhere on the news and social media. Surely you remember."

Fianna ran a hand across her brow. Why did everyone seem to know Niall but her?

Dahlia's bow-shaped lips parted in surprise. "Don't tell me you don't know who Niall is."

"He said he writes music." Fianna rested her chin in her hand, remembering the sensuality in his rich voice.

Verena laughed. "Just a little." She shot a look of disbelief to Dahlia. "I forgot. You don't listen to rock music, do you?"

Fianna shook her head. Jazz, opera, classical—she'd picked that up when she lived with Davina. She'd never been a celebrity fan either. She'd met plenty of them in her store and had become accustomed to their eccentricities. Some were lovely, normal people, like Maude Magillicutty, a 1960s siren who'd invested in Bow-Tie, but others, like the recently indicted Gina "Fleur" Georgopoulos, who'd once been a law client of Scarlett's, had let fame go to their heads.

"Unbelievable." Dahlia swung her dark hair over a shoulder. "Niall Finley managed to find the *only* woman in town—and an Irish woman, at that—who doesn't know who he is."

"Then enlighten me." How could she be so out of touch? She'd been working nonstop in her business for years, immersed in fashion. She certainly didn't have time to stay abreast of the latest gossip or television shows. Or rock stars, evidently.

"He was the lead singer of Finley Green." Dahlia explained. "The day his wife died, he walked out."

"Well, I doubt he'll ever want to see me again." Fianna remembered how she'd left him; she recalled the despairing look on his face in her rearview mirror. Maybe she'd been wrong about him. But a dead wife didn't make him a saint.

Fianna winced at her thought. She wasn't really that callused. What was she thinking? She twisted her napkin. She'd been protecting her heart for so long that her shield had become nearly impenetrable.

"Ladies, your fresh-squeezed, ruby red grapefruit juice." Johnny filled their glasses with a pitcher and sat down. "I hope you're hungry. Lance is whipping up a new recipe, and Scarlett's mother is experimenting with a new empanada: Asian fusion."

"Yum, sounds good. I'm starving," Dahlia said. "Johnny, can you believe Fianna had no idea who Niall was?"

Fianna drew a hand over her face, slightly embarrassed.

Johnny looked quizzically at her. "That's right, you're the Enya fan. And opera."

"I'm afraid I might have insulted him." Fianna blinked at the memory. She often spoke before she thought. She was working on that.

"He's had a rough time of it." Johnny ran his knuckles against his dark, day-old stubble. "Decked a paparazzi at his wife's funeral. Practically became a hermit after that."

"I don't blame him," Fianna mumbled. Last night, trapped among the rocks in the black raging water, he'd been willing to give his life so she could live. Niall was far more complex than she'd given him credit for.

"He used to stay at the Beverly Hills Hotel and take meetings in the Polo Lounge," Johnny said. "That's how I got to know him. He's a really good guy."

"It figures, doesn't it?" Fianna twisted a wavy red lock of hair around her finger, guilt consuming her. *I mistreated a man who offered to give his life for me. And I wouldn't even listen to him before I roared away.* Should she call and apologize?

"*Hola, mi amor.*" Scarlett walked up behind Johnny, slid her hands across his broad back and kissed him. "Smells like Mama is in the kitchen."

Johnny rose and hugged her, ruffling Scarlett's coppery blond hair. "I'll see what's ready. Take over for me here."

Fianna grinned at Scarlett, who'd become her business attorney. "You look like you've been at the beach."

"I had a long walk this morning," Scarlett said, rubbing her bare arms, bronzed from the sun. "It was warmer than I thought it would be."

Verena and Dahlia quickly filled in Scarlett about Niall and Fianna.

"That's enough," Fianna said, laughing in protest. "I just met the guy, and knew him for what, ten or twelve hours, at the most?" She tossed her twisted napkin on the table.

"You're right, let's change the subject," Verena said. "Fianna, with the exposure in the newspaper, it might be a good time to call the buyers from Saks and Barney's. I know them, so you can use my name."

Scarlett nodded. "Verena's right. If you can get your line in the stores, even a few pieces on consignment, that will go a long way in forming the licensing program we've been

56

talking about. With your red carpet exposure in magazines, you have a good publicity foundation, but distribution is so important. Shoppers have to find your work in the stores."

"They do, but it's not mine." She made a face and shook her head in disgust. After the Grammy Awards last year, two of her designs had been knocked off by a mass ready-to-wear manufacturer within the month.

Fianna had a dream she'd harbored since she was a girl and that was to delight as many people as she could with her whimsical, flattering designs. Later, when she started her business, her long-term goal was to sell her lines into the most exclusive stores, and then engage licensees for accessories, such as handbags, sunglasses, and shoes.

Scarlett's specialty was intellectual property licensing in cosmetics and fashion. In fact, she'd been instrumental in recommending and negotiating Penelope's recent deal with High Gloss Cosmetics. Now, Penelope was a spokesperson for the company and had her own branded line with them. Ever since Scarlett left the large law firm she'd been with, she'd been working with a number of entrepreneurial clients.

"And I have another show coming up," Fianna said, thinking about her trip to Ireland. Her aunt Davina had arranged a runway show for a major charity event in Ireland. The event showcased a top designer every year, and Fianna had been chosen because of her Hollywood red carpet connections. She'd dressed many stars for televised award shows. She didn't make money from loaning cocktail dresses and evening gowns, but the exposure was valuable to her growth. Her trip to Ireland would be expensive, but it could be an important stepping stone in her career.

"Who's hungry?" Wearing chef's whites, Lance appeared at the table holding a tray of food, dished up family-style in large bowls and platters. "Today we're trying an Asian theme, with Asian fusion empanadas—vegetarian or seafood—and a new garlic lemongrass crab recipe I'm testing. *Bon appétit*, and let me know what you think." He placed the tray on the table, and then sat next to Verena, giving her a sweet little kiss before he began serving.

Johnny and Scarlett joined them at the table. Scarlett's mother, Isabel, who had come out of retirement to assist in the kitchen, sat down, too. Wine and champagne bottles were passed around, and everyone was happy to catch up with friends and eat delicious food.

These lazy Sunday afternoons were the high point of Fianna's social life. Only when she met someone like Niall— which wasn't often—did she wonder about the choices she'd made in her life. As she took a bite of a steaming empanada, the lightly fried pastry pocket burst with flavor. "This is fabulous, Isabel," she said, enjoying herself.

Bow-Tie was known for its food and ambiance, and today, Fianna was simply happy to be eating delicious food and laughing with friends. *Niall is too complicated anyway.*

That's what she told herself. She sighed. Still, she couldn't deny the effect he'd had on her. She wondered if she'd ever see him again.

5

NIALL RESTED HIS hands reverently on the piano keyboard, glided them over a few keys, and then paused to pick up a pencil. He changed a line on the notes and lyrics he'd scribbled down. Satisfied, he started again, spreading his long, agile fingers over the keys, singing to himself as he did.

"Hmm, I love that song, must be new," Kaitlin said, sliding onto the piano bench beside him. "I haven't heard you play in forever." She wore a tank top and short white shorts, which showed off long legs tanned from the California sun. Clutching a cup of coffee in her hands, she bobbed her head, keeping rhythm with his tune.

"It's been a long time. Guess I felt inspired." He hadn't touched this piano in three years, not since Laila died. But today, something in him had shifted. Maybe it was because of the cool ocean breezes blowing the scent of jasmine through the open doors, or the birdsong he'd woken to, or the tinkle of the wind chimes he and Laila had found in an artist colony in San Miguel de Allende.

Or maybe…

"And I know why." She nudged her brother in the side.

"When I came home, you and Fianna were curled up on the chaise lounge on the balcony, snoring away."

Feeling self-conscious in front of his younger sister, he pushed a hand through his hair. "We weren't snoring. Well, I'm sure *I* wasn't."

Kaitlin poked him again. "How rude!" She laughed. "Actually, there was no snoring. The two of you were sound asleep. You didn't hear me come in, so I left you alone. Besides, you looked awfully sweet together." She winked at him.

"Yeah, well, that's about it, I'm afraid." Disappointment settled heavily on his shoulders, as it had this morning when he'd watched Fianna drive away. He'd felt a distinct sense of loss again, though he'd only known her a short time. And there was only so much loss a man could take. Just the whiff of it again had been enough to send him scurrying back to his cave like a hermit crab. There, he'd admitted it. His heart had already been shattered once. And that was enough.

"What do you mean?"

"She saw the painting of Laila." He nodded to the large picture that hung over the white travertine fireplace. "She thinks I'm still married."

Niall slid off the bench and picked up the guitar he'd brought with him. He sank into a white sectional sofa positioned to look out over the Pacific Ocean through walls of glass. "When I took her back to her car this morning, she roared off and left me in the dust." He quirked his mouth to one side as he strummed the guitar and tuned the strings.

"You know, she'd never heard my music. Had absolutely no idea who I was."

Kaitlin spun around to face him. "You mean, she liked you for *you*? How bizarre, bro." She laughed and mussed her hair. "So, are you going to call her?"

Niall smiled at his sister. She was a younger, lankier version of himself, with long, lean limbs, a quick smile, and tousled blond hair. Like him, she had a romantic soul, but he hoped the world wouldn't hurt her as it had him. He'd been devastated over Laila's untimely death. When he'd met her a decade ago, he'd had a moment of clarity. He saw that the life he was leading was no longer for him. The travel, the groupies, the drugs—being on the road had been far too much for him. He'd never wanted to be a rock star. He'd only wanted to write songs and play his music. And be with the woman he loved.

Laila.

All his life, he'd never been happier than when he was playing his music, dreaming up a new song, or perfecting one he'd been working on. He loved playing for people and seeing the joy on their faces. But he didn't need to fill an arena anymore. An audience of one was fine with him.

But there was something about Fianna. Not that she could replace his wife, no one could. Still…

An audience of one…

Like the special one he'd had last night. He glanced up. Kaitlin was staring at him, waiting. He shook his head in answer to her question.

Kaitlin watched him. "Why don't you call her?"

"You know why. Besides, I don't have her number."

"You're lonely."

"I don't get lonely." At least, that's what he told himself. And for the most part, it was true. However, last night he'd felt an emotion stir within him, a flutter of the heart he hadn't felt in years. Was Fianna different?

But it was impossible.

Kaitlin glanced at the portrait of her brother and his wife, and then gazed at him with sad, luminous eyes. "I loved Laila, too," she said softly. "But I worry about you."

"You're too young to worry. You should be out having fun today, doing all the things our father is afraid you might do." He grinned at her. She was a good kid, and he trusted her, although he always kept an eye out for her. There were some creepy guys who went after models.

"I'd rather hang out with you." She finished her coffee, and then plopped on the sofa beside him. "I hardly ever hear you play. What are you working on?"

"I had a couple new ideas last night."

Kaitlin chuckled. "See, I knew she was special."

Niall lobbed a pillow at her, and she ducked. "I'm not calling her. She's probably a wacko, anyway." Whether it was the brush with danger when the high tide came in, or the soulful expression in Fianna's eyes, he had to admit, something had dislodged the creative block he'd had. "Did you see those crazy eyes of hers?"

"Oh, it was her eyes, was it?"

"Hey, knock it off. But really, she has one marine blue eye, and the other one is ambery brown. A mismatched set. I've never seen that before." And the way she looked at him... Not since Laila had he seen such honesty in a woman's eyes. Most of the women he met were more interested in his bank account, or in being with a famous man, or in bringing him back to the world of the living, as if he were a near-hopeless cause. They all thought he jetted around from one party to another. At one time, he had.

Being with Laila had changed all that, though the demands of his work had tested her patience. If he'd known she only had a few years to live, he would have spent every precious day with her. *But we never know.* Did she truly forgive him? He strummed the guitar a few times, aching at the thought.

Kaitlin stretched. "I'm starving. I heard Johnny from the Polo Lounge opened a new restaurant in Beverly Hills."

He shook his head. "Long trip from Malibu." And he didn't want to run into Fianna. But even as the thought of that possibility flashed through his mind, his heart beat quickened.

"I just remembered they're closed on Sunday." She paused. "Let's call for pizza."

"You don't have any shows lined up?" Though Kaitlin was naturally slender, he knew she watched her weight when she'd committed to a show.

"Not for a while. I thought I'd leave a few weeks open. Maybe go back to Ireland with you for that wedding."

"Sure, you're invited, too. You'll be my date." A close friend from years ago had asked him to sing at his wedding to surprise his bride.

Lately, all his friends seemed hell-bent on breaking him out of his depression, as if there was a universally allowed time frame for grief, and the alarm had gone off.

Maybe Fianna was that wake-up call.

After spending the afternoon with her friends, Fianna left for her apartment, which was on a residential street within walking distance of her boutique on fashionable Robertson Boulevard. Now that she was alone, thoughts of Niall intruded once again. *What is it about him that I can't get out of my mind?*

She stopped at a news kiosk to see if any other newspapers had covered her show. As she was thumbing through the papers, the grainy cover photo of a tabloid caught her eye. She snatched it from the rack and peered closer. A man and woman clutched each other in an embrace, and they were both dripping wet. The headline screamed: *Niall Finley Seduces Mystery Woman in Malibu.*

She was that mystery woman. Glancing from side to side, she tucked it under her arm and paid for it. The kiosk seller paid no attention to her.

On the way home, she opened the paper, eager to see if a story had been written about Niall. But there was nothing else, only the photo splashed on the cover. She let out a breath of relief. She couldn't imagine leading a life where every movement was chronicled in the news.

After she came to her apartment complex, she walked down a red brick pathway dusted with red bougainvillea flowers and ducked around a sprawling bougainvillea plant vining across the arched white stucco entryway to her apartment, one of just eight units in the vintage Spanish complex. The scent of sun-warmed, antique lavender roses perfumed the air.

She opened the door, slipped off her shoes, and padded across the wooden floor. Built in the late 1940s, the cozy apartment was perfect for her. A fireplace warmed the living room on crisp winter evenings, a patio off the kitchen was the perfect place for morning coffee, and a tiered fountain from Mexico outside her bedroom trickled water in an endless melody.

Fianna sank onto a shabby chic, white canvas-covered sofa. Niall's house in Malibu was incredible, but she didn't need any more than this. Besides, she liked to keep her personal expenses low so she could plough profits back into the business to keep up with growth.

Only her close friends understood how difficult it had been to start and grow her business. Verena, Dahlia, and Scarlett had their own businesses, too, and they often traded contacts and helped each other.

She brewed a cup of tea and curled her legs under her on the couch. She checked her phone messages, but then remembered she hadn't given Niall her number. *Not that I care*, she reminded herself.

At that moment, her phone buzzed in her hand and the caller ID appeared on the screen. "Hello, Aunt Davina."

Her aunt's melodious voice rolled across the phone lines. "Darling! I heard your show was a smashing success! Why didn't you call to tell me? I've been dying to hear how it went. I got a media alert on my phone. Sounds like it was fabulous!"

Fianna grinned. Davina often spoke in exclamation points. Her gaze fell on a grouping of antique, silver-framed photos on a table. A svelte, stylish woman in a variety of high fashion poses stared back at her. *Davina.* "I know I promised to call you right after the show, but something happened last night."

"Really? Do tell, darling! A new man?"

"Well, yes, but not exactly. Anyway, doesn't matter. Won't ever see him again."

"Plenty more where that one came from, I'm sure. Oh, we're going to have such a grand time in Ireland. I can't wait to see you, darling!"

Her aunt had always been an exuberant, Auntie Mame sort of woman who lived life with gusto and style, regardless of her circumstances. Since Fianna had been a little girl, everyone had said she took after her gregarious aunt, much to her mother's consternation. She smiled to herself. In Mary Margaret Fitzgerald's eyes, her daughter was too much like Davina.

"I'm organizing the outfits this week. I'd love to have you walk, Davina."

"No one wants to see me on the runway again. Think of

those horrible magazines that run the side-by-side, look-what-happened-to-her photos. We age, for heaven's sake. Even Dorian Grey didn't get out of this life alive."

"You look fabulous for a woman half your age. Come on, haven't you always told me to grab life with both hands?"

Davina sighed. "Yes. Wasn't I was a greedy girl back then?"

"No, you lived. And lived well. And you still are." Fianna paused. "Sounds like you've been speaking to Mam again."

"Fair warning. Mary Margaret is expecting of lot of you when you return."

"The answer is no." Her mother was forever trotting out suitable young men from what she called the "right families" for her. And Doyle O'Donnell was at the top of the social ladder. They had once dated, and her mother was still holding out hope for a reunion. The fact that her younger sister was marrying before her had her mother quite grief-stricken.

Davina's laughter burst across the distance. "There's my girl. Live your life well, my dear. Every day is a gift; who knows how many we'll receive?"

"Seems I need twice as many as I've got. I'm not complaining, but there's so much to running a business."

"The beginning is always the hardest. Stay focused and dedicated. I have a feeling a big break is just around the corner for you."

Fianna smiled. Davina was always making grand predictions, and everyone would laugh along with her. Oddly enough, they often came true. "I will, Davina. And I'll send some press clippings on the show to you."

Fianna clicked the phone off. After butting heads with her strict Mam, she'd lived with her aunt in New York through most of her high school years. Her mother had never supported her creative dreams and ambitions, and she had actually torn up her fashion sketches, calling them childish. Her dad had intervened, and suggested she spend the summer with her aunt. Once in New York, Fianna had spent as much time there as she could.

She sipped her tea as she remembered living with Davina. Every day had special moments, from the flowers her aunt chose at the market, to the wine and cheese she arranged for her impromptu, let's-toast-the-sunset gatherings from her balcony. Anything was a reason to celebrate.

All manner of people congregated, drawn at first to Davina's beauty, and then to her sparkling eyes, musical laughter, and genuine empathy. Her high sculpted cheekbones were legendary and had graced many a *Vogue* and *Harper's Bazaar* cover. Her flaming red hair had been her trademark, along with her shimmering azure eyes.

Davina had just turned fifty. *Certainly not old*, Fianna thought. And yet, her aunt maintained otherwise. "Definitely past my prime for modeling," Davina had said. She'd even let her hair turn silver, but it was the most gorgeous mane of platinum hair Fianna had ever seen. She hoped she'd age just like her aunt.

Maybe she could talk her into walking again at her show

in Dublin. It was for charity, after all. Would her aunt come out of retirement for her?

Her phone rang again and she checked the number. *Dahlia.*

"Hi, what's up?" Her adrenaline rose as she listened. "Thanks, Dahlia. I'll meet you at the Beverly Hills Hotel tomorrow."

She clicked off and pumped her fist in the air.

Dahlia's grandmother Camille—the legendary perfumer—wanted to meet her for lunch.

6

FIANNA FIDGETED WITH a pink linen napkin on her lap. The open air café at the Beverly Hills Hotel was a popular power lunch spot. She and Dahlia were waiting at the table for Dahlia's grandmother, Camille, who'd established the family perfume company decades ago. Fianna wore a supple matte jersey dress with a flared skirt and sleeves, and draped lace accents. The peach shade set off her hair. It had been one of her most popular designs for her cruise collection last year.

"I have to admit, I'm nervous, Dahlia." Fianna and Dahlia had been talking about branding a perfume for her line for a long time, but Camille had not been supportive of the idea. Would she be now?

"Relax, she's always curious," Dahlia said. "She likes to keep track of new talent. Plus, you look splendid. Every woman in here is wondering where you got that dress."

"I'm more than happy to tell them." Fianna grinned at her good friend. "Do you know why she wanted to meet?"

Before Dahlia could answer, Camille Dubois swept into the elegant dining area, a tuxedoed maître'd leading the way. "Bonjour, Fianna, I'm so pleased you could join us."

Fianna and Dahlia stood to greet her. Camille was a well-known doyenne of perfumery who'd garnered all the top industry awards for her perfumes. She still oversaw her company, even into what was rumored to be her eighties. She was an elegant, impeccably coiffed woman. Though petite like Dahlia, Camille had a commanding presence.

After exchanging kisses on the cheek with Fianna, Camille sat down, nodding to other diners as she did. "I had to have a word with Mia and Pierre. They're at their table inside. Mia is always protective of her skin, you know."

Mia was Verena's grandmother who had started the Valent Salon, and she had been dating a widower for a few months. *Even the grandmothers have a better love life than I do,* Fianna thought wryly. She leaned across the tablecloth and brushed away deep pink bougainvillea petals that had drifted onto the table in front of her from the bracelets of flowers suspended overhead.

Camille's gaze roved over Fianna's slim-cut dress, which was a buttery shade of rich duchess satin with a paler shade of lace just visible from beneath the wide, expertly draped neckline. Resting on the shoulders, the cut framed the face and skimmed the hips, showcasing Fianna's lean figure without hugging too tightly. She'd swept her hair in a sleek style from her face, and accented her look with four-inch Manolo Blahnik pumps the designer had sent her before the show, insisting she keep them.

"Exquisite dress," Camille said. "One of yours, I hope?"

"Yes, one of my most popular."

"Stunning work. A modern, classical point of view." Camille seemed to ponder this. "And how is Davina?"

"She's doing well, still living in New York. But I'll see her soon in Ireland." Fianna told her about the upcoming show. She'd known Camille for years as Dahlia's grandmother, and Mia's closest friend, but when it came to backing a new designer for their brand portfolio, Camille was strictly business.

They spoke a little longer, until a waiter appeared at their table.

"I suppose we should order," Camille said, making a little moue. She still spoke with a French accent, though she'd come to America in the 1950s. "I miss having Lance in the kitchen, and Johnny at the front."

"Their new restaurant is awfully popular," Dahlia said. "Fianna, I've seen several celebrities there wearing the signature bow-tie you designed for them."

"That's why it's selling so well at the restaurant and in my shop."

"No, dear, that's not why," Camille said, arching a brow. "It's because of *your* design. Never forget that. Celebrities will give your brand a moment of exposure, but it's your work that keeps clients returning. Publicity has its place, but it doesn't replace ingenuity, innovation, and quality."

"That's true." Fianna nodded. *Camille didn't miss a beat.*

Camille placed a finger alongside her jawline in thought. "Lance and Johnny have done a marvelous job with Bow-Tie.

Excellent branding. I'm glad for them. I'll just have to get to know the new faces here." Even as she spoke, the maître'd brought a bottle of French champagne to the table.

"Madame, allow me to welcome you back," he said, pouring the golden bubbles with a flourish. "I believe this is your favorite, isn't it?"

Camille tilted her chin. "Very nice, indeed. *Merci.*" She lifted her glass and Fianna and Dahlia followed suit. "To new beginnings.

As Fianna drank, tiny bubbles exploded against her nose like little firecrackers. Dahlia had told her that Camille had been very circumspect about this meeting, so Fianna waited for her to broach the subject.

She didn't have to wait long.

After they ordered, Camille talked about the runway show and how Fianna's designs had matured. "I'm glad to see that the fashion press is covering your work. Dahlia tells me that Scarlett is representing you for licensing."

"Yes," Fianna replied, quelling her nerves. "I know it's premature. As you said before, I need more exposure in the media and broader distribution." Recalling their last meeting, she didn't want to appear too eager this time.

Camille held up a perfectly manicured finger. "But not too broad. Maintain the appearance of exclusiveness, without actually committing to exclusivity with a retailer, if you can help it."

"Verena is making introductions for me to buyers at Barney's and Saks Fifth Avenue." Fianna had worked out a plan with Scarlett. Once her line was in a major retailer, Scarlett would approach manufacturers for distribution of ancillary products Fianna would design.

"At Parfums Dubois, we're always interested in keeping our portfolio of fragrance brands fresh, aside from our original iconic line."

Parfums Dubois still sold perfumes dating from the 1950s, the earliest ones Camille had blended, which still dominated the market. But Camille hadn't stopped there. Once she'd established relationships with retail stores, she used these channels of distribution to sell more perfume brands into them. Fianna knew that was the real brilliance in her plan.

"You have an enviable portfolio of well-established designers," Fianna said. Parfums Dubois worked with leading fashion designers to translate their artistic vision into perfume. Camille and her staff created the perfume, coordinated the package design, and handled sales, distribution, advertising, and marketing.

In return, the designer made a small percentage override, which often equaled millions of dollars. More important, it was the best marketing a designer could have. Their names were prominently displayed on perfume counters across the U.S. and around the world, which in turn sold more of the designer's clothes and accessories. As long as the brand sold through at retail, everyone was happy with the arrangement.

Camille held her champagne to the light. With a nearly imperceptible nod, she brought it to her lips and sipped.

Satisfied, she trained her gaze on Fianna. "Perhaps someday we could create a branded line for you."

"I'd be honored." Fianna held her breath, trying to keep questions from tumbling out and appearing too excited.

Camille peered at her, seeming to weigh her words. "But not until you're ready. I wouldn't want to bring you to market too early. Trust me; that would be the worst thing I could do for you."

"Why is that?" Fianna would jump at the chance if offered.

"Because your brand *must* sell through at retail. If it doesn't, the product is returned, and you seldom get another chance. The timing must be perfect. You're like a sister to my Dahlia. I have your best interests at heart. Believe me, I have enough money."

Dahlia shot Fianna a look. "But Grand-mère, we've already talked about creating a new line, remember?"

"Of course I do, *ma chère*. Which is why I asked Fianna here today." She turned her gaze to Fianna, studying her.

Fianna straightened her posture, met Camille's gaze, and held her breath. A signature perfume could send a designer's career into the stratosphere. It was what every designer secretly hoped for. Many would fight to have this seat at the table with Camille Dubois.

Fianna was lucky, and she knew it. But having a connection only took a designer so far. Her designs had to be excellent. Unique. A forward point of view. And so much more. Her brand had to be focused, her publicity pitch perfect.

A smile crept onto Camille's face. She removed a card from her purse and handed it to Fianna. "Call my friend at Neiman Marcus. She should see your line now."

Fianna stared at the name on the card, and her heart dropped. The woman was a vice president in Dallas. "Actually, I've spoken to her." *Very briefly.*

"But has she seen your new line?"

Fianna shook her head. She couldn't even get in the door. The woman had practically hung up on her when she'd finally gotten through.

Camille inclined her head. "Then you must call her again. Use my name and tell her *I* said she needs to see your work. She'll see you."

Fianna glanced across the table at Dahlia, who winked at her. Fianna could hardly breathe she was so excited. This is how business at the highest levels was done. It was driven by relationships and trust. And if you were adequately prepared, you might just get lucky.

Fianna thanked Camille and tucked the card into her purse. As she did, she realized the bar had been raised. She *had* to be brilliant now. Nothing less would do.

A waiter arrived bearing three bowls of tortilla soup, a specialty at the Polo Lounge.

"Enough business," Camille announced, picking up her spoon and ending the conversation. "Let us dine."

The next morning, Fianna opened the boutique. She

turned on jazz music, lit soothing aromatherapy candles, and brewed a fresh pot of organic, fair trade coffee.

She'd built up a devoted clientele who delighted in discovering her unique styles. Even on her most constructed designs, a flounce of lace might peek from beneath a sleeve, a whisper of chiffon might trail from a hem. She ran her hand across a rainbow display of her retro flapper girl cocktail dresses. Hers were sensuously cut to flatter the body, fun and flirty, and made of sumptuous silks and lace with exquisite beading.

Other styles, like the one she'd worn to meet Camille, were quietly luxe in shades of sherbet and vanilla, but still made a statement. Top stylists who created looks for some of Hollywood's biggest names had taken these dresses. They were perfect L.A. looks, though she wanted to design a similar line in shades of eggplant and black for winter. She sighed. She had so many ideas, but she had to focus on creating a unified look for each seasonal collection.

"Good morning, Fianna." Her intern from the Fashion Institute was right on time. Her best salesperson, Evangeline, was right behind her. "Have you checked the clothes from the show yet?" the younger woman asked.

"On my way," Fianna said. Thanks to the newspaper coverage that had also buzzed through social media, they'd been nonstop busy yesterday.

"Give her a hand, Tiffany," Evangeline said. "I've got this." She poured a cup of coffee for Fianna.

Fianna gratefully accepted it. "Thanks, I needed another

cup."

They'd been swamped with curious new shoppers. It was exactly what Fianna had hoped for, but after she'd returned from lunch with Camille and Dahlia, she hadn't been off her feet until nine o'clock that evening. She'd kept the shop open for late arriving VIPs and their stylists, which she often did. She would open an excellent bottle of wine, champagne, or sparkling water, and the restaurant down the block would deliver delicacies whenever she wanted. It was part of what set her boutique apart.

Fianna walked through the shop to the storeroom. Tiffany hurried to keep up. "We'll need to inspect all of these clothes," Fianna told her. The young woman began sorting through the clothes.

Fianna removed a sleek sage green evening gown from the rack and checked it. The delicate beading and chiffon godets, or flared skirt inserts, were still perfect. She swept through the collection, satisfied. Most of these items would travel with her to Ireland, and she was relieved the models had been careful with the garments.

She stepped back to look at her collection. She couldn't get the meeting with Camille out of her mind. Camille was right; her style had evolved, but she knew she had to raise her work to an even higher level of excellence if she wanted to step onto the world stage.

And that's exactly what she wanted to do. New ideas had been swirling through her mind, and she needed to capture them.

Fianna picked up her sketchpad and settled into her favorite overstuffed chair. Depending on her mood, she had different ways of working. Most often she liked to sketch by hand, but she also used computer design software to test her ideas on virtual models in different colors and patterns. It saved a lot of time and mistakes, and it helped her create prototypes faster.

Her intern peered over her shoulder at a design she'd been working on for a while. "Wow, that's amazing."

Fianna smiled. She remembered how eager she'd been in school, just like this girl with the short black hair.

"Can I help with anything?"

"Sure," Fianna said. "Can you bring me those samples on the desk? And the trend report. It's on top of that stack."

Tiffany delivered the fabric samples Fianna had gotten from a manufacturer at a recent show. The trend reports covered colors, patterns, and fabrics that were projected for an upcoming season. Textile manufacturers worked from these reports to create fabrics. She flipped through the samples and settled on a lightweight violet crepe. "What do you think about this?"

Tiffany ran her fingers over the material. "It's beautiful. Can I help you cut the pattern?"

"Sure, when I'm ready. This still needs quite a bit of work, but the next step will be to make a toile."

"We just learned about that in school," Tiffany said, her kohl-lined eyes widening. "You make samples out of a fabric like muslin, right? To see how the design drapes on a mannequin."

"That's right. I usually do everything myself, but last year I was so busy I engaged a pattern-maker and a tailor to help create the prototypes." And she probably would again. As her business expanded, she needed to be smart about her time and get the help she needed. Hence, the new interns. If they worked out, she might have jobs for them on graduation.

"How do you know when a design is right? When it's ready?"

"Good question." Fianna ran her fingers across her sketch, and then she touched the fine fabric. She could see it in her mind's eye, knew how it would drape, and imagined how it would hang on an actual person. "I have to be a perfectionist. Nothing is just good enough. I always have to take it to a high level, and then another. That's what sets my work apart."

She'd always been a hard worker, and her runway show had been well-received, but was she capable of advancing? Camille had noted her progress, but could she really handle the pressure that went along with a successful, high-level career?

Tiffany gazed at her with earnest eyes, enthusiasm shining in her face.

Fianna brushed her thick hair back and tucked it behind her ear. "Want to help me drape and pin? I'm feeling creative. Bring the muslin, and we'll work with that."

No doubt about it, if she wanted a shot at the big time,

she'd have to up her game. She barely had time to add to her collection before taking it to Ireland, but she had a couple of new ideas. Each show she did was more important than the last. Someday soon she hoped to show at Fashion Week, when all the media and buyers converged to see the next season's offerings in major cities from Paris to New York, and from London to Los Angeles. A big show was a major investment, but new designers also showed in smaller venues.

Fianna twirled the mannequin around and Tiffany unrolled the bolt of material. As Tiffany handed her the edge of the fabric, Fianna caught a glimmer of a new ring on the young woman's hand. "Are you engaged?"

Tiffany's eyes twinkled as she grinned with glee. "I got engaged last week."

Fianna felt a stab of... *what*? Not jealousy, no, she was pleased for Tiffany, but she had a flashing thought that she was missing out on a part of life that she really didn't want to forgo.

Niall had stirred feelings in her she'd never known. He was different. Or had it been the champagne, the evening, or the high tide? None of it mattered now, not after the way she'd treated him.

Still, her work meant everything to her. She stuck pins in her mouth and swept the lightweight fabric around the mannequin, pinning as she went, feeling the design emerge under her hands. A tuck here, a shift there.

When she was in a creative mode, the world around her faded away, and she became entirely focused on her work.

Fianna draped and pinned, stepped back to analyze, and then knelt to drape and pin again. Tiffany worked patiently alongside her, assisting her with tools, taking photos, making notes.

Fianna didn't know how much time had passed when Evangeline appeared at the doorway. "Fianna, there's a man here to see you."

She glanced up and removed the pins from her mouth. "Can you take care of him? I'm pretty busy."

"I'd sure like to, but he said he's a friend of yours. Niall Finley." Normally unruffled, Evangeline grinned with delight this time. "Some friend you have."

Tiffany dropped the bolt. "Wow. Niall Finley from Finley Green?"

Fianna raked her teeth over her lower lip. What could he want after she'd stormed off in a misinformed huff? Furthermore, she hardly had time for a relationship with a man who was moving away. What good could possibly come of seeing him right now? She'd save him the trouble. Still, an inexplicable wave of sadness filled her with regret.

"Tell him I'm out."

7

NIALL SHIFTED FROM one foot to another, waiting. Fianna's small boutique was stylish and welcoming. The scent of verbena and the sound of a jazz saxophone filled the air. Mirrors lined one wall, and zebra striped chairs sat on ebony wood floors. An Art Nouveau, curved burl wood bar stood to one side. Several bar stools sat in front of it, and men's magazines were displayed to one side. He thought of how he used to wait for Laila to try on clothes, and an ache of longing filled him. He turned away.

Niall ran his fingers over a long silk dress the color of butterscotch, appreciating the way the skirt flared. "Beautiful," he said to himself, recognizing and appreciating the creativity and artistry in the garment. He'd been drawn to Fianna's designs when he'd first seen them, and then when he met her, something in him had shifted. He wasn't sure what it was, but he'd been on his way to meet Johnny at Bow-Tie before the restaurant opened, when he'd suddenly decided to stop at Fianna's shop.

He'd received a call from his realtor saying she had a cash buyer for his home in Malibu and asking how soon he could leave. They wanted to move in immediately.

Though he probably wouldn't see Fianna again, he didn't want to leave her with the wrong impression of him. He was so used to dodging the media and questions about his wife, or why he'd left the group, or when he was making a comeback, that he'd been astonished to meet someone who knew nothing about him or his past. He had to clear things up with her.

He caught a glimpse of himself in the mirror. His blond hair brushed his collar, mirrored sunglasses obscured his eyes, and the old black T-shirt he'd found in a drawer was stretched across his shoulders. The past few years he'd spent a lot of time with his thoughts, on long runs or swims or rides on his horse, assiduously avoiding people. And his music.

Now, he was unable to halt the melodies that ran unbidden through his mind. The last couple of days, words had started to mold themselves to the tunes.

Was Kaitlin right? Was it Fianna who'd opened some shuttered part of his mind? He shook his head. He wasn't looking for a woman to replace Laila, though well-meaning friends invited him to parties he never attended. He'd only gone with Kaitlin to the fundraiser last weekend because he'd promised his father he'd look after her. She was his kid sister, and L.A. could be rough on young girls, although she was smart.

Bells on the door tinkled when two young women with long hair, blue jeans, and high heels strolled in. He angled his face from them. They were chatting and laughing, and they paid no attention to him.

The saleswoman who'd introduced herself as Evangeline reemerged with an apologetic look on her face. "I thought she was here, but she must have slipped out the back."

Disappointment filled him. "Thanks for checking." He turned to leave.

"Do you want to leave a note for her?"

A note. He'd already written a song in his mind about her crazy eyes, without really meaning to, but he couldn't imagine scribbling a few words on paper to her. What would he say? *I stopped by to say I'm not married. I'm really not a cheating husband.*

Right.

Who was he kidding? In his heart, he was still committed to Laila.

"No, thanks." He walked toward the door.

"Shall I tell her something for you?"

He paused, his hand on the door. "Just tell her I'm sorry I missed her. And I'm leaving L.A."

"Niall, come on in." Johnny opened the back door to the restaurant for him. "Good to see you, bro."

Niall slapped him on the back and stepped inside. The stainless steel kitchen gleamed under bright lights, and the prep crew was so busy they didn't notice him. It was such a sunny day he'd put the top down on his vintage Thunderbird, but he'd pulled on an old baseball cap to keep from being recognized.

"Smells fantastic," Niall said. The aroma of fresh baked bread hung in the air. The rapid staccato rhythm of a knife clipped against a board as a man chopped through a mound of chives, releasing a scent that reminded him of Laila's herb garden.

Johnny grinned. "Today's bread is rosemary. You have to try it." He grabbed a black jacket from the back of a chair and slung a swath of red and black silk around his neck.

"Still wearing the bow-ties, I see."

"Fianna designed this one for me. Got the wait staff wearing them as well."

A broad-shouldered man in a white chef jacket rounded the corner, his arms laden with fresh produce. "Niall, my man. Heard you were in town. It's been too long."

They spoke for a few minutes, and then Johnny led Niall through the restaurant, showing him around. "We've been lucky. Business has been good."

"Lot of hard work, too, I'll bet. You and Lance make a good team." He glanced outside. "The patio in the front looks great." Ivy climbed the brick walls, and yellow umbrellas shielded the tables and lounging sofas beneath.

"It's always packed. I should warn you, the paparazzi hides behind the privet hedge over there. I think some of the guests tip them off. Probably Fleur. She's out on arraignment." Johnny grimaced. "Ever met her?"

"No." And he had no desire to. The celebrity's wild outfits and pending trial kept her on the covers of the tabloids. Not that he read them, but they were at every grocery checkout and carwash. He'd learned how to go incognito. Sometimes people even told him he looked a little like Niall Finley, leaner and with longer hair, of course.

"I shouldn't complain. The coverage brings in even more people."

"That's good for you guys." Niall looked outside again. He'd like a leisurely dinner on a patio like that. Without the paparazzi.

"If you're going to be in town for a while, you should join us on Sunday afternoons. We're closed, but family and friends gather, and we try out new dishes." Johnny paused. "Fianna comes around sometimes."

Niall shot him a look. It had been a long time since he'd been among new people, but if Fianna was there, the idea was more appealing. "Does she ever come here for lunch?"

"Sometimes she meets Scarlett and Verena here." Johnny perched on a bar stool and Niall joined him.

A server appeared with a silver coffee pot. "Got your morning juice, boss."

"Want some?" When Niall nodded, Johnny pushed a coffee cup toward him. "Black, as I recall."

"You got it."

Johnny looked up. "Here comes Lance. Hope you're hungry."

Lance placed a tray in front of them. A small loaf of rosemary bread, a slab of butter, a saucer of green olive oil and herbs, crunchy marcona almonds with sea salt, thin shaved parmesan cheese, and other delicacies tempted him.

"The bread is just out of the oven," Lance said. "You have to try our empanadas, too. They'll be ready soon. Scarlett's mother makes them from her family's authentic Spanish recipes." Lance tore off a hunk of crusty bread for him before hurrying back to the kitchen.

The scent of rosemary teased Niall's nose. "That's delicious." As he ate, he couldn't remember the last time anything had tasted so good. Laila used to bake, and he missed that.

Johnny dipped a piece of bread in olive oil and took a bite. "So how long are you going to be in town?"

"I'm leaving tomorrow. The house in Malibu sold, and Kaitlin wants to go to the island." By the island, he meant Kauai, where he had a house on the beach. It was a classic Hawaiian style with rooms that opened to the outside. "Thinking of selling that one, too." He'd only agreed to go because he'd made an appointment with a realtor. They'd have a week before his friend's wedding.

Johnny raised his brow. "I thought you loved that house."

"I do, but with Laila gone, why do I need it? Why do I need anything anymore?"

"Even the Thunderbird?" Johnny punched his shoulder. "I'll take that off your hands."

"Hey, that baby stays. I'll put it in storage." It was a wreck when he'd bought it, long before he'd made his money. When his music was topping the charts, he'd restored the car while his accountant and business manager were busy investing his share of the profits for him. From houses and real estate to Apple stock and private equity funds. He'd never want for money again, but without Laila, none of it mattered.

"Think of the Hawaiian luaus you used to throw." Johnny wagged his head. "I think you spent too much time at the ashram."

"Maybe so. The food's definitely better here." *The luaus.* Johnny and other friends used to visit him and Laila on Kauai, and they'd thrown parties for everyone. Laila had loved dressing up. He would hire local musicians, and they'd all eat and dance on the beach. He could just imagine the smell of her suntan oil, the taste of the fresh pineapple, and the sound of the Hawaiian music he loved. Music in all its forms intrigued him.

"Kaitlin should liven up the place for you."

"Oh yeah, but she's a kid sister, you know." A memory of Laila running on the beach flashed through his mind. Maybe he hadn't spent enough time at the ashram. He'd tried everything after his wife's death. From the ashram in India to the Benedictine monks, from meds for depression to psychological counseling. From spending time at home to traveling. In the end, none of it had mattered. Laila never left his mind.

"Still, Kaitlin's fun to have around." Johnny topped off his cup. "She's sure grown up."

"Hard to believe. She's not old enough to order a glass of wine in L.A., but she travels all over the world. Our dad's decided I'm her chaperone here."

"That's good. Gets you out." Johnny nodded to an employee who was unlocking the front door. He slipped into his jacket and knotted the silk that hung around his neck into a bow-tie.

Out of habit, Niall angled his back to the door. "Some, anyway. Kaitlin's a sweet girl, and has a good head on her shoulders. She doesn't need me. She's got her own life to live."

"And so do you. Planning any new projects with Finley Green?"

"Come on, Johnny. Not you, too. Everyone wants us back together, the music label, my agent, even the guys. Especially the fans. But I can't live that life anymore. It was wild and crazy, and I'm just not that guy anymore." Had he known what the future held, he would've spent less time on tour and more time with Laila. Another one of his many regrets.

Niall popped a few almonds into his mouth. Lance had warmed them and added sea salt and herbs. "Besides, the guys are doing great without me. Their last single spent weeks on the charts." They were still recording music he'd written, so his royalties kept rolling in. He funneled a large portion into the scholarship fund for the arts that Laila had suggested they set up right before she died.

Johnny leaned over, snapping him from his thoughts. "So what *are* you doing?"

Niall shrugged. "I haven't written anything in a long

time. Not until last weekend." He could hear people filtering into the restaurant, and the buzz of conversation began to rise behind them.

"That's good. What got you going again?"

He sat back and blew out a breath. "I guess it was that girl with the crazy eyes." *Fianna*. Walking on the beach with her and waking up beside her had somehow energized him. She'd dislodged some creative blockage in his mind that nothing had been able to clear, not even the monks, nor the psychologist. But was *he* ready for someone like her? He still spoke to Laila every day, at least in his mind, or in his dreams.

Johnny laughed. "So why not hang around a while? You know, for more inspiration." He winked.

"I can't. Kaitlin has a break between jobs." Niall had promised her, and Kaitlin had been looking forward to the trip. "Maybe I'll come back soon."

A woman's squeal erupted behind them. "Look, Niall Finley is here!"

Niall squeezed his eyes shut. This is why he didn't go to Beverly Hills or Hollywood. There were too many tourists hoping to catch a glimpse of stars. He'd never dreamed of stardom; he'd only wanted to play his music and watch people enjoy it. Still, the adulation came with the territory. He'd learned how to handle it with grace, but since Laila's death, he'd found it impossible to plaster on the smile for very long.

"I love, love, love your music," gushed a young woman about Kaitlin's age. "Can we take a picture together?"

It wasn't really a question for permission. She was already hanging onto his shoulder and vamping for her friend, who'd whipped out her cell phone and was flicking photos.

"Ah, sure," Niall said, tugging his mouth into a half smile while her girlfriend kept snapping.

"Let's go over there, the light's better." She pointed to a spot at the front and pulled on his arm.

"We're fine here." He enjoyed his fans, and he was trying to be amiable, but he wouldn't be posed like a wax museum statue.

Johnny was watching him.

"One more, and that's it, ladies," Johnny said. A note of authority underscored his gracious host persona.

"Okay, okay." *Snap, snap.* "When are you going back to Finley Green?" she asked. *Snap, snap, snap.*

"That's in the past."

"I know you left the group because your wife died, but come on, it's been *years*. You *have* to get back together!" *Snap, snap.*

"Alrighty, ladies, I think your table is ready now." Johnny wrapped his arms around the pair and escorted them toward a woman at the front. He jerked his head toward the patio. "Don't we have a table outside for these two lovely women?"

Niall let out a guarded breath.

"Hey everyone, Niall Finley is here!" The girl was determined to broadcast his whereabouts. "Look, over there!

Get your picture with him."

Heads swiveled in his direction, and a couple of people started toward him. Niall tugged his baseball cap over his forehead and slipped on his sunglasses. Holding up two fingers in a V-sign of peace, he headed for the kitchen door, nodding to Johnny as he left.

He jogged through the rear exit and slid into his old Thunderbird. He was still too raw for the questions, even if people meant well. Most of them did, but others, like that girl, were just selfish, and they didn't even realize it. His remote house in Hawaii looked pretty good after all.

He might even write down some of the lyrics running through his mind.

If only Fianna were there, too.

Whoa, where did that come from? He shoved the car into reverse.

8

"DARLING, OVER HERE!"

Limping out of the international customs arrival area at the Dublin airport, Fianna turned in the direction of her aunt's voice and waved. She missed Davina and couldn't wait to show her the new designs.

Davina wore a flowing blouse of deep purple over her slender frame, and her stylish, wavy platinum hair stood out in the crowd. Her aunt towered above everyone. Fianna grinned to herself. She must be wearing platform shoes, she thought. Maybe she could still talk her aunt into walking the runway.

A woman with gray, blunt-cut hair in a brown tweed jacket stood next to her aunt. Fianna's heart sank at the expression of disapproval on her mother's face. Her eyes were glued to Fianna's bare shoulder. She hadn't even said hello, and already Mary Margaret Fitzgerald had found displeasure in her daughter's traveling outfit. Fianna pushed her black jersey blouse up over her exposed shoulder, wincing at the movement.

She'd worn a comfortable jersey outfit from her

sportswear collection for the twelve-hour trip. She had twisted and jammed her long frame into a coach seat all the way from Los Angeles. It would take at least a day to stretch out and adapt to the time change. She angled through the crowd, rolling her suitcase behind her.

"Hi Mam," Fianna said, bending to hug her mother and kiss her on the cheek. Their relationship had been strained for years, but Fianna hoped they could improve it during this visit.

"My, look what Los Angeles has done to you. You're so thin." Her mother rubbed her arm, inching Fianna's blouse even higher on her shoulder.

Davina wrapped her arms around her and swayed back and forth. "What do you mean? She looks fabulous, Mary Margaret."

"Hush, Dervil Nora. She's my daughter and I'll decide how she looks."

Fianna watched Davina bristle. The two sisters could not be more dissimilar. Davina had changed her name from a traditional Irish name, Dervil Nora, to Davina when she'd started modeling.

"It's Davina, I'll thank you. Has been for years."

"You're still Dervil here," her mother shot back.

"I'll not answer to it. My name was legally changed years ago."

"And from a fine name, too, it was," Mary Margaret said with a huff.

Fianna had heard this argument all her life. "Seems they

ran out of names by the time they got to you, Aunt Davina." Her mother and Davina were the oldest and youngest, respectively, in the family, with six others in between. She could hardly remember all the names of her cousins. The babies just kept coming, while she and Davina were the single hold-outs.

"You must have a lot of luggage," Davina said. "I can't wait to see your collection. The photos from the show were a little dark."

"I shipped the collection ahead. It arrived yesterday, and I'll have it delivered to the hotel."

"Well, come on, then," her mother said. "We haven't got all day. Your father is waiting outside and I have a corned beef cooking. I can't understand why you're not spending more time at home with us."

Davina winked at her. "She'll be fine with me, Mary Margaret. We'll be like two girls at a slumber party in a hotel room."

They made their way to the car, and when Fianna saw her father she fell into his arms. "Dad, I've missed you terribly."

"Fianna, my flower, sure and it's good to see you." He swung her off her feet and twirled her around as he had when she'd been a little girl. Ryan Fitzgerald was tall and barrel-chested, a tree-trunk of a man, as Davina often said. Fianna's height came from both sides of the family.

Her father lifted her suitcase into the boot with ease, slid into the Audi, and started for the family home in the country.

Davina had booked into a hotel in Dublin, where the runway show would be, and insisted Fianna stay with her.

Fianna was relieved. Her family house was bursting with younger siblings, and her older sister Emily had moved home with her four children while her husband looked for work. She'd visit, but it was more family closeness than she wanted with the runway show so close at hand. Besides, her sister Lizzie was bound to be frazzled over the wedding.

Although Fianna had offered to create Lizzie's wedding gown, their mother had overridden the decision and chosen a different bridal designer. From the photos Fianna had seen, the dress was like a fluffy meringue pie, which wasn't her style anyway. Fianna had been a little hurt until she'd seen the dress, and then she was glad her name wasn't on such a creation.

The runway show was to be first, followed by the wedding. After that, as long as she survived, Fianna would be on the first flight back to Los Angeles. She loved her family, but she'd always been the artistic loner, sketching and sewing while her brothers and sisters were outside playing and roughhousing.

Fianna gazed out the window and watched the windswept countryside fan out before her. As they drove south toward County Cork, she took in the sights and smells and sounds of her early childhood. Her father fiddled with the radio. It had been several years since she'd heard the lilting accents of her homeland on the radio.

Sprawling hillsides covered with emerald green moss

waved across the edge of the horizon, with the occasional tree hardy enough to sink its roots silhouetted against the cloudy sky. Sporadic rain showers swept across the roads. She inhaled the sweet scent of peat moss burning in fireplaces of thatch-roofed cottages.

Her father wheeled onto the graveled road that led to Fitzgerald Manor, which had been in the family for generations. Built in 1798, the three-story stone home sat on a grassy rise, which made it look all the more imposing. Centuries-old ash, beech, and oak trees dotted the lawn, a badminton court was set off to the side, and a lake sparkled in the distance. In many ways she'd had been a magical childhood, exploring secret caves in nearby mountains, gamboling across the hillsides, and running free with her siblings under wide Irish skies.

Until she and her mother began to butt heads, and she'd moved to New York with Davina.

An extra wing had been added in the late nineteenth century for the expanding family, and Ryan, as the oldest heir, kept it open to all Fitzgerald family members in need. As long as they could tolerate the rigidity of Mary Margaret, that is.

With her sister and husband in residence, and their four children, plus wedding guests, tonight Fianna and Davina would share a bedroom the little girls usually slept in.

Fianna walked past a low rock wall and stepped through the red front door. An arched Palladium window stretched overhead. The house was never locked. "What if someone wanted to call by and we weren't home?" her father would always say. "Sure, and they're welcome to stay and have a cup of tea or a pint before they go on their way."

Not much has changed, Fianna noted. Inside were polished wood floors and colorful floral rugs. The Fitzgerald family crest hung above a marble fireplace. Next to that were photos of the Pope and Mother Mary, as well as John F. Kennedy, thirty-fifth president of the United States and a favorite son of Ireland. The Kennedy family hailed from County Wexford. They shared a lineage with an old clan, the FitzGeralds of Desmond, a fact that Mary Margaret made sure everyone remembered.

Her father had managed the family's funds well, and her family seemed comfortable, but the upkeep and repairs on the rambling manor home were expensive.

A commotion sounded on the staircase. "Fianna!" Her name was screamed out as "fee-ina," in the Irish way, instead of "fee-ahna," as was customary in America, and to which she'd grown accustomed.

"Lizzie!" Her younger sister flung herself into her arms and the two girls spun around.

Her sister was a smaller strawberry blond version of herself. Growing up, Lizzie had always been the pretty, angelic one, and Fianna had been the angular, gangly redhead with dramatic tendencies.

"Are you nervous yet?" Fianna asked, laughing.

Lizzie's aquamarine eyes widened, and Mary Margaret answered for her. "Of course not. Lizzie was born to this match."

Fianna lowered her eyelids and waited a beat.

Her mother wasn't wasting any time. "Shane's cousin Doyle is still asking after you. What a fine family they have."

"Well, that didn't take long," Ryan said with a chortle. "I thought he was seeing another girl."

"That little tart?" Mary Margaret waved her hand, dismissing the idea. "Lots of girls would be happy to have Doyle, but he's always had his eye on you, Fianna."

"Mam, we've been over this. I'm no longer interested in Doyle." The heir to a fortune, he was from a long line of O'Donnells, descended from an ancient, powerful family that included Kings, Dukes, Earls, and Barons. Doyle had an assortment of inherited titles, but to Fianna, there was something distinctly less than stately about him.

They had dated when they were younger and again during her return visits to Ireland, but the last time she'd seen him, his intensity had unnerved her. "You should spend some time with Doyle," Mary Margaret said, brushing a speck of lint from her tweed jacket. "You're not getting any younger. Look at Lizzie here, younger than you, and already starting her life."

"My life *is* in progress, and I'm quite happy with it." Fianna bristled and turned to Davina for support. Her mother was like some 1950s relic, only concerned about making good matches for her daughters and carrying on family names with titles and fortunes and scads of children. Mary Margaret had been disappointed with their eldest sister,

Emily, who had run away to marry to her childhood sweetheart. Everyone loved her husband Charles and their four adorable children, but her husband had fallen on hard economic times.

Her mother seemed determined to make up for Emily's mistake and see Lizzie and Fianna married into top families. They had four younger brothers, too.

"When this fashion phase passes," Mary Margaret said, "you'll wish you had taken the O'Donnell name, you will."

"It's hardly a phase," Davina said. "It's her profession. And she's quite good."

Lizzie shot Fianna a look, and she could see terror in her sister's watery eyes. "Lizzie, let's take a walk. I've got to stretch my legs after that plane trip, and I can't wait to hear about your wedding plans." She steered her sister through the house and out the rear door.

"Let's walk by the water," Lizzie said, hurrying toward the lake. "No one will bother us there."

Fianna glanced at Lizzie, who wore her wavy hair loose around her shoulders. She wore an ivory sweater with slim green plaid pants and loafers. She'd always been her sweet, kind little sister, the one who always tried to keep the peace in the family, and as a result, the one who often acquiesced to their mother's desires. Her normally smooth forehead was furrowed.

As they approached the lake, Fianna asked, "What's wrong, Lizzie? Aren't you happy?"

"I've been too busy to think about it. Shane and I have

known one another forever, but the engagement happened so quickly. It was at Christmas time, and it was so romantic."

"Are you having second thoughts now?"

"It's too late for that. Our mams are in high gear planning this wedding. I guess it's just a case of nerves. It'll pass."

Fianna knew it was a big bash. *The wedding of the season*, her mother had said. "And what if it doesn't? It's not too late, Lizzie."

A wan smile softened Lizzie's knotted forehead. "Not for someone like you, Fianna. You've always spoken your mind. It wouldn't surprise anyone. And you live in America. But me... what would I do?"

"Exactly what you want to do." Fianna hooked her arm through her sister's as they skirted the small lake.

"I don't even know what to want, besides get married and have children."

Fianna paused. "I thought that was what you wanted."

Lizzie blew out a breath. "Sure, someday. But all of a sudden, the wedding is here, now, expected, and I feel like I'm suffocating. I know there's more of life to experience. Will I ever get that chance? Or will I become an instant baby-maker like Emily?"

Lizzie kicked a stone with the tip of her tasseled loafer. "I'm scared of being stuck here forever, raising the next generation of O'Donnells before I ever get to do anything, go anywhere, or discover who I am. And his mother is worse than ours, if you can believe it. She's a world-class screamer."

"Have you thought about postponing the wedding until you're certain this is what you want?"

"But I'm really fond of Shane." Words tumbled from Lizzie's mouth as her luminous eyes widened even more. "I'm so confused, I adore him, really I do, but I don't know if this is love. If I call off the wedding, will I regret it later?"

"Maybe it's a chance you have to take."

"I want to know for certain." Lizzie stared into her eyes. "Have you ever been in love?"

Fianna shook her head. She'd dated other men, but she'd never experienced the jolt of electricity and awareness that had coursed through her when Niall's lips touched hers. Was that love?

Or merely emotional relief? They'd nearly died, after all.

Fianna had the same question Lizzie did. All across the Atlantic, Niall had crept into her mind. While she was sketching, or gazing across the clouds, or trying to sleep. She could close her eyes and feel the length of his body curved into hers, the night air cool on her skin, the sound of his steady breath warm on her neck. She could still taste his kiss while they were waist deep in frigid salt water, the current threatening to yank them apart and pull them under.

She hadn't even known Niall a day. Who was he? She'd never met anyone like him before. Was that the thunderbolt that lifelong partners often spoke about?

And would she ever see him again?

A gust of wind caught her hair, slapping it across her face. Fianna brushed away unruly strands tangled in her lashes and gathered her thoughts. "Honestly, Lizzie, I don't know. Only you can make that decision. But if you have doubts—"

A deep voice boomed behind them. "Doubts about what?"

Fianna and Lizzie whirled around.

"Shane, what are you doing here?"

A lean, well-toned red-haired man with an engaging grin caught Lizzie by the waist and kissed her. "Hey Fianna, we heard you were arriving today." He jerked his head behind him toward a dark-haired man with hooded eyes. "Doyle wanted to see you," he added with a grin.

"Fianna, it's been too long." He stepped forward to hug her.

"Hello, Doyle." She quickly offered her hand.

A slow smile spread across Doyle's face. He took her hand and held it. Too long, in fact. "Still friends, Fianna?"

"I don't see why not, Doyle." Friends, but nothing more. Doyle had a way of suffocating a woman. He'd never supported her decision to pursue a career in fashion.

"So what doubts are you having, love?" Shane wrapped his arm protectively around Lizzie.

Lizzie shot a look at Fianna before answering. "Doubts about... my dress. It's so... voluminous."

Fianna squeezed her hand. "I'm happy to help any way I can."

"Thank you, Fianna. I know I can always count on you." Lizzie's eyes were pleading.

Shane's eyes lit up. "Could you fix it for her, Fianna? You're a designer."

"Um, I can look at it."

Doyle fell into step beside them. "So you're still sewing, are you? That's a fine skill to have."

Fianna shot him a frown, and then lifted her chin in defiance. "It's more than that. I have a runway show planned in Dublin. And lots more after that." Why did most men assume she was a seamstress who took in mending?

Her words barely registered with Doyle. He shook his head. "How will you do that and have a family?"

Fianna just stared at him. *Have I stumbled into the last century?* She knew plenty of successful women who had careers and families.

"Well, I'm impressed." Shane kissed the top of Lizzie's head. "If Fianna is going to fix your dress, you should get started today. We haven't long until the wedding. And we have the rehearsal dinner and party to think about."

"Rehearsal?" Fianna glanced at Lizzie.

"Didn't you know?" Lizzie scrunched her nose. "I thought Mam told you. It's the entire wedding party."

"You can be my date again," Doyle said, a grin spreading across his face. "I daresay we'll pick up where we left off."

"Why, that's perfect." Shane gave Fianna an enthusiastic hug before she could protest. "Won't that be grand, then? The four of us can ride together. Just like old times."

9

LATER THAT AFTERNOON, after Shane and Doyle left, Lizzie begged Fianna to look at her dress and give her an honest opinion.

"What do you think, Fianna?" With great effort, Lizzie swung around in her bedroom. As she did, the full, tiered skirt and train of her blindingly white wedding gown swooshed behind her and caught on an occasional table.

Fianna lunged and caught an antique Tiffany lamp before it tumbled to the hardwood floor. "It's enormous. It reminds me of Princess Diana's wedding dress. Remember the trouble she had with her gown?"

Lizzie's lower lip trembled, giving her the appearance of a fidgeting rabbit. Her eyes were rimmed in pink and her pale golden strawberry hair was piled onto her head in a messy bun. She sank to the floor and covered her face with her hands. "It's horrible, isn't it? Our mam chose it. She was so certain it was perfect." The dress billowed around her, engulfing her in tall peaks of shimmering white satin.

"It's what *she* wanted, not you." Fianna knelt beside her sister. "Lizzie, where's your backbone?" she asked. Her tone was playful, but her words rang with truth. "Do you want to fix this travesty, or not?"

Lizzie sniffed and peered through parted fingers. "Can you really do it?"

"Sure, I can fix almost anything. In fact, there's enough fabric here to make several dresses."

"I wanted something slim and elegant." She swatted the skirt back as it rose again of its own accord. "And it's such a bright white. Can you dye it?"

Fianna chewed her lip. She didn't have much time. "Is there anything you *like* about it?"

Lizzie thought for a moment and spread her hands over her torso. "I suppose the bodice fits well."

"Actually, it does." Fianna unzipped the back and looked inside. The silk interior had finished seams and was constructed with foundational stays and underpinnings. The gown was well made, but it would be complicated to remake on such short notice. "So, we have to deal with the color, and this giant skirt and train."

"And the headdress and veil are far too heavy," Lizzie added, pointing to a hat stand swathed in tulle and lace and satin. "I'm not sure I could make it down the aisle without tipping over. I'd feel like a Las Vegas showgirl wearing that."

Fianna laughed. She stood and measured lengths of the veil by stretching it from her fingertips to her nose. "This is several yards long." What had their mother been thinking? Poor Lizzie, who favored sweaters and slacks and tailored dresses, had been swallowed in enough satin and tulle to clothe an entire family.

Rubbing her hands together, Fianna stepped back to consider her task. She could redesign and trim it down, fit it to Lizzie, and use her mother's sewing machine, but she was awfully short on time. "Do you have a pencil and paper? I'd like to sketch a few ideas for you to see."

"In my vanity." Lizzie struggled to her feet, but lost her balance and plopped back down. "I can't even get up in this thing." She fell to one side, and started laughing so hard tears came to her eyes.

Fianna reached out to help her, but she stumbled on the train and fell into the mound of fabric alongside her sister. "Whoops! It's like I fell into a lemon meringue pie."

"Can you see me tumbling and rolling down the aisle, strangled in tulle?"

"Strangled in Tulle, sounds like a murder mystery." Soon they were both howling with hysterical laughter and rolling on the floor.

"What's going on here?" Mary Margaret flung open the door. "Girls! What in heaven's name are you doing to that dress? You'll ruin it!"

Davina looked over her sister's shoulder, clearly amused at the antics.

Lizzie sat up, her blond mane in wild disarray, and wiped tears of laughter from her cheeks. "Don't worry, Mam, Fianna's going to fix it."

Their mother's face grew ashen. "You will not touch a stitch on that beautiful gown."

Davina smothered a laugh. "She could only improve upon it."

"See? I told you it was hideous." Lizzie threw a look at Fianna and then turned to face her mother. "Fianna offered to redesign it for me. This is *my* wedding, and I'll wear what I want. If I have to wear *this*—" She flounced the fabric over her head for effect. "I'd sooner call off the wedding."

"Lizzie, you don't know what you're saying. Why, I'm sure Fianna has—"

"Told me the truth," Lizzie finished. "But I already knew it was ghastly."

"Fianna *is* an expert," Davina said.

Mary Margaret sputtered in anger. "Do what you want, you willful child. But don't come running back to me when that gorgeous gown is ruined beyond repair. It's *your* wedding."

Fianna gazed at her mother, saddened. "Thanks for the vote of confidence, Mam."

"Mary Margaret, your daughter is a talented designer," Davina said softly. "I wouldn't have brought her collection in for the event if it weren't. And her last runway show was covered in both the *Los Angeles Times* and *Fashion News Daily*. Why don't you give her a chance?"

"She'll have to do something. Look, the train is torn." Mary Margaret turned and huffed down the hallway.

Lizzie flung her arms around Fianna. "Thank goodness you're here. I've missed you so much."

Fianna hugged her sister. "You did that all by yourself,

Lizzie. I'm proud of you."

"Yes, indeed, you spoke your mind." Davina stepped inside the bedroom and helped the two girls to their feet. "I'd love to hear how you plan to salvage this, Fianna."

"I have some ideas." While Davina helped free Lizzie from the confines of her wedding dress, Fianna opened the white vanity festooned with hand-painted roses and found a pencil and paper. She perched on a pink velvet stool and quickly drew a few lines on the notepad.

"Here's a simple, lean silhouette." She added more strokes. "Or I can gather material in the back, and twist or weave it into something interesting…" Another quick sketch.

Davina peered over her shoulder. "That reminds me of an old 1950s design by Charles James, the British designer who worked in the States. It was called the Butterfly, with wings of tulle flowing from the back." She waved graceful hands to her sides, and then arched her arms in back of her, striking a model pose.

"Wait, Davina. Hold that." Fianna studied her for a moment, and then made a rapid sketch. Her aunt still had a dramatic sense of style, and she'd certainly maintained her figure. Fianna wished she'd wear one of her designs in the upcoming show, but Davina had been steadfast in her refusal. "What about this?" She spun the notepad around to Lizzie, who'd slipped on a thick terry cloth robe.

"It's a smooth silhouette that skims the body in front, with a slim skirt affixed to the existing bodice so that it appears as one elongated line. I'll widen the neckline to showcase your long neck. In the back, the fabric can be draped from the waistline in graceful folds to form a modified bustle. The flowing line will be elegant, and the cut will be supple enough to move with you."

"Will I be able to dance in it?" Lizzie asked, her aquamarine eyes shimmering.

"All night, if you wish. I can make the back section detachable."

"Bravo," Davina said. "What do you think, Lizzie?"

Lizzie's smile grew wider. "That's exactly what I've dreamed of. But what about that hideous shade of neon white?"

Fianna grinned. "Leave that to me."

After a boisterous supper with all the siblings, nieces, nephews, and neighbors, Fianna's energy was ebbing due to the time difference and long distance travel.

After they'd helped clear the dishes, Lizzie asked, "Join me for a nightcap? It's not often I see my sister."

"I'm exhausted, how about we talk in the morning?" Fianna yawned and slung her arm around her sister as they climbed the stairs. "Lizzie, you're trembling. Still nervous?"

"It seems like the world is spinning faster every day, and I wish I could slow time. Shane is just the opposite. He's impatient; he can't wait for us to be married."

"Shane is a good guy, Lizzie. You two have always been close."

They reached the top of the stairs and Lizzie turned to Fianna. "Sure, but is he the one?"

"Only you can make that decision."

Lizzie's wide eyes grew glassy. "I wish we were having a smaller, more intimate wedding." Her voice dropped to a whisper. "I don't know if I can go through with this. Sometimes I wish I could find that escape hatch we always imagined, and drop through the earth to the golden sands of Tahiti. Remember that?"

"I sure do." Now at a loss for words, Fianna wrapped her arms around Lizzie. She couldn't encourage her sister to walk away from her wedding now, but neither could she suggest she go through with a marriage she had doubts about. Would Lizzie bolt?

Fianna framed Lizzie's pale face in her hands. "Search your heart, Lizzie, and block out the noise around you. Think about what *you* want."

"I look at Emily and her children, and while they're precious, I don't know if I'm ready for a family."

"You don't have to have children right away. Or at all. But you should talk to Shane now and share your feelings. Before the wedding. Promise?"

Lizzie blew out a ragged breath. "Guess I should."

"And remember that I'm always here for you." Fianna hugged Lizzie again and wondered what her sister would do.

The next morning, Fianna slept in, intent on recapturing the sleep she'd missed on the trip from California. But with the runway show and the wedding both close at hand, she had precious little time to waste.

She tugged on the red silk kimono she'd found in Little Tokyo near downtown Los Angeles and wrapped a swath of black satin around her waist before making her way downstairs.

Fianna padded across the newly modernized kitchen. Stainless steel appliances sparkled in the morning light. It wasn't at all as she'd remembered it, another reminder of how long she'd been away.

When the large pine table in the kitchen came into view—the old table where they used to eat breakfast every morning—she saw her mother and Davina sitting together, their voices low, their heads bent so close their hair was touching. "Morning Mam, Davina."

They immediately stopped talking and looked up in surprise. Her mother spilled her tea, and Davina quickly sopped it up with her napkin. Her mother seemed flustered, though she managed to raise her eyebrows at Fianna's robe. "Why, would you take a gander at that? Well, I never."

"Maybe you should, Mary Margaret," Davina said, winking at Fianna. "I think that kimono is utterly marvelous. Where did you find it?"

Fianna shared a knowing look with Davina. "It's vintage. Next time you're in L.A., I'll take you to Little Tokyo. You'd love the silks and slippers and sushi bars." Fianna reached for a cup, poured milk into it first, and then added strong black tea. She slid into a wooden chair at the table, keeping her eyes on her mother. She started to ask what was wrong when Davina cut in.

"I've been meaning to visit you, dear. Tell me, how is my old friend Camille?"

Her aunt had smoothly changed the subject. Fianna took notice, though she went with the flow. "As active as ever, and still running Parfums Dubois." Davina had been a spokes model for the perfume company years ago. "I had lunch with her and Dahlia. We've been talking about branding a perfume at some point."

Mary Margaret bustled into the kitchen as she had for so many years. "Fianna, if you're hungry, we have pinhead oats and boiled eggs. You should eat something."

Fianna started to protest, but caught Davina's eye and changed her mind. "Thanks, Mam, porridge sounds good." Fianna watched her mother's familiar motions in the kitchen. As she did, she noticed lines on her mother's face where once there had been none. Her usually pink skin was ashen. Something was definitely amiss in her life.

Her mother looked tired and stressed. The pending wedding was surely an enormous strain, of course, but Fianna sensed something more. Perhaps it was the life her mother had led, one of constant worry, responsibility, and rigidity. Emily was living there with her family, and Mary Margaret was helping look after her four toddlers, as well as her own brood.

In contrast, Davina was as bright as ever, her shiny platinum gray hair full of waves, her face wreathed in a smile. All her life she'd done what she loved, traveled, and lived the life she'd wanted.

Two sisters, who'd led such different lives. What had they been like at her age? Did Mary Margaret have unfulfilled dreams? Something had changed, and Fianna decided to find out what it was.

Lizzie's frightened words from last night came to mind. Would her sister become like their Mam someday? The notion startled her. No wonder Lizzie was nervous.

And then Fianna thought of her siblings, her father, and the large house that always seemed to be in need of repair. Her mother was strict, but she probably only wanted what she thought was best for her children.

With Fianna's change in perspective, the wide rift that had once divided Fianna-the-rebellious-teenager from her mother narrowed.

Fianna got up and went into the kitchen. "I can make the porridge, Mam. Why don't you sit down, have another cup of tea, and visit with Davina." She took the wooden spoon from her mother. She was no longer a child. Maybe they could mend their differences during this visit.

Mary Margaret blinked in surprise and stepped away from the stove, albeit with some hesitation. After a moment, she poured another cup of tea and sat at the table beside Davina.

Davina nodded her approval, almost imperceptibly, but Fianna caught it. "What will you do today, Fianna?"

She lifted the pan from the flame. "I'll keep Lizzie company. Mam, would you like to join us?"

"I've so much to do, you know." Mary Margaret shot a

look at Davina as she stirred her tea. "Fianna, you're not really going to touch her wedding dress, are you?"

Davina put her hand over Mary Margaret's. "It's what *Lizzie* wants. That's what counts, isn't it?"

"I promise it will be stunning," Fianna said. "I wouldn't let her walk down the aisle any other way." *If she makes it down the aisle.*

Davina rubbed her hand in circles on her sister's back. "Relax. Your girls are grown now. They can take care of themselves. Emily and her husband will bounce back soon enough."

Mary Margaret ran a hand over her salt-and-pepper hair. "I suppose they are, but the boys are another story entirely."

Their rowdy, boisterous brothers were still young. After Emily, Fianna, and Lizzie were born, their father was anxious for a boy. Patrick was next, a gangly young teen now, while Dermot, Quinn, Riley, and James were stair steps in grammar school.

Though her mother passed her hands over her face, she seemed to accept the fate of the wedding dress.

Fianna smiled. "After breakfast, I'll get to work. May I use your sewing room?"

"Of course," Mary Margaret replied, the briefest of smiles touching her lips.

After finishing breakfast and changing clothes, Fianna made her way to the third floor sewing room. Sunlight poured through the French-paned windows. Fianna stepped inside and opened a window, letting the scent of fresh spring leaves and blossoms filter in.

Outside, birds trilled in the tall swaying trees, just as they had when Fianna was a girl. This is where she'd first learned to measure, cut, and sew, long before she'd moved to the U.S. and enrolled at the Fashion Institute for Design and Merchandising. She and Emily had made all their own clothes, and they took turns dressing up fair, blond little Lizzie like a precious doll.

She ran her hands lovingly along the long cutting board, which was padded and covered in muslin. Behind it, a rainbow of thread hung on tiny dowels affixed to the wall. She opened a sewing box that contained the sharpest of scissors, dressmaker's chalk, steel pins, and other tools of the trade. She smiled as she sorted through them. She'd learned how to sew with the items in this box.

A commotion sounded outside the door.

"Here's the dress." Lizzie bustled in, dressed in the leotard and yoga pants that Fianna had insisted she wear. Fianna wore similar yoga pants and a white cotton blouse, and had pulled her thick curly hair into a high pony tail.

Lizzie was nearly obscured by the voluminous gown. "Let the surgery commence." She dumped it on the cutting table.

Fianna spread out the dress, inspecting it. She glanced at her sketches, and back at Lizzie. "I'll need all my magical powers and some sleight of hand, but I think you'll be pleased."

Lizzie rested her chin in her hand. "I took your advice and called Shane this morning. We're going to meet for lunch and talk." She flipped the switch on an old radio their mother kept near the sewing machine and turned the tuning knob, searching for a more contemporary channel.

"How's this?" Lizzie stopped on a pop channel, where a song about heartbreak was playing. She swayed and snapped her fingers.

"That's fine." Fianna didn't listen to much music besides jazz and classical music, mostly out of habit now. She'd always liked instrumental music when she was studying, and then when she was working. Her friends had always had crushes on boy groups, but not her.

"This song reminds me of Shane," Lizzie said. "I really love him, but I hardly slept last night, thinking about us."

Fianna hugged Lizzie. "You're doing the right thing." She couldn't help but wonder if the wedding dress would even be necessary, though she didn't want to jinx their meeting. Besides, if the dress were going to be ready on time, she'd have to start today. "I'll need your measurements before you leave."

The song on the radio ended, and Lizzie stood up straight, tightening her tummy, ready to be measured.

Fianna was rummaging through the sewing supplies looking for a measuring tape when another song began and a deep, familiar voice floated through the air. Startled, she whirled around, her heartbeat quickening. She jerked her head toward the radio. "Who's singing that?"

"Wow, you're sure out of touch. That's Finley Green. It's one of their older songs, too."

Fianna stepped toward the radio, mesmerized by the slow ballad. She turned up the sound, thinking about the man who sang to her one balmy night, not too long ago. "The man who's singing, isn't that…"

"Niall Finley. What a sexy, gravelly voice, huh? Too bad he left the group."

"Mmm." Fianna ran her fingertips over her lips, remembering the kiss they'd shared, and the magic that had flared between them.

"His wife died, and he hasn't done anything since." Lizzie squinted at her sister. "Hey, are you okay?"

Fianna drew a breath and turned to Lizzie. "That song does something to you, doesn't it?" Ignoring Lizzie's puzzled look, she added, "Now let's get your measurements so you can meet Shane for lunch."

After Lizzie left, Fianna switched the radio to a classical station and breathed a sigh of regret. The last thing she needed was a reminder of Niall Finley and her massive error. What an idiot she'd been to accuse him of being a philandering married man. She'd always been quick to speak her mind. *Maybe too quick.*

10

NIALL EASED INTO a lounge chair, adjusted his dark Maui Jim sunglasses against the sun's bright early rays and gazed over crystalline waves lapping sandy, vanilla shores. He kept an eye on Kaitlin, who was jogging along the water's edge in a white bikini.

Kauai was less crowded than Oahu, or even Maui, which was why he and Laila had chosen this particular Hawaiian island. Kauai received a great deal of rainfall, so tropical plants proliferated. Spiky hala trees with aerial roots and lacy palipali ferns grew wild. Pikake flowers sweetened the light breeze. Vanda and dendrobium orchids bloomed in abundance, dotting the jungle-like landscape with vivid shades of purple, pink, and white.

Niall loved this island, which held some of his most cherished memories. He and Laila had often hiked through thick botanical vegetation, intent on discovering spectacular waterfalls and obscure swimming holes, where they'd had the freedom to frolic without the long invasive lenses of the paparazzi.

Their home here was a modest Hawaiian-style house, or

hana, a single story family home that was nothing like the sleek, modern Malibu home he'd just sold.

The sprawling ranch property was gated at the road, but once inside, wide pocket doors slid into the walls and the house stood open to the natural surroundings. All around the house, white plumeria blossoms scented the air, the sound of running streams trickled over moss-covered rocks, and palm trees swayed in the onshore breeze.

Niall picked up a glass from the low table next to his chaise lounge and sipped fresh pineapple juice. His chest was already bronzed from three days in the sun. He was fortunate; his grandmother was of Italian heritage, and he'd inherited her deeper skin tone. Unlike his fair, freckled cousins who burned bright pink, his skin tanned to a rich golden brown—unless he stayed too long in the sun—while his dark blond hair gained streaks of light.

The waves were relentless in their rhythmic dance, arching, curling, crashing, and receding, only to begin anew. As he watched the sea, a nascent melody emerged in his mind. To his surprise, music had returned to his dry, desert-scape soul, taking root again in moist, fertile ground, sending up tender new shoots and unfurling like the hapu'u ferns that grew wild on the island.

There was only one explanation for it.

Fianna.

The night he'd met her, music had returned to his soul.

Kaitlin had wanted to come here to relax and recharge before returning to work. "I need a holiday," she'd pleaded.

He couldn't deny his sister, and it wasn't as if he had pressing business or a busy social schedule.

But as soon as he'd turned the key in the front door, he'd heard Laila's laugh, the slap of her bare feet on the bamboo floors. This had been their hideaway, their most personal residence, where they'd come to disappear from the world. He remembered the songs he'd written for her here, the last ballad he'd recorded with Finley Green, as well as those he'd never shared with others.

Her presence was still here. Though her perfume had long since vanished, Niall could close his eyes and conjure the scent of island jasmine in her silky hair.

The squawking of shorebirds erupted on the beach. He watched as they sailed low across the sand, their wings spread like gliders, sunlight glancing off their white feathers. He and his wife used to sit for hours watching the ocean. The surfers, the sailboats and catamarans, the creatures of the sea. The warm Pacific Ocean was inviting, and they often jogged on the beach or swam in the morning before breakfast.

Niall breathed in the subtle, spicy aromas of lantana and red ginger wafting on the morning breeze. Glossy green plumeria leaves swayed slightly and the scent of jasmine blossomed in the air. He'd had strangely fitful dreams last night. Under the warmth of the sun, his eyelids grew heavy. He shifted on the chaise lounge and dozed off.

Soon a whisper of breath touched his shoulder, distinctly different than that of the ocean breeze.

Hello, Laila.

He drank in her presence.

Your music is returning, Niall. You can hear it again, can't you?

His chin dipped against his chest.

It's been a long, long time.

A melody wound through his mind. *I was afraid it might never return.* His neck prickled again, as if brushed with her gossamer touch.

It never really left you, Niall. I've been watching over your gift.

Gratitude filled his heart, and warmth spread through his chest. Since the first time he'd seen her, she'd been his muse. *We need to talk, Laila.*

A silence. *Not yet, Niall.*

He imagined her fingertips caressing his cheek and turned into the feeling, needing to summon the love he'd shared with her for so many treasured years. *No, not just yet, my darling.*

"Niall, wake up." A hand—a real hand—rested on his arm.

"Hmm?" Niall slit open an eye, squinting against the brilliant reflection of the sun's rays on the sea.

Kaitlin stood in front of him to block the glare. She wore a gauzy white sundress over her bikini, and her feet were bare. "You've been sleeping, but you're starting to look like a lobster."

He sat up, pushing his hair back from his forehead. His

foggy thoughts were clearing, but he was reluctant to leave the dreamland he shared with Laila.

"Come inside. I have aloe vera gel in the refrigerator." She held her hands out to him.

Niall grasped her strong, slender hands and pulled himself to his feet. He felt a vacuum forming in his mind where Laila had been.

"I've made fruit salad with avocado, lychee, mango, papaya, and lilikoi."

Niall closed his eyes and smiled. "Passion fruit. That was Laila's favorite." He tried to summon his wife again, but she was gone.

Kaitlin drew her brows together. "Yes, it was." She started across the warm sand, still holding his hand.

"You know what else she liked?"

Kaitlin sighed, and a wistful smile flickered across her face. "What, Niall?"

A smile tugged his lips. "This place. It was her favorite. We were happier here than anyplace else."

Kaitlin led Niall through the opening by the kitchen. Bamboo floors and cabinets created a warm ambiance, and Kaitlin had bought fresh orchids as soon as they'd arrived. She'd give them to the caretaker when it was time to go.

On the walls hung Hawaiian artwork, which glowed with the natural shades of Hawaii—golden sunrises, an azure sea, scarlet hibiscus, and jade-colored tropical palms. A plumeria candle Laila had bought burned on the table, filling the air with its sweet floral scent.

Kaitlin reached into the refrigerator. "Here's the aloe vera gel." She handed him a green tube.

As Niall smoothed the gel onto his warm skin, he felt immediate relief.

She served the fruit salad and poured a vanilla protein shake into two tall glasses. Kaitlin sat beside her brother and unfurled a napkin.

"Ah, Laila would have loved this."

"Yes, she would have." She put her napkin down and turned to face him. "You know I love you, but I'm worried about you, Niall."

"Worried? About what?" Outside, a pair of wind chimes tinkled in the breeze. "Listen to that, would you? Laila bought those at the local market."

"I remember. Niall, I loved Laila, and so did you. But since I've been around you, I've noticed it's as if she's still with you."

"She is, Kaitlin." Niall's voice was low and reverent. "She's in every breath of wind, every note of music, every sunrise. Don't you see that?"

As she took this in this truth, Kaitlin's eyes rimmed with tears. "What I see is a man who loved his wife very much." She wrapped her arms around him. "I miss her, too, Niall. After we eat, let's go out. I met a man on the beach. He's a musician, and he invited us to visit him on the beach this evening."

Later, as the sun swept low in the sky, Niall heard a

soulful Hawaiian tune rise from the shore. He stepped outside. Kaitlin was skipping toward a rotund, mahogany-skinned man, whose glossy dark hair flowed down the back of his white linen shirt. A bright floral Hawaiian wrap encircled his waist and hung to his shins. He sat on a rock and strummed a guitar, and his voice was one of the most mellow Niall had ever heard.

The man raised his hand in greeting. "Aloha," he called, a smile wreathing his welcoming face.

"This is the man I as telling you about, Niall. While you were sleeping, we talked on the beach." She tipped her head toward him. "His name is Eli, and he's very wise."

"Aloha," Niall replied. He gestured toward the guitar, which was scratched and battered, but had a rich patina and an astounding sound. "That was a beautiful song. I love Hawaiian music."

"Do you play?"

Niall raised his brow and gazed at Eli, but the man's question was an honest one. "Yeah, but I haven't played much in a long time."

Eli smiled, his white teeth sparkling in the fading light. He handed his guitar to Niall. "Then you must play again, man."

Niall shook his head "I'd like to listen to you for a while. You have such a unique voice."

Eli plucked a few strings and sang, "Oo-ooh, oooh."

Kaitlin clapped her hands. "That's 'Somewhere Over the Rainbow', isn't it?" she asked.

Eli's face lit with pleasure, and his sweet voice soared as the sun slipped beneath the horizon, washing the sky with streaks of pink and orange and purple. As he segued into "It's a Wonderful World", Niall began to sing softly with him, and Kaitlin moved her shoulders with the music.

After they finished singing, Niall said, "That's the version IZ recorded."

Kaitlin stretched out on the sand on her stomach, digging her elbows into the soft sand and cupping her chin in her hands. "Who's IZ?"

"Israel Kamakawiwo'ole," Niall said. "He was called IZ for short. He was one of Hawaii's most beloved singers."

Eli nodded, and began another song. Tiki torches flared against the darkening sky, illuminating the night with flickering amber light.

After a while, Niall took the guitar and played a few of his old songs that had never been recorded, songs he'd kept for himself and Laila. Eli listened with his eyes closed, swaying in rhythm.

When Niall finished, Eli opened his eyes. "That was beautiful, man. Laila loved those."

Kaitlin's mouth opened. "Did you know Laila?"

Eli only smiled. "Play the new music that's filling your soul, man." His words were deep and rounded, and his voice reverberated in his broad chest.

Niall didn't ask Eli how he knew about Laila, or the new melodies he felt in his soul. After all, Niall was from Ireland, the land of fairies and leprechauns, with tales as tall as the mountains. To him, Laila might have easily been dancing barefoot in the sand behind them. He swept around. He didn't see her, but her felt her silky breath on his neck.

Slowly, he drew his fingers across the strings, trying out a new sequence of chords that had been running through his mind.

Eli rocked back and forth, listening with closed eyes again.

When the last note faded into the night, Eli locked his gaze on Niall. "You created that for a special woman."

"I did," Niall said softly. He handed the guitar back to Eli.

Eli focused on a spot just beyond Niall's shoulder. "Laila says you must play that for your new woman." His eyes misted. "She says it is time."

Niall and Kaitlin glanced back, and saw a mound of sugary sand ruffle and gather and swirl into the air, glittering like diamonds against the golden torchlight. Higher and higher it went, until the twirling helix finally subsided and fell back to the soft dune.

Niall sucked in a breath. He turned back to Eli.

But his new friend had vanished.

11

FIANNA SWEPT TENDRILS of hair from her face with the back of her hand. On her other wrist, she wore a red pin cushion, which held an assortment of steel head pins. She'd spent the day marking and pinning and cutting. White satin, silk, and tulle formed a fluffy mound in the corner of her mother's sewing room. She felt like a sculptor, whittling away the excess to find the true work of art within.

Davina sat beside the window, which was speckled with afternoon raindrops. She was sipping tea in a thin china cup imprinted with the Fitzgerald crest in red. They'd been discussing details about the fashion show. "Are you absolutely certain the trunks with your collection arrived?"

"I checked this morning. The hotel received them, and now they're locked in storage. But I'll have to open the trunks soon and hang the clothes."

"The staff can steam or iron for you."

"I'd rather do it myself." When Davina shot her a look, she corrected herself. "This is important. I'd like to be present at least. Believe me, if I'm going to grow this enterprise, I realize I can't do everything myself."

"That's better," Davina said with a decisive nod. She crossed her legs and adjusted the Pucci turquoise and lime green print dress she wore. It was a relic from the 1970s that she'd found in the attic. "I gave this to Mary Margaret after I walked the runway for Pucci. She never wore it. Can you imagine? It's like new." She had a blueberry-colored scarf wrapped around her hair, and an assortment of gold chains and beads dangling around her neck.

"I can't even imagine her in that," Fianna said.

"Maybe not now, but there was a time Mary Margaret would've worn this. When she was at university in Dublin before she married." She shook her head. "But she never did. What a waste."

Fianna wasn't sure if Davina meant the waste of a dress, or the waste of a moment in time. Mulling this over, she inspected a seam, recalling how her mother had looked at breakfast. She wondered if she might be ill. "Davina, is there anything wrong with Mam?"

"Wrong?" she echoed.

Before Fianna could elaborate, Lizzie poked her head in the door. "How's it going?"

Fianna clipped a stray thread and looked up. "Fairly well. I have something for you to try on. The dress is still in progress, but I want to see how it falls on you."

Lizzie slipped out of her sweater and skirt, and Fianna helped her into the reconstructed dress. "Careful, it's held together with pins."

Fianna stepped back and folded her arms, assessing the

work she needed to do. She knelt and adjusted the hem.

"This is amazing." Lizzie ran her hands over the new wide neckline and the slim silhouette. "What do you think, Davina?"

Frowning, Davina said, "The dress is looking much better, but why the long face, Lizzie? I've never seen such a sad expression on a girl who's about to be married. How are things between you and Shane?"

Lizzie blinked several times. "We talked at lunch, but now I'm more confused than ever."

Fianna rocked back on her heels. "Why?"

"He understands why I'm freaked out, from this wedding that's grown completely out of hand, to wanting to wait before I start popping out babies like Pez candy. The problem is that I think he's being *too* accommodating. I don't know whether he's just trying to placate me before the wedding, or if he has the spine of a jellyfish. Either one is unacceptable."

Davina drew a finger along her smooth, well-defined jawline. "Maybe he actually agrees with you. Shane O'Donnell has always seemed like a good egg."

Lizzie blew air into her cheeks and shook her head. "What could you possibly know about marriage, Davina?"

"Just because I've never been married doesn't mean I don't know about men. Believe me, I've sampled the selections. And unless I'm mistaken, which I doubt, that man would lasso the sun to make you happy."

Fianna grinned at her aunt's colorful expressions as she

made a chalk mark on the dress. "There, now step out of it. I know what I need to do."

"It's still that awful shade of bright blue-white. It's horrible against my skin tone. Is there anything you can do about that?"

"You could dye the dress," Davina said. "We used to do that all the time."

Fianna glanced at a Degas ballerina print that hung on the wall. "I have an idea. How much tea do we have in the kitchen?"

Davina arched a brow, but she was clearly intrigued. "Whatever for?"

"In ballet class we once tinted our shoes and tights with tea. I could try a science experiment." She picked up a length of discarded fabric and inspected it.

"Oh, no. Imagine the perfume I'll have to wear to offset that scent," Lizzie said.

"Dior, darling. Or maybe Chanel. I'll help you with that." Davina waved her wrist under her nose for emphasis. "The age-old question is, which tea is better, Barry's or Lyon's? You'll have to have a tea-off."

Lizzie groaned at Davina's little joke. "I can see it now; I'll be walking down the aisle with a red or green tea bag poking out of me bodice."

"No, you won't. Not on my watch, Lizzie." Fianna quirked a corner of her mouth. "Maybe I'll try something else. But trust me, this is going to be gorgeous."

Lizzie zipped up her beige woolen skirt while Fianna

hung up the dress. "Oh, Fianna, we saw Doyle at lunch. He asked after you. Wouldn't that be interesting if—"

"Absolutely not."

Davina's eyes lit up. "Didn't you and Doyle used to date?"

Lizzie pulled on her nubby Aran sweater. "He's quite the catch. Heir to an old family fortune, and all that."

"Mam said he's seeing someone else."

"Brona, but she's docile as a mouse. Makes me look like Joan of Arc."

Fianna chuckled. "He can't stand the idea that a woman might actually want to have a career, or even her own interests." She eyed her sister's old-style fisherman's sweater. Davina cast a pleading expression in her direction. "Lizzie, we've got to do something about your wardrobe. You're dressing like Mam."

Lizzie beamed. "Would you help me? I'd really love to update my look."

Fianna threw herself onto a silk duvet-covered, fluffy down comforter. "Ah, this is wonderful, Davina." After spending two nights at Fitzgerald Manor cramped in a twin bed that normally housed a seven-year-old, she stretched her legs in luxury, her toes barely reaching the end of the enormous bed. Davina had booked them into one of the most posh hotels in Dublin, which was also hosting the fashion show for the charity event Davina had arranged.

Davina wore a casual orange twill Tory Burch dress and

was perched on a mahogany chair reading messages that had been delivered. "Your friend Penelope Plessen is on her way here. She'll check in tomorrow and would like for us to join her for dinner."

"I can't wait to see Penelope again. And it's so good of her to donate her time to the cause."

Davina gazed through the tall French-paned windows in the Georgian hotel, which overlooked a manicured park. "What a lovely lass she is. I remember her first major show in Paris. She was nervous, but no one would have guessed from the way she owned that runway. I knew she was going to be a star."

"With Penelope here, we'll probably make the pages of *The Irish Times*." Fianna rolled onto her side and leaned on her hand. "Of course, if you'd walk the runway, Davina, the show would hit all the major newspapers in the world."

"Don't be silly. Who wants to see me anymore? Modeling is a young woman's game. Like Greta Garbo, I retired while I was still on top. Leave them wanting more, that's what I always say."

"I thought you always said *more is never enough*. Come on, walk one more time? In your niece's Irish debut?"

Davina fluffed her platinum white hair and laughed. "You're not playing fair, appealing to my emotions. No, darling, my detractors—and yes, I have quite a few critics— would gleefully point out how decrepit I've become, as if models shouldn't age."

"Hardly! And I thought you were proud of your age.

You'll look fabulous at a hundred, Davina. Look at Carmen." Still working in her eighties, the silver-haired Carmen Dell'Orefice had first appeared on the cover of *Vogue* magazine at the age of fifteen. She was a muse to artist Salvador Dali, and she and Davina had been photographed by Richard Avedon, Irving Penn, and Francesco Scavullo.

"She's marvelous, isn't she? But I have my reasons." Davina sorted through the messages. "Here's a note from Scarlett. She says to tell you that a gentleman by the name of Niall dropped by Bow-Tie to visit Johnny and Lance, and then left for Hawaii. He asked after you." She lowered the note. "Niall—that's a fine Irish name, isn't it?"

Fianna bolted up. "I met him in Malibu at my first show."

"Nice fellow, is he?"

"As it turns out, he probably is. Of course, I accused him of being a philandering married man and stormed off."

"Well, that doesn't sound good. But it makes you terribly memorable, doesn't it?"

Fianna blew out a breath. "No, it wasn't good, because he's actually a widower."

"Oh, dear. That's even more tragic." Davina grimaced.

"Me and my big mouth." She stood, brushing off her black jeans and silvery gray silk turtleneck. She pushed up her sleeves. "It's time to go to work on this show anyway. I'll have the suitcases delivered and have someone sent up to help steam the clothes."

"Good, you need to begin delegating so you can grow

your business." Davina paused. "Have I told you lately how proud I am of you?"

Fianna hugged her aunt. "But if it weren't for your encouragement and support, I wouldn't have made it this far." She kissed her on the cheek. "I love you, Auntie." She cherished her relationship with her aunt and wished only that she had the same with her mother.

Davina kissed her back. "And I love you, my darling. Isn't it grand that we share such a passion for style, too?"

Fianna made a telephone call, and a little while later, several rolling racks with clothes and accessories were set up in their suite. A maid arrived to help her unpack and steam the garments. The woman knew exactly what to do, and set to work immediately. As she unpacked the sumptuous clothes, Fianna checked her list and organized the outfits in the order in which they'd be sent down the runway.

Fianna was grateful for the assistance, and the work went quicker than planned. Minutes later, steam was hissing from a handheld steamer, and the clothes came back to life.

She still had to finish Lizzie's wedding dress. She'd had a brilliant idea, and Mary Margaret had given her their grandmother's fine Irish lace to execute it. When, or *if*, Lizzie walked the aisle, she'd be one of the most stylish brides of the season. Fianna had been trying to reach her sister ever since she'd left the manor, but Lizzie's phone had gone straight to messages. She'd have to work on her wedding dress in the evenings. Lizzie could have her final fitting before the rehearsal dinner next week.

As Fianna was thinking about the dinner, a knock sounded on the door. When she opened it, a smartly uniformed butler stood with a colossal floral arrangement that nearly eclipsed his portly frame.

"What's this?"

"Compliments of a gentleman, Ms. Fitzgerald. Where shall I place them?"

"In the sitting area," Davina said.

The maid quickly cleared a low table by a sofa. The butler hefted the arrangement onto the table. The sweet aroma of stargazer lilies and white roses immediately filled the room.

The butler presented a card, before closing the door behind him.

Davina cupped her hands around a rose and inhaled. "Aren't they lovely? Could these be from your Niall?"

Fianna held her breath and slid a monogrammed card from the ivory envelope. Upon reading it, her heart sank. "Doyle O'Donnell sent them."

"Shane's cousin, right?"

"Exactly." Before Davina could say anything, she added, "No, he's definitely not my type." He was the type of man whose attributes looked good on paper, but there was absolutely no chemistry between them. At least, not on her part.

"Young, handsome, rich. And madly in love with you." Davina placed a finger on her cheek in mock thought. "You're right, he won't do at all. So what *is* your type,

Fianna?"

She laughed, but she knew precisely what her type was. "Someone who's genuine. Who's passionate about life and what they do, as well as their contributions to the world."

She closed her eyes and pictured Niall curved around her on the chaise lounge, his breath warm on her neck. She could still hear his rich, gravelly baritone echoing in her mind, and it touched her to her core. But now that he'd sold his home in Malibu, would she ever she him again?

"That's a lofty pedestal, darling. Not many men like that around." Davina sighed. "I should know. I've looked long enough. Those men get snapped up in a hurry."

"I'll have to talk to Doyle and make it clear that we're just friends." Fianna tossed the card into the trash bin. "He asked me to go to the rehearsal dinner with him, and Shane suggested we make it a foursome. Lizzie can't understand why I'm not mad about him."

Fianna turned back to her collection, which the maid was de-wrinkling to perfection. Fianna couldn't have been more pleased. She returned her attention to her checklist. "Penelope is bringing her new makeup line from High Gloss, and I have a team of makeup artists and hair stylists scheduled. The models' show sizes are confirmed, and shoes are matched with the outfits."

She ran her finger down the list. "I'd like to check the venue, and make sure the runway is stable."

"Please do," Davina said. "Once I was in a show and the runway collapsed. The models weren't injured, but there were plenty of frightened girls and nasty bruises. Not to mention dreadful reviews."

"I hope the room will be nice." Fianna knew Davina had worked with the charity on a choice of venue, but she was still nervous about it.

Davina arched a brow. "I think you'll like it."

After the maid finished her tasks to Fianna's exacting instructions, Fianna thanked her and made arrangements for her to be on call.

Fianna slipped her feet into a pair of cherry-red patent, Jimmy Choo heels, and then she and Davina stepped into a gilded elevator that whisked them to a lower floor where the show would take place.

As she opened the door to the grand ballroom, Fianna felt as though she had stepped into a jewel box. Waterford crystal chandeliers sparkled overhead, their fiery brilliance reflected in a vast array of mirrors. Mauve-tinted walls with ivory architectural mouldings created a stunning setting that Fianna thought would perfectly showcase her lyrical collection.

"This is magnificent," Fianna said, hardly believing her good fortune. "Davina, you couldn't have chosen a finer venue."

Davina's eyes twinkled. "I'm glad you like it."

The elevated runway had already been set up. Fianna tested it, striding across the platform and bouncing to make sure it held. Next, she checked the undercarriage. Finally satisfied, she pronounced it sturdy enough.

Davina watched her, nodding her approval, and jotting points on the checklist. Together they marked the runway, timing the models' revolutions. They checked the dressing room, and Davina made a note to add more tables, stools, and mirrors for the stylists and models. "It's vitally important to have a smooth flow backstage. Eliminate the chaos, or at least keep it to a minimum."

"We make a good team," Fianna said, draping an arm around her aunt.

Davina beamed at her. "What kind of music do you have planned?"

"A friend gave me some music to use for the show in Malibu. It was perfect, so I'll use it again." *Niall's music.* Fianna liked to think it was lucky. It had definitely contributed to making the show a success. She ran a hand over her collarbone, reliving his touch. Meeting him the night of her first show was something she'd never forget. She only wished he could be here for this show, too.

This was an important professional step for her. Davina had friends attending from top fashion magazines in Dublin and London. A buyer from Harrods would also be in the audience.

The charity benefited pediatric medical research, so it was well supported. While the show was an excellent opportunity for Fianna, it was also a cause she was pleased to support. She had donated her cost of travel, along with the cost of engaging makeup artists, hair stylists, and models. Penelope was contributing her time and covering her own expenses, too.

Fianna let out a sigh of relief. "Everything looks fine, Davina. We've checked and double-checked. I can't imagine anything that might go wrong."

Davina sucked in her breath. "Don't jinx it, dear."

12

THE HOTEL LOBBY lounge was crowded with a stylish crowd of young people wedged onto eggplant-colored leather banquettes, martinis and cosmopolitan cocktails in hand. The lights were low, and candlelight flickered on the tables. Overhead, chandeliers reflected the radiant glow, casting rainbow prisms on the glass table tops. Fashionable people milled about, as if waiting for a party to begin. Some looked vaguely familiar, but Fianna had been gone a long time. She couldn't place any of them.

Doyle O'Donnell sat next to Fianna and clutched her slender fingers in his beefy hand. "When I heard you were coming home, I said to myself, 'it's your lucky day, Doyle,' sure and it is. The stars aligned again for us, Fianna. We're meant to be. I'm sure of it."

Yesterday after they'd arrived, Doyle had called to see if she'd received the flowers. Fianna had thanked him for the lavish bouquet, but she also wanted to make him understand that they were only friends. He wouldn't hear of it and insisted she meet him for a cocktail today. In fact, the more she resisted, the more persistent Doyle became, as if the challenge excited him.

She could see his dark eyes flashing, and truth be told, she was glad they were in a public place.

Doyle had greeted her with a kiss, which surprised her. They had dated years ago, but as far as she was concerned, their relationship was firmly in the past.

However, Fianna wasn't getting through to Doyle. She tried again. "Doyle, I've always been fond of you as a friend, but I don't think we're meant to be anything more than that."

"We've known each other a long time, Fianna. Every couple should be so lucky to call each other friend."

Why was he doing this now? The runway show was tomorrow, the rehearsal dinner was shortly afterward, and Lizzie's wedding was that weekend. Her head was spinning, and she still had to finish her sister's dress. Worse than that, Lizzie was becoming increasingly harder to reach. She'd been vague and evasive on the phone, and Fianna thought she might be on edge of calling the wedding off. She had no idea what to do, except support Lizzie's decision, whatever it might be.

"Doyle, you're not listening to me. We haven't been a couple for a long time."

"You're not listening to me, lass. I'm talking about our future, not our past. Maybe I should try a different language."

Doyle reached into the jacket of his Savile Row suit and brought out a velvet box. "Shane and Lizzie, you and me, we'll make a grand family, we will. Imagine all the wee ones we'll have, growing up together, uniting our families. It's what our ancestors couldn't have imagined, but here we are, erasing old feuds and starting a millennium with a clean slate. Marry me, Fianna Fitzgerald." He snapped open the lid to reveal a dazzling emerald-cut diamond ring flanked with baguette diamonds. She gasped. Doyle never did anything halfway.

"Doyle, you really shouldn't have..." People at surrounding tables were now taking interest in them. A ring like that was hard to ignore, however, she had no intention of ever becoming Mrs. Doyle O'Donnell.

"Would you look at the size of that ring?" one woman said.

A man turned around. "Well, if it isn't Doyle O'Donnell, making a proposition."

Fianna wanted to sink through the floor. This was not going to go well, she just knew it. It was one thing to turn him down, but quite another to do it in front of witnesses and friends—*his* friends.

She lowered her voice. "Doyle, not here." She needed to leave. Fast.

"Let's make an announcement at the rehearsal dinner."

"No, that's not a good idea. Doyle, I can't..."

"Of course you can."

To her horror, he took the ring and slid it onto her finger.

Cheers broke out around them from people in the entryway, at neighboring tables, and at the bar. With a sinking feeling, she realized he'd set this up. He knew everyone here. He probably thought the pressure would sway her.

Fianna's skin burned with a mixture of anger and embarrassment. This was his own doing, but he'd blame her for spurning him. And right before the rehearsal and wedding. *How could he?*

She drew a breath. "Doyle, everyone knows I speak my mind." She darted a glance at his friends, many of whom she now recognized as old friends of her family, too. No doubt she'd see many of them at Lizzie's wedding. How could she be graceful about this?

"That's what I love about you, Fianna. That's why we're so good together."

She shook his forearm to get his attention. "Listen to me. While I appreciate your offer, I must decline it." There, that was as graceful as she could be. She tugged the ring off and handed it back to him.

The gathering crowd booed with dismay, and it was Doyle's turn to flush beet red. "What's the matter with you?" he sputtered, his eyes darkening under drawn eyebrows.

She stood up, anxious to make a break for it. "Sorry, Doyle. I don't doubt you'll soon find someone who loves you." She paused. "I'll make my own way to the rehearsal dinner."

A woman's voice rang out. "Why, you ungrateful bitch." From the direction of the bar, a plump young woman with mousy brown hair wearing a tweed jacket and skirt raced toward them, her sensible low-heeled Ferragamo shoes clicking on the hardwood floor.

Must be Brona. Fianna ignored the woman and strode toward the exit, though it was all she could do to keep from sprinting though the crowd. Clearly Doyle had thought they were going to have celebration party. *What's wrong with this guy?*

A chill coursed through her. Something told her this wasn't over.

Niall made his way through the crowd at the international arrivals terminal at the Dublin airport. He wore a vintage Hawaiian shirt and sunglasses, and his sun-streaked hair brushed his upper shoulders. He kept his head down and no one recognized him, though the government agent who checked his passport couldn't help but jerk his head up in surprise.

Niall lowered his sunglasses. "Yeah, it's me." He grinned, and the agent waved him through. "Welcome home, Mr. Finley."

Home. Niall hadn't been back in ages. He climbed into the back of a black limousine.

Kaitlin slid in after him. "Thanks for meeting us, Jimmy." Her white linen jacket and slim skirt looked good with her newly acquired bronze tan.

"Shall I head for Finley castle?"

"Sure, Jimmy, we've got a bit of jet lag to shake." Niall rested his head against the black leather seat. The limousine was a little ostentatious, but if he stood in a taxi line, he'd be mobbed in no time.

Though he appreciated his fans, it could be overwhelming: autographs, photos, people insisting he join them for a pint, women writing their phone numbers on his arm, leaving lipstick kisses on his face and neck. Some of his old band members thrived on the attention and found a different woman every night, but he'd never desired that kind of attention like some rock stars. All the money in the world couldn't buy what he often craved: Anonymity.

When they were on tour, he preferred to stay in the hotel room, strum his old guitar, and dream up new songs. When he was home, he liked to jam with a few friends at home, or on a beach.

Like Eli.

Niall drew a hand over his mouth. For the life of him, he couldn't figure out how such a large man had disappeared so quickly. He expelled a breath.

"What's wrong?" Kaitlin asked, snapping her seatbelt.

"I was thinking about Eli."

"It was so strange that I couldn't find anyone who knew him. Not on the beach, not in town."

Niall buckled up, too. He'd really wanted to see Eli again, have him to the house for supper, and share their love of music. But he'd vanished like the morning dew.

Or he'd never existed in the first place. "We didn't imagine him, did we?"

"I don't see how. Neither of us had a drop of alcohol.

No Mai Tai, no Blue Hawaii, not even wine."

They'd tried to follow Eli, but he hadn't even left footprints in the sand. Niall glanced at his sister. That's what had really spooked Kaitlin.

As for him, he wondered how Eli knew Laila's name. Maybe he'd met her on a previous visit. Everyone who'd met Laila had remembered her.

Who was he kidding? *No footprints.*

Jimmy pulled away from the curb and Kaitlin shifted in her seat. "If the man didn't exist, then what did we experience?"

Niall stroked the stubble on his jaw, thinking. He'd been through counseling for grief, and was well acquainted with the cycles: denial, anger, bargaining, depression, and eventually, acceptance. He'd been through them all. But he still couldn't explain why a beautiful, full-of-life woman was here one moment, and gone the next. Life wasn't fair. Intellectually, he knew that, he accepted that, but his heart still ached. "There are a lot of things I can't explain, Kaitlin."

"Like what?"

He didn't want to tell her about his conversations with Laila, because he knew it sounded crazy, even though his wife hadn't returned after Eli left. Had he fabricated Laila in his mind, or was there really a connection? Instead, he said, "Sometimes I wonder where creativity and imagination comes from. How does this wellspring within us work? Why does it ebb and flow?"

Kaitlin touched his shoulder. "I've thought about that,

too."

"You have?"

Kaitlin's cheeks reddened. "At the *hana*, sometimes I actually imagined Laila was still present. I'd turn around to say something to her, and then realize she wasn't there. I can't explain the sensation. Even so, I'm glad you decided not to sell that house. It's such an amazing place."

Niall squeezed Kaitlin's hand. "And I'm glad you're coming back to the castle with me." They had grown up in nearby Dublin, where his parents still lived. Niall had bought the castle after the owner died and had no family left to take it on. He'd built a recording studio there, and he and Laila had hosted music debuts for Finley Green and other musicians.

"Until the next job takes me away," she said. "So have you decided which songs you're going to play at your friend's wedding?"

"He has a couple of requests, and I have some new ones I'm working on that I think they'll like." This was the new music that Fianna had inspired. He wished he'd been able to see her again before he left Los Angeles. As it stood, he didn't know when he'd return. He didn't have any pending business there. Or anywhere, for that matter. "Maybe it was time I put out a new collection."

"Are you going to contact your old music label?"

"No, I think I'll do something different this time. I could form an indie label, and distribute it digitally online."

"You could. You're completely set up at the castle. You

could call it Castle Green Music, or something like that."

"That's a good name." Niall lifted his gaze to the ceiling, imagining the possibilities. Returning to work on his terms would give him deep satisfaction. Not everyone liked his music, but he knew it brought joy to many. "I could arrange a few intimate performances. No giant tour, though. Small salons, nightclubs. In Dublin, New York... Los Angeles."

Delight spread across Kaitlin's face. "That's a grand idea. Maybe you could see Fianna again in L.A."

The driver wound into Howth Head, an old fishing village outpost on the eastern side of Dublin, where Niall could rise with the sun shimmering on the bay every morning. *Howth, rhymes with booth,* he always told visitors from overseas. Lately, a number of other musicians had moved into the area because of the privacy. Niall welcomed them into the studio over pints of Guinness ale and glasses of wine. He loved hearing his friends create new music, though he hadn't joined in for several years. Now, that would change. He was itching to return to the studio.

The Howth Lighthouse stood at the northern tip, and the Baily Lighthouse stood at the southernmost point. They drove past the market and the ruins of St Mary's Abbey, and turned into the grounds of the gray stone castle that had been built in the 1700s. The original structure had been built six hundred years ago, but it had been rebuilt after having been destroyed by a fire.

The grounds were a carpet of emerald green, and migratory birds took up interim residence on the surrounding ponds. The ocean lapped the shore at one end of the property, and from the third floor, Niall could see all of Howth Head.

After Laila died, he'd spent time working on some of the renovations they'd planned, but the old structure still needed work. He had a small staff to watch over it, and they provided company, too.

Jimmy pulled the car near the front and cut the engine. "No worries, Jimmy, I've got the luggage," Niall said. He and Kaitlin didn't have much. He'd shipped a few personal belongings from the Malibu house back, and he had a small suitcase. The advantage to having several residences was that he seldom had to pack clothes or toiletries, and consequently he could speed through the airports. Traveling was even easier when he flew private planes, but he wasn't traveling as much as he had when he'd been performing with the group.

Commercial flights were fine with him now, and he often met interesting people onboard. Most of the older people in first class had no idea who he was. The first class flight attendants were accustomed to having celebrities in their section, so they hardly took notice of him.

They climbed the semi-circular stone steps that led to the front door, which was a welcoming shade of carnelian red. Three stories above them, turrets spiked the cloudy sky.

The castle had come with all the original furniture, paintings, books, china, and silverware intact. It was rare to find a castle so well preserved with its original contents, and Niall felt it was his duty to maintain the integrity of the collection. He'd added his own mark in some rooms, such as the master bedroom, the studio, and one of the salons, decorating them with vivid, striking paintings from talented young Irish artists.

They walked through a gallery lined with John Carver and James Barry landscapes, John Lavery's romantic portraits, and Susanna Drury watercolors. Sarah Purser's large stained-glass window at the end of the gallery was breathtakingly brilliant. The only piece he'd parted with was a Francis Bacon portrait that he'd donated to the museum so that everyone could enjoy it.

When he wasn't in residence, he allowed visitors to the gallery and salons so that others could enjoy the incredible works of art, too. Everyone was welcome, and if they could afford a donation, the funds collected went to a local school for musical instruments for kids who couldn't afford them.

They passed the formal dining room, which was a jewel box of hunter green with white architectural mouldings and an ornate ceiling, from which hung fine Waterford crystal chandeliers. A long mahogany table and chairs graced the room. He and Laila often had their family and friends join them here for holidays. Niall appreciated the craftsmanship and liked preserving history.

"I can't wait to fall into a warm bubble bath in that giant claw foot tub," Kaitlin said. "I'll call our parents to let them know we're home."

"I'll pop into the studio," Niall said. "There's something I want to work on." For the first time since Laila had died, he planned to record some new songs.

"Can't wait to hear it." Kaitlin raced up the carpeted stone staircase, easily taking the steps two at a time.

Niall dropped his bag at the foot of the stairs and went the other way, descending into the basement level where he'd built the recording studio. It was perfectly soundproofed. He'd also built a kitchen and pub-like tavern room for his friends. A grand, carved stone fireplace anchored the room, while dark red leather chairs on flagged stone floors created a relaxing vibe that everyone enjoyed.

Niall opened a guitar case and lifted out his favorite guitar. He plucked the strings. It had been so long since he'd played it was out of tune. He'd need new strings, but he tuned it by ear. Once he was satisfied, he played a song that had been running through his mind. "Fianna's Song" is what he'd decided to call it.

He was seldom happier than when he was creating and playing. He'd forgotten how satisfying it was. The self-styled music critics could be brutal, but most of them couldn't carry a tune anyway, so he'd learned to ignore them. Though it still hurt him that people could be so crass and cavalier when his music didn't suit their taste anyway. He played the music that welled up in his soul. He knew it gave plenty of people joy. Those were the people he played for.

He flicked the record switch and strummed the opening chords, adding his deep gravelly voice to the music. After the acoustical guitar segment, he turned to the keyboard and ran his fingers over the keys. He'd work on that tomorrow, he decided, as his stomach growled. He always lost track of time on travel days. He closed the studio and climbed the stairs to find Kaitlin.

He rapped on the door to the bedroom suite she'd claimed as her own. "Hey sis, if you're not submerged, want to cycle over to the tavern? I'm feeling a little peckish, and I could use some good pub food."

Kaitlin opened the door, and the scent of lemon verbena wafted out. "Great idea. I'm starving."

As they tromped down stairs, Niall noticed that what was distinctly absent from the house was the sense of Laila. There was no breath on his neck, no silage of jasmine perfume. He'd taken comfort for years in her lingering presence—real or imagined—but he hadn't felt her impression since leaving Hawaii. Since Eli.

He ran a hand over his hair, pushing a lock from his face. Would she ever return to him?

13

THE MORNING OF the fashion show dawned with a drenching downpour. Fianna stood at the window with a cup of hot tea watching sheets of rain sluicing across the window pane. In the sun-loving city of Los Angeles, many people wouldn't go out because of the rain, but in Ireland, rain was hardly an excuse. She doubted it would deter attendance.

A rap on the door broke her reverie, and Fianna turned the shiny brass handle. "Penelope, I'm so glad to see you," she said, throwing her arms around her dear friend. "Are you ready for this today?"

Penelope hugged her back. "It's what I do. The question is, are you?"

"Everything is set. I can't think of anything else to check."

"Then let's get ready to rock that runway." Penelope was dressed in black leggings and boots. A Louis Vuitton tote was flung over her shoulder.

"It means the world to me that you're here." Penelope had arrived after the Doyle debacle last night, and Fianna had never been so glad to see a friendly face. Along with Davina, the three of them had a light dinner and retired early to be well rested for the big show.

"I support my friends, and this is an important day for you," Penelope said. "I just passed the *Vogue* editor in the hallway, and she seemed excited." Penelope told her that she had sat next to the woman on the plane, who'd told her she was coming to attend Fianna's show. "Between the media coverage on the Malibu charity show, the *Los Angeles Times* piece, and the Emmy Awards, you're becoming hot, hot, hot. Are you nervous yet?"

"I haven't *stopped* being nervous," Fianna replied, laughing. "But I've learned to hide it." She pressed a hand against her racing heart. It was finally her turn. She'd been studying and working for ten years and dreaming about this day since she was a little girl. Her first fashion show in Ireland, attended by international fashion editors and media—she'd finally hit the professional jackpot.

She could hardly imagine what might happen next. Before she'd left, Fianna had placed a call to the Neiman Marcus buyer that Camille had shared with her, and she'd actually received an appointment for when she returned. Back in Los Angeles, Scarlett was standing by, ready to field calls and work on whatever licensing or retail offers that might come in.

"Right before I left, Dahlia gave me something for you," Penelope said. "She said to give it to you before the show for good luck." Penelope fished a small package from her bag.

Fianna opened the padded envelope and withdrew two

plain perfume sample bottles. Each one had a label with a name and version number written on it by hand. Fianna turned them around.

"Runway and Catwalk," she read, smiling with delight. It was common practice for perfumers to assign working names to samples. She slipped the caps off and sprayed them into the air. "There's a note, too." She slipped it out. "These are our first ideas for a new Fianna Fitzgerald line." Fianna could hardly believe it. She let out a little squeal. She couldn't wait to talk to Dahlia and thank Camille.

"Congratulations! It's all coming together, isn't it?" Penelope pointed to the bottle marked Runway. "I like that one best."

"So do I." Fianna sniffed the air. "It's whimsical; it smells like orange blossoms and seashores." *And Hawaii*, she thought, with another pang over Niall. She spritzed some on her wrist and neck, and Penelope held her wrists out, too.

"For luck," Penelope said with a wink. "Have you triple-checked everything at the venue?"

"Everything I could think of. I went there early and tested the lights, music, and runway again. The clothes, shoes, and accessories are organized. All the models have checked in, so we're ready to go." She'd been over every detail, and Davina had been with her to manage the checklist and make sure nothing was overlooked.

Davina emerged from the bedroom, looking elegant in one of Fianna's slim, plum-colored cocktail suits. She wore an elaborate Philip Treacy hat, which she'd worn to the wedding of Prince William and Kate Middleton. Flowers and netting topped an angled crown and brim that framed her face. It paired beautifully with Fianna's design. Treacy often coordinated with designers, and Fianna hoped to meet him someday.

"Davina, you look magnificent," Fianna said. "You should be walking the runway. That plum color is gorgeous on you."

"I've had my turn," Davina said.

Fianna clasped hands with Davina and Penelope. "Are we ready to go?"

When they arrived, Penelope went backstage, Davina found the fashion editors, and Fianna paused for a moment to take it all in.

The buzz of conversation, the tinkle of laughter, the flash of jewels—Fianna stood to one side of the hotel ballroom enjoying the moment she would surely remember for a long time to come. This was the show she'd been waiting for.

She fixed the scene in her mind. The ladies, the hats, the sumptuous venue. The media seated at prime tables to cover the show.

Fifty round tables covered in pink tablecloths seated ten guests at each one. This luncheon was the highlight of the season, and funds raised would benefit pediatric research. Every year a top fashion designer was brought in to show their spring collection. Davina had put forth Fianna, and the committee approved her because she had a Hollywood connection, having recently dressed stars for the Emmy,

Academy, and Grammy award shows.

The opportunity to dress celebrities for these events came about because Fianna was friends with several high profile stylists. Their famous patrons often relied on their personal stylist to find lesser known designers, so they wouldn't be compared to another star wearing the same outfit a week later. Many stars borrowed clothes for the events, and then there were those who had modeling contracts with fashion houses, such as Chanel, Dior, or Saint Laurent, and had clothing provided to them.

The publicity was fabulous, but Fianna still had to make sales. Usually celebrities were happy to mention Fianna's name on the red carpet, but some, like Fleur, treated Fianna's boutique like their personal closet and rarely acknowledged her. Those relationships didn't last long.

Today Fianna wore one of her own designs, a butterscotch yellow silk dress with an asymmetrical neckline and hem. She wore mid-height heels so she'd be comfortable on her feet backstage. The hair stylist had arrived early to style her hair. To keep Fianna's hair out of the way while she worked, the woman had swept her hair from her forehead with a thick braid and left curls cascading past her shoulders.

Fianna pressed her hands together, and made her way to Davina.

"Fianna, I'd like you to meet some of my long-time friends," Davina said, introducing her to the fashion editors of *Vogue*, *Women's Wear Daily*, and *Harper's Bazaar*, as well as the buyer for Harrods in London. The attendance by media was even better than Fianna could have hoped for.

A photographer she'd hired for the event snapped photos while she spoke with the group.

The buyer from Harrods asked, "What's your point of view for this collection?"

"Modern luxury with an emphasis on casual elegance. Luxury is inherent in the materials and finishing employed," Fianna replied. She fielded other questions about plans for her next collection, where her line was sold, and which celebrities had worn her designs.

After excusing herself, Fianna hurried backstage. Makeup artists were busy with models contouring and applying false eyelashes for dramatic effect, while manicurists were dabbing on color. The hair stylists were giving the models sumptuous, flowing hair styles, and one was adding a hair piece to Penelope's cropped auburn hair. Some were working simultaneously on the models.

"We're looking good, ladies," Fianna said, clapping. She switched on music backstage to put everyone in the mood. It was Niall's music, and as soon as she heard his voice, her heartstrings cracked. She'd give anything to have him here, but he was thousands of miles away in Hawaii. Which, she had to admit, sounded awfully enticing.

A seamstress was making last minute adjustments, while other models were listening to music, taking photos, texting, or playing solitaire and waiting their turn at the makeup station. Others lounged in dressing robes, or grazed at the refreshment table, which was loaded with fruit, yogurt, and vegetables, and plenty of coffee, tea, and bottled water. The scene might appear chaotic to the uninitiated, but to Fianna's eye, everything was under control.

Fianna had made photo boards for each outfit, just to make sure that the models didn't grab the wrong pair of shoes with an outfit. She also had a board of all the models with their names. The show would go fast, and there was no time for mistakes.

The models began to change into their first outfits, and Fianna checked every article of clothing, making minor adjustments as needed.

Fianna peeked out across the audience. She spied André Leon Talley, a legend of the fashion industry, towering above the crowd. At the table next to Davina she saw her sisters, Lizzie and Emily, and her mother and father. This was the first time they would really see the breadth of her work, and she was glad they were here. She caught a glimpse of Doyle with the woman in tweed from the bar in the back, and briefly wondered why he'd come. A moment later the lights were lowered, and the announcements began.

She turned back, and saw Penelope perched on a stool near the exit. "Penelope, I'd like you to lead off again."

"I'm ready, boss." Penelope swayed to the music. She was already in her Zen mood—cool and calm, unaffected by the commotion around her. She had a look that was both unique and chameleon-like; furthermore, she could always be counted on, which was why she was in such demand.

After the speeches concluded, the lights were lowered

again, and Niall's music blared across the ballroom.

It was time.

Other models had taken their places behind Penelope. Everyone's adrenaline was surging. Some of the long-legged beauties jiggled a leg, while others tapped a shoe, or snapped their fingers.

Fianna drew a breath and waited for a beat in the music. "And...go," she said to Penelope, who stepped out into the spotlights, attitude in place, and pranced across the runway.

"Next," Fianna said. A floor manager sent the models out in measured paces.

The first round of applause filled the air, and Fianna breathed a sigh of relief. She saw the editors and buyers nodding and making notes.

One after another the models went out, and the applause grew. Fianna felt the show take on a life of its own as the returning models hurried to change into the next outfits. They were thrilled with the response they were getting from the crowd.

"Okay, next segment," Fianna said, and a new group of models stepped up in line. Everything was going according to plan. It was absolute perfection.

An elegant model from London stepped out and glided down the runway. Fianna was watching, pleased with her performance.

Then the model turned, and in a flash, Fianna saw her stumble. A gasp of concern rippled across the room. Fianna's heart nearly stopped, but she knew this model was a pro, and she'd recover. It wasn't the worst thing that could happen. Models often tripped, or even fell, but they'd pick themselves up and the show would go on.

The model regained her balance and took another step, and then… it happened again. This time she fell to her knees, and Fianna saw the heel separate from the shank of the shoe. The model calmly picked up the shoe and the heel. She walked on with a shoe on one foot, tiptoeing on the other. The crowd applauded her cool and bravery.

But the applause was short-lived. Another model went down and fell into the willowy woman who was passing her on a turn. Both tumbled onto the runway. A third model approaching them also stumbled, and Fianna could see that her shoe seemed to have malfunctioned, too.

"It's the shoes," she said, her heart racing. "Check the shoes, all of them, right now!"

As she was speaking, another model fell and slid off the runway. Several men leapt up to help her.

Fianna was mortified. "Someone find a doctor." She feared the model might have been injured, and she wanted to get help right away.

A model limped backstage, cursing under her breath. "These damn shoes. My ankle is toast, I can't walk."

"Fianna, the shoes have been tampered with." Her assistant held up a mangled shoe. The heel was separated from the main body of the shoes and rigged with a small piece of tape and a tack. It was clearly designed to give way under force of walking.

"Inspect all the shoes. Don't wear any that haven't already been worn." She stopped the next model poised to go out. "Take those off. Here, put these on instead."

Fianna turned to her assistant. "This is serious. Put in a call to the police. Someone has intentionally tried to cause these models harm."

Another model returned backstage barefoot, holding a broken shoe. "What's happened? We're all going down out there. It's a disaster."

Fianna ran a hand over her face. She felt like crying or screaming, but she couldn't do either one. She had to put the show back on track and do it fast. "We've been sabotaged. But we have some shoes that are okay. Find the shoes from the first segment and check them."

Her floor manager stood next to her. "Fianna, we're short three models now. Should we cut some outfits?"

"No. I'll help."

Fianna whirled around. "Davina, am I glad to see you."

Her aunt was already removing her hat and clothes. "Give me something spectacular to wear. André Leon Talley is out there, and I want to knock off his fancy socks. Let's get this show back on."

Fianna could have kissed Davina, but instead she snatched a diaphanous, plum-colored dress that was sure to garner applause. And Davina was making a comeback. The crowd would go wild. "Put this on," she said.

"My own shoes will go with this," Davina said, shimmying into the dress. "Close me up, there's no time to waste." A hair stylist hovered with a brush and hairspray, while a makeup artist hurried to refresh Davina's lipstick and blush.

Penelope rushed into place behind Davina. "I'll follow her in case anything happens."

"Okay, on the beat," Fianna said to Davina.

Her aunt raised her chin, tossed her hair back, and straightened her frame.

"Now go."

Davina stepped onto the runway, stopped, and raised her arms, commanding attention. The diaphanous sleeves and gown undulated around her. Spotlights danced on the iridescent fabric and her platinum hair.

The noisy chatter that had been rolling across the ballroom in waves died. A silence fell across the room.

The announcer said, "Today we give you the one and only Davina, returning to the runway for the first time since her retirement. She is here for her niece, Fianna Fitzgerald."

Cheers rose and applause thundered through the room. Davina milked it for a moment, and then she began her famous prance down the runway. Photographers snapped wildly as their digital cameras whirred hundreds of shots.

Tall and confident, Davina strode to the end of the runway, paused, executed her turns, and started back.

Fianna had never thought she could love her aunt more than she already did, but at that moment she was overcome with adoration for Davina. Her aunt had put aside her desires to come to Fianna's aid. Her eyes welled as she watched

Davina. She hadn't seen her aunt on the runway in years. Davina was as marvelous as she'd always been.

"You were smashing," Fianna said when Davina arrived backstage.

"Looked like you needed a miracle, sweetie. We'll talk later. We have a show to finish now." She hurried to change into another outfit.

Penelope was carrying on the enthusiasm, and Fianna readied the next model. "Go, be confident and shine."

The rest of the show was a blur to Fianna, as model after model walked the runway without incident. Penelope, and then Davina, wore the last two magnificent outfits, the stars of the show.

All the models returned to the runway for a final walk. At the end of it, the applause rose, and Fianna knew that was her queue. She stepped onto the stage, blew kisses, and pressed her hands together in appreciation to the models and the audience.

Davina took one hand and Penelope the other, and then the three women raised their clasped hands in victory to the audience. They'd suffered a major catastrophe, but had rallied together to overcome it. Some media would undoubtedly publish photos of the models who'd fallen. Fianna felt bad for those models because it hadn't been their fault.

But who *was* responsible?

14

AS SOON AS she woke, Fianna slipped into her robe and picked up the newspaper outside the hotel suite door. Utterly exhausted from the stress of the fashion show and the ensuing calamity, she'd slept late.

Before she read the news, she made a call to check on the model who'd been injured. The young girl sounded good, but Fianna knew she'd be out of commission for quite a while to heal from a broken ankle.

She sank onto the sofa and curled her legs under her, mentally steeling herself for the reviews of yesterday's show. She opened the newspaper. There on an inside cover was a photo of her runway show with models stumbling and falling. The headline read: *Fianna Fitzgerald Struggles*. She went on to read a blow-by-blow account of the disaster. The anguish she'd felt yesterday returned with full force.

She pressed a hand to her head. She turned on her laptop to check other news outlets online, which she immediately regretted. One headline screamed: *The Fitzgerald Flop*. Fianna winced; that sounded like a bad dance routine from the 1920s.

Fianna clicked another link. Evidently she had already been fodder for late night talk shows, with Conan O'Brien staging a stumble as he walked out. Jimmy Fallon had guest models who tried to teach him how to walk in high heels, and then they re-enacted her runway show. She'd never been so embarrassed. This was far, far worse than she could've imagined.

She corralled her nerves and kept reading: *The Crash of the Giraffes* read another headline. A knot tightened in her gut.

Davina Rescues Fashion Show. That wasn't so bad. At least Davina received good press.

Unable to stomach any more, she flicked off her computer and checked her phone. She listened to several messages from tabloid reporters who wanted comments about the debacle. *Who might've done it? Was this in retaliation for something she'd done? Did she have a jealous husband, or an angry ex-employee? Might it have been a sort of fashion terrorist?* Fianna pressed her fingers to her throbbing temple. *Delete, delete, delete.*

The last one was from the Neiman Marcus buyer canceling their appointment.

Davina swept into the living room, dressed in a blue satin dressing gown that matched her eyes. "I can see from your face that you've seen the news. How bad is it?"

Fianna blinked back hot tears. *It's just business,* she told herself. But it was *her* business, *her baby* that she'd given everything she had to. "The reviews are awful. People are calling it the Fitzgerald Flop." She swallowed against a hard lump in her throat. "But I'm more concerned about the injured models."

After the show, the police had arrived and questioned everyone backstage who had access to the shoes. The model who had fallen from the stage had broken an ankle, and Fianna had immediately arranged for her to be transported to the hospital for care.

The police confiscated the shoes as evidence—the Manolo Blahniks, the Jimmy Choos, the Pradas—and promised to look into the matter, but Fianna understood they had more pressing issues than malicious acts at a fashion show. Nevertheless, someone had tampered with the shoes and intended to cause harm. A six-foot tall model falling from a six-inch heel on a raised runway was a formula for disaster.

The model who'd fallen from the platform was fortunate she hadn't been more seriously hurt. *What if she'd hit her head?* The fall might've killed her. As it was, the poor young girl had a compound fracture. She wouldn't be able to work for some time, possibly a year. After all, a model's job required the ability to strut with purpose in five or six-inch heels.

A tray of tea, yogurt, and fruit was delivered to the door. "I ordered breakfast. Figured you'd need a strong cup of tea as soon as you got out of bed." Davina poured milk and tea into a china cup and handed it to Fianna. She settled on the sofa next to her. "About that model who slipped from the runway—you'll probably hear from her attorney. She's sure to suffer lost wages."

"Undoubtedly." Fianna had no idea how much that would be, but it was sure to be quite a bit. "I was awake half the night thinking about her. I feel awful about it, and I'm furious with whoever did this. They clearly wanted to inflict as much pain on the models as they could." A mixture of emotions coursed through her—anger, worry, concern, embarrassment.

"Or on *you*. Can you think who might have wanted to sabotage your show?"

"The police asked the same question." Fianna shook her head. "Maybe a competitor, but I can't imagine who." Whoever did this, she'd want punished to the full extent of the law. What they'd done was absolutely reprehensible.

"Do they have any leads?"

"None that I know of. The police collected data from security cameras in the hotel to review." She'd given a statement to police. They'd told her to stay close. An investigator would be calling to follow up. She groaned. On top of everything else, she'd have to handle a police investigation.

"Let's hope they find something."

Fianna quirked a corner of her mouth. "Your quick thinking salvaged what was left of the show. The only good review I've seen was about you." She was so grateful to Davina. The fiasco—the Fitzgerald Flop—would have been far worse if not for her aunt's rapid action. At least the audience had been concerned and appreciated efforts to salvage the show.

"I'd never planned to go back to modeling, but I have to admit I enjoyed being back on the runway." Davina cradled Fianna's face in her hands. "There's nothing I wouldn't do for you, dear. You've always been like the daughter I never had. When I saw that you—and the show—were in trouble, I didn't hesitate for an instant."

"Everyone enjoyed seeing you again." Davina had a fresh glow in her cheeks this morning, and her blue eyes were brighter than Fianna had seen in a long time. "Have you thought of having a second act to your career?"

"Not until yesterday. In this business, when you're aging in front of the camera, people can be so cruel. Once you've been away for a while, I suppose they're glad to see you again. With the aging demographics, there's actually a need for older models." Davina inclined her head. "You gave me the kick I needed—unintentionally, of course."

"Have you missed working?" Fianna couldn't imagine what she'd do with herself if she weren't pursuing her dreams, but her aunt had already done that. What would she feel like at Davina's age? Not that her aunt was old; Davina was still a stunning woman in her fifties. However, many women in the beauty industry found their careers stalled at her age.

"At first I didn't. Retiring at forty is what many people aspire to, but the truth is, I loved what I did. Besides, there's only so much traveling and volunteer work I can do." Davina shook her thick silver hair back. "As long as I'm in a class of my own, and not competing against the twenty-year-old girls, then I'd like to work again."

Fianna rubbed her fingers along the smooth skin on Davina's hand. "Well then, as awful as the show was, I'm glad something good came out of it for you."

"For both of us, dear."

"What do you mean? The press has completely trashed the show."

"The tabloid and entertainment media, perhaps. But now, everyone knows your name."

Fianna shuddered. "I never thought I'd be known as the Fitzgerald Flop."

"Now, now," Davina said, holding up a manicured finger, "a wise publicist once told me there's *almost* no such thing as bad press." A slow smile crept onto her face. "What I haven't had a chance to tell you is that I received calls this morning from my editor friends. They thought your collection shows a lot of promise."

Fianna sat up so quickly she spilled tea on her robe. "Are they going to mention it in their magazines?"

"I wouldn't be surprised if they did. And I doubt if they'll use the unfortunate shots the tabloids chose, so you shouldn't worry about that. They have a different audience. Their readers want to know about the clothes. In fact, they could spin the story to your advantage."

"I can't imagine that." Fianna ran a hand across her forehead. How could they possibly find a positive side to such a travesty?

Davina patted Fianna's hand. "Let me deal with them."

Aside from the disaster, Fianna still had to focus on business, which was the main reason she'd agreed to do the show. "Have you heard from any of the buyers who were present?"

"Unfortunately, no."

"One step at a time, I suppose. I'll follow up with them soon." Publicity was welcome, but what Fianna really needed was sales. She chewed her lip as she thought of how much this had cost her. She'd drained her savings to put on a first-class show, hoping to gain retail orders and expand distribution, which would in turn drive licensing opportunities. This had been a monumental gamble for her. And now she was on the losing end. Her head throbbed at the thought.

Davina rose regally from the sofa and started for her bedroom. "I plan to have a swim and massage before the rehearsal dinner tonight. I'm booking a massage for you, too, and I won't take no for an answer."

"You'll not hear that from me." Fianna rotated her aching neck. She also had to work on Lizzie's dress to have it ready for the final fitting she'd promised her sister today.

Would Lizzie actually go through with the wedding?

Fianna gathered her violet pashmina shawl around her against the evening chill and gazed at the stately home before her, silhouetted against the clear night sky. The rehearsal dinner was being held at Shane O'Donnell's family home. She had Lizzie's wedding dress covered in a protective plastic bag flung over her arm. She'd finished it just in time before leaving the hotel.

The O'Donnell House, as it was known, was surrounded by a thicket of trees and set on a high promontory overlooking the ocean. A golfing club was located nearby, where the O'Donnell's were members. They were quite well to do, though Gerald O'Donnell's eldest brother had inherited the majority of the vast wealth and land holdings of their father and his ancestors.

Therefore, Shane's cousin Doyle stood to inherit one of the largest fortunes in Ireland—a fact that didn't escape Mary Margaret Fitzgerald.

"Fianna, must you wear those high heels? Goodness, you'll tower over Doyle." Her mother walked beside her, reciting a litany of instructions.

"I don't want to discuss this, Mam." As if the embarrassment from the fashion show disaster wasn't enough, she also had to face Doyle and his friends this evening. She'd give anything for an escape hatch right now. If Lizzie disappeared, she was definitely going with her.

"The entire county knows you rebuffed him, but I know there's still hope." Mary Margaret gave a sharp nod. If nothing else, she had faith in Fianna's ability to land Doyle O'Donnell.

Fianna stopped on the stone path, letting the rest of the family walk on without them. "I've told you I have absolutely no interest in Doyle. We are *not* getting married."

"You should reconsider. A woman has to look out for

her future. As your mother, I must guide you in these matters." Mary Margaret pressed a hand to her chest and took a series of short, sharp breaths.

At first Fianna thought her mother was merely acting, but then she saw the gray pallor in her face. "Mam, are you all right?"

Her mother turned her face from her. "I'll be fine, I'm sure."

Something in her mother's voice registered an alarm.

Ahead of them Davina turned around. She hurried back to them and touched her sister's arm. "Mary Margaret, do you need to sit down?"

Fianna took her mother's other arm. She and Davina guided her mother to a bench on the lawn.

"I don't know what came over me. Give me a moment."

Fianna shot a glance at Davina. "This is not about Doyle or Lizzie. Which one of you is going to tell me what's going on?"

Davina rested her hand on her sister's shoulder and spoke softly. "Do you have something you want to say to your daughter?"

Mary Margaret raised watery eyes to her. "Why don't you tell her while I catch my breath?"

Fianna's heart raced as Davina pressed her lips together. "Your mother has been recently diagnosed with hypertension. Her doctor is trying to get her blood pressure under control with a new medication, as well as dietary and exercise changes. She's scheduled to see a cardiologist for more tests after the wedding. But right now, stress is a large issue she must learn to manage."

"Oh, Mam, I thought there was something wrong. I wish you'd told me sooner." Fianna was crushed with a combination of concern for her mother and guilt over the way she'd spoken to her. "I'm so sorry for what I've said. Why, the strain you've been under…" She shook her head, feeling ashamed of her part in the arguments they'd had.

"I'm sorry, too, my dear. I've meant well, really, but I guess I've said harsh things to you, and I regret it. It's just hard to control my feelings." Mary Margaret began to weep. "I've always been the sturdy one in the family, able to take care of everything and everyone. Now look at me, falling apart."

"You *have* taken care of us, and it hasn't gone unnoticed." The stress of the wedding couldn't be good for her mother.

Her mother went on, catching her breath between soft sobs. "But now, I realize I won't live forever. All I want is to see my girls settled. Emily has her family, and I'm sure they'll get back on their feet someday. Lizzie and Shane are soon married, but I'm so terribly worried about you, Fianna. Have I let you down?"

Davina slid her arm around Mary Margaret. "Shh, that's enough worry for you. Fianna's a smart one, she is. No need to worry."

Fianna blinked, and as she did, tears spilled from her eyes. She brushed them away with an unsteady hand. Never had she imagined that her capable mother would have issues such as this. Not yet, anyway. Not until they'd made their peace. Fianna took her mother's hand and stroked it. She was still far too young.

"I know you want what you think is best for me, Mam. But I'm happy with my choices, and I won't settle for a husband like Doyle who'd try to squash me under his thumb. I don't love him, and I wouldn't be able to keep from telling him exactly what I thought of him."

Mary Margaret laughed softly through her tears. "You've always been my outspoken, headstrong girl, you have."

Fianna wrapped her arms around her mother, and Davina did the same. The three women comforted each other. Mary Margaret sniffed. "I tried to be strong for you, and for everyone in my family."

"You were, but it's our turn now," Fianna said. "You taught us well."

"I want you to know how proud I was of you yesterday. What a show that was—without the disaster, of course. And your designs! Why, they're stunning. I never dreamed you were so talented."

"Thanks, Mam," Fianna said, her words catching in her throat. Her mother's words touched Fianna deeply. She realized she'd been yearning for her mother's approval all her life. Fresh tears sprang to her eyes as she listened.

Mary Margaret caught her breath and went on. "I hate to admit it, but for years I've been envious of the bond that you and Davina have with regard to fashion. I could never understand it. I thought fashion was frivolous, and yet, you've both made a living from it. Fianna, I saw how good women feel when they wear your clothes." Mary Margaret drew her hand across her daughter's damp cheek.

"That's exactly what I want for them, to make them feel good about themselves and to give them confidence and creative expression." Several women at the show had worn Fianna's earlier designs. She'd been surprised to see that in Ireland.

"And Davina, how happy people were to see you on the runway again. People love to see you wear beautiful clothes. I think it gives them something of beauty to dream about. I could see it in their faces at lunch. For women our age, especially. You're their champion."

Davina rummaged in her vintage Dior handbag and withdrew a packet of tissues and passed it around. "I thought we might need these tonight. I just didn't know we'd need them before we reached the house."

"I'll stay and go with you to the doctor, Mam." Fianna thought about her friend Verena, who'd lost both her parents in an accident. Fortunately, Verena still had her grandmother, Mia. And then there was Scarlett, whose father had passed away. She thought of Niall, whose wife had died so suddenly. She closed her eyes, wishing that she'd seen him when he came to visit her at her shop.

This was the first time she'd had to face a parent's mortality, and it scared her. Fianna prayed her mother would be all right, but she now understood that life held no promises. It could be sliced short at any moment. Fianna was no longer a rebellious teenager; it was imperative that she make peace with her mother, especially because she lived so far away.

"Promise me one thing, then," Mary Margaret said, dabbing her eyes.

"What's that, Mam?"

Her mother managed a wan smile. "That you'll forget everything I said about Doyle." She gazed up at the imposing house. "And now, let's go see if Lizzie actually made it."

15

AFTER FIANNA HAD collected herself upon hearing her mother's sad announcement about her health, she made her way into the O'Donnell House with Mary Margaret and Davina. Inside, Fianna gazed around. She'd been in the house many times over the years, but now she looked at it with a fresh designer's eye.

The large Georgian-era home had cherry red walls and dark polished wood floors over which hand-woven rugs were arranged. Flowers graced the entry and living room, and in the dining room an extended cherrywood dining room table was set with vintage Waterford crystal and china that Fianna knew had been in the family for generations. The sweet spring scent of white lilies permeated the rooms.

"Fianna!" Lizzie rushed to her side and hugged her. "I'm so relieved to see you," she whispered in her ear.

"How are you doing?" Fianna asked. Davina and Mary Margaret greeted her sister, and then were swept into the welcoming arms of family and friends. She saw Doyle across the room. He waved and smiled—a little too broadly, Fianna thought, for a man who'd just been jilted. Was her mother right? Was he not ready to give up? She sighed in exasperation.

Their families had known one another for centuries and their ties dated back to a lingering feud over horses or land or someone's wife. So many ancient stories floated around. Who knew what had really happened?

Her father and the O'Donnell clan had met in school and played sports together. They'd become friends and tried to heal the wounds of the past in the family—a task that hadn't been easy with the older generations. Lizzie and Shane were the first to join the families together. For as long as Fianna could remember, her mother had talked about what a fine match she and Doyle would make, too.

Lizzie nodded toward the staircase. "Let's go upstairs and I'll tell you about what's happened. Is that my wedding dress?"

"It is." Fianna whispered back, "Are you still planning on wearing it?"

Without a word, Lizzie clasped her hand and Fianna followed her. On their way, a plain brown-haired woman of about their age stepped in front of them.

"Hello, Lizzie."

"Hi, Brona." Lizzie turned to Fianna. "Have you two met?"

Fianna remembered the woman from bar. She'd called her a bitch. "Not by choice." She gave her a tight smile.

"Brona is Shane's cousin," Lizzie explained.

"Cousin by marriage," Brona said with words so sharp

they could've sliced through them.

"I'm sure we'll see you around later," Lizzie said.

They hurried away. Fianna whispered "She's dreadful. I hate that you have to pretend to be nice to someone like that."

Lizzie shrugged. "Comes with the territory." She pushed open a door to a guest bedroom splashed with pink cabbage rose wallpaper and decorated with an overstuffed floral headboard and chairs.

Lizzie sank onto the bed, her mint green lace dress flaring around her, and sighed. "I've been talking to Shane."

A clock next to the bed ticked loudly in the silence. Fianna placed the dress on the arm of a chair and sat beside her. They might never get around to trying on the dress she'd worked on, but Lizzie's happiness was far more important. "That's good. Do you want to tell me about it?" Better they talk now about their desires and differences, rather than after the wedding.

"Shane doesn't want all this," Lizzie said waving her hand to indicate the house.

"It's a responsibility, that's for sure. Is it what you want?"

"No! What a heavy anchor this is. Actually, I don't know what I'll want ten or twenty years from now, but I don't care about it today. We're young and we've got time before we think about settling down and having a family. I just need time, Fianna. I need to find out who I am and what I want to spend my life doing. Do you understand that?"

"Of course I do." Fianna thought about her life, and her

mother and Davina, and how the choices they'd made when they were younger had set in motion the course of their lives. "Life goes quickly. Does Shane know what he wants to do?"

"Yes, and there's the problem." Lizzie leapt to her feet and paced the room, tossing her wavy blond hair back from her face and pressing the palms of her hands against her temples.

Fianna waited for the story to unfold. She had a feeling this rehearsal dinner was going to take quite a turn.

"Shane doesn't want to follow in his father's footsteps in business. He wants to study medicine. He feels a calling to be a doctor."

"A calling is a noble thing. Would you have a problem with that?"

"The problem is *where* he wants to do it."

"Not in Ireland?"

Lizzie slowed her pacing by the window and stared into the distance. "He wants to practice in Africa, or India, or even South America—wherever doctors are needed to administer to and raise those on the lowest rungs of the world's society."

Fianna released a slow breath. "I see."

Lizzie turned back to her. "He says there are already so many children who need attention. Why should we bring more into the world?"

"I can just imagine what his parents will say to that." The O'Donnell's were a traditional family, and Shane had been groomed to take over the family business when his father retired. "What do you think, Lizzie? Is that a life you'd want to share?"

"I don't know," she whispered, twisting a tissue she'd drawn from her pocket.

"That's honest. Getting married is a life changing decision. This new information must be staggering to you."

"I had no idea Shane was thinking about like that. Med school, the travel, leaving our families. Would he ever want to have children of our own? And what would I do?"

"It would be awfully daunting. That's not just a job, it's a passion. A *calling*, to use his words. You have to decide if you can share that dream or not." What would she do in Lizzie's position? She could hardly fathom it. Falling in love was more than kisses and sex and holidays. It was the building of a life with someone and the sharing of dreams. If one partner's dreams were fulfilled, but the other one's were not, could the marriage survive? Was love *really* enough?

The thought of Niall drifted into her mind. He had a gift, a passion, a calling, too. Should she have been so quick to label him and leave him? She swallowed a lump lodged in her throat. Would the path not taken haunt her forever?

Lizzie sat beside Fianna and rested her head on her shoulder. "I followed your advice, Fianna. We had dinner and wine—okay, a lot of wine—and I asked him what secret desire for his life he harbored in his soul. But now that his dream is out in the open, it changes everything. I love Shane, and the only thing I wish for him is his happiness. He should have a right to do what he wants in his life."

"We only get one shot at it, that's for sure. But what

about you? You're my sister, and I want the same for you."

Lizzie didn't answer. In the silence, the ticking of the bedside clock grew louder, warning of the need to make a decision soon. Lizzie's gaze traveled to the dress resting on the chair. "Do I really need to try on the dress?"

"No." Fianna held her sister and rubbed her shoulder. "It's finished, and I'm sure it will fit. You're free to do whatever you want with it."

Lizzie raised her face to Fianna's. "Thank you for understanding. I don't know what I'd do without you."

Niall sat in an old wooden chair with his feet propped on a weathered table and gazed over the stone walls of the turret rooftop to the endless sea beyond. Shorebirds and hawks circled at eye level, hunting for prey. Clouds were gathering in the west and the moist air was laden with the scent of rain.

He strummed the guitar he held in his lap, working out the words to the last of his new piece. The music that had poured out of him after he'd met Fianna was some of the best he'd ever written, and he wished he could share it with her.

He'd been thinking about returning to Los Angeles to see her. He could stay at the Beverly Hills Hotel, like he used to before he and Laila had bought the house in Malibu. He liked the little village of Beverly Hills, especially the cafes and the family run shops that hadn't yet been bought out by Gucci, Chanel, or Cartier.

Not that he didn't like to pop into one of those stores

and buy a special gift for Kaitlin or his mother, but his style was more Gap than Gucci, though he remembered Gucci did have leather goods that lasted forever. He was a man who appreciated quality, especially in music. And women.

Fianna. How could a woman with crazy eyes have beguiled him so quickly? He grinned to himself. That was a good title for a funny little song for her. He thought of the song Willie Nelson had written, "Crazy". Maybe he *was* crazy for feeling what he did for her. He'd been through a lot of expensive therapy after Laila died. Was he on the rebound?

He chastised himself for not waiting at her shop the day he'd dropped by. He probably could have gotten her phone number from Johnny, through his girlfriend Scarlett.

Johnny. That's who he needed to call. But it was far too early in California to call yet.

Niall continued working on the words to the music he'd composed. He had to finish it today. His friend's wedding was the next day, and he'd promised to sing to surprise the wife. Evidently she was a long-time fan.

Niall tried a couple of new versions of the love song he was working on, but he couldn't seem to get the words quite right. What would he really like to say to Fianna someday?

Kaitlin stuck her head through the door on the turret rooftop. "I think we're going to have to cancel that bike ride this afternoon. Smells like rain is on its way."

Niall swung his legs off the table. "Then let's go to the pub for a pint. I need to take a break anyway."

16

DRESSED IN YOGA pants and a T-shirt, Fianna paced in Lizzie's room, wondering how much longer her sister would be gone. She should be back by now. The wedding was in mid-afternoon.

Emily stopped in the doorway holding her carrot-topped, two-year-old daughter, who was complaining about being carried. Her four-year-old son was tugging on her hand, whining about a toy his older brother had taken from him. "Any word from Lizzie yet?"

"Mam said she went out for a run almost two hours ago." Fianna turned a cotton scarf in her hands, twisting it in into knots, which was exactly the way her stomach felt. Had something happened to her sister? "I'm worried, Emily."

"Did she take her phone?"

"No, it's here." If Lizzie was planning to skip the wedding, she would've taken her phone. Wouldn't she?

"Maybe she just kept running," Emily said, glancing at her children. "Sometimes I'd like to do that."

"You don't mean that." Fianna took her niece from Emily and swung her in the air. The little girl started giggling, and the boy clamored to be next. "I'd better take the car and look for her. She could be injured on the side on the road with no way to call for help."

"Now you sound just like our Mam. Where is she, by the way?"

Fianna eased the little girl down, and then whisked up her nephew, who squealed with glee. "She's having a long bath. I told her not to worry. She doesn't need the stress."

Emily shot her a look. "She told you, didn't she?"

"You knew?" Fianna was a little hurt by this, but Mary Margaret and Emily had always been close. As the oldest child, Emily had been a helpmate to her mother with the younger children.

"That's why I've been taking on more of the duties around here. I know we're a burden with our little ones under foot, but Mam seems to enjoy her grandchildren. Once we're back on our feet, we'd like to move into old man Finn's cottage down the lane. He'll be moving in with his son soon. But Mam will still need help here. The manor house is too much for her to care for by herself, so our father wants to bring in a housekeeper for her."

"What will she say to that?" Mary Margaret had always been a thrifty, industrious woman who took pride in doing everything herself.

"Oh, she'll make a fuss all right, but secretly I think she'll be relieved. She'll never let on that she likes the idea." Emily peered out the second story window and frowned. "You should look for Lizzie. I'd come with you, but I have to feed and bathe the children for the wedding."

Fianna flipped the little boy onto his feet. He flung his arms around her neck and she gave him a kiss on the cheek and a playful tug on the ear. "Back to your mam now." She straightened and put her hands on her hips. "I'd better go."

Driving slowly down the lane, Fianna searched for any sign of Lizzie. She looked for a spot where her sister might be resting, a swath of broken brush, anything. *Has she been hurt?*

A thought occurred to her. Had she intentionally left her phone at the house so no one could reach her? If that was the case, then the wedding was probably off.

She wondered if she should call Shane. She didn't want to worry him unnecessarily, but if Lizzie didn't surface soon, she'd have no choice.

Fianna swept a hand across her neck. If Lizzie had decided to forgo the wedding, why didn't she tell her? Or leave a note? With that thought, Fianna pulled to the side of the road and checked her phone. But there was no text, no email, no voice mail. No calls at all.

Lizzie had disappeared.

Soon she'd made a full circle, and the manor house was up ahead. She squinted against the sun as it rose in the sky.

Where is Lizzie?

As she drove, she thought about a swimming hole nearby where she and Lizzie used to swim when they were young. She pulled over, got out of the car, and maneuvered down a steep tree lined slope.

She gripped a tree, steadying herself, searching the grassy slope. Her heart thudded in her chest. Lizzie's running shoes were sitting neatly near the water's edge.

"Lizzie!" She tore away, frantically racing down the hill. "Lizzie!

The surface of the water broke. "Fianna? What are you doing here?"

Fianna skidded to a stop near the water. "You've been gone more than two hours. Emily and I were worried. Are you okay?"

Lizzie treaded water. "I had a good run, and stopped here to cool off. The water's lovely. You should come in."

Relieved to have found her sister, Fianna sat down on the soft spring carpet of grass and rested her elbows on her knees. "So do you think you'll wear your wedding gown today?"

Lizzie arched her neck and floated on her back. She still wore her tank top and running shorts. "I always loved coming here with you. This spring so natural and beautiful just as it is. I don't need all the latest technology, or the latest fashions."

Fianna knew her sister well enough to know she was winding her way around to a point.

Lizzie fluttered her feet. "The water is so cool. I'm virtually weightless."

Fianna could feel the seconds ticking away. Birds called from a tree overhead, and the sun passed behind a whipped meringue cloud.

"Shane could be here beside me, and we could be anywhere." Lizzie lifted her head. "Do you understand what I'm saying?"

"I think so."

"The family is going to hate me for leaving, but Shane and I have decided that being together, and following our dreams together, is what will make us happy."

"So what's your dream, Lizzie?"

Her sister dove through the water, her body a rippling mirage under the surface. Moments later, she was in front Fianna, blinking water from her wide aquamarine eyes. "My dream is to *find* my dream. Isn't that what this journey of life is about?"

Lizzie had a point. Fianna nodded.

"Shane and I plan to explore the world and help as many people as we can." Lizzie brushed water from her eyes. "So how much time do we have before I have to put on that amazing dress you made for me?"

Fianna grinned. Lizzie had made her decision. "We have time for a swim." Fianna tore off her shoes and dove in after Lizzie, and the two sisters splashed and laughed like they had when they were children.

Niall turned off the main road onto the lane that led to the church. He and Kaitlin had left early, but he'd still managed to miss a couple of turns.

"You're sure this is the right way?" Kaitlin looked doubtful. She was a vision in a blush pink lace dress.

Niall tugged the collar of the gray afternoon suit he wore. "Now I am."

"I hope we're not late."

"I think we'll just make it. But weddings seldom start on time."

Kaitlin tugged her dress over her long bronzed legs. They'd both gotten a tan in Hawaii. "I can't wait to hear you perform your new songs."

Niall winked. "It's my best work in a long, long time. These are pretty special songs."

Suddenly the car emitted a grinding noise and shuddered to a stop. "No, no, no," Niall muttered.

"That can't be a good sound."

Niall tried to start the engine, but it failed to respond. He looked around, but no one else was on the road. "I've got to push it out of the way."

He shoved the gear in neutral, opened the door, and heaved his shoulder against the frame. Kaitlin jumped out to help in her heels, and together they steered the car to the shoulder of the road.

"Now what?" Kaitlin asked.

Niall pulled his phone from a pocket. "Now we call for help. We're not that far away." He punched a number and spoke to his friend, explaining what had happened. "Can you send someone to give us a lift?" They talked a little more before Niall hung up.

He turned to Kaitlin. "Help is on the way."

Fianna peered into the church. Spring hats of every pastel macaron-hue bobbed among the pews, which were filled to capacity with family and friends.

She ducked back in to the outer chamber where the bridal party was waiting. Lizzie looked so beautiful, but she was so happy she would've been radiant in a burlap bag.

"I love what you did with the dress." Lizzie ran her hands over the slim silhouette, which flared in the back beneath the hip, giving her an elegant, graceful line.

Fianna had draped antique lace of candlelight white over the bright white, softening the shade and illuminating Lizzie's fair complexion, which had a healthy glow after their swim. With a pearl choker and her blond hair brushed into soft waves, she looked a little like Princess Grace, the American actress who'd married the Prince of Monaco.

"You're a master, Fianna." Mary Margaret touched her arm.

Fianna and Davina had helped her mother and Emily coordinate their outfits. They all wore dresses in shades of delicate pink and spring green in keeping with the colors Lizzie had chosen. Fianna had brought a soft, pistachio green silk dress of her own design. She was the only one standing up for Lizzie.

The church bell tolled on the hour. The wedding was supposed to be starting now, but they hadn't received a signal from her father.

Lizzie drew her delicately penciled brows together. Davina had created a smooth, flawless makeup look for her niece that enhanced her natural glow.

"Weddings never start on time," Fianna said.

The door opened and their father stepped inside, looking handsome in a light gray afternoon suit. "Lizzie, my darling. Have you heard from Shane?"

"Not since last night. It's bad luck to talk on the day of the wedding. Why?"

Ryan Fitzgerald fidgeted with a button on his jacket. "He was here, but he seems to have gone missing. His car isn't here either. Do you know where he might have gone?"

Mary Margaret looked shocked. "Or if he's coming back?"

Lizzie lowered herself onto a chair and the color drained from her face. She closed her eyes and shook her head, unable to speak.

Fianna placed a hand on her father's shoulder. "How can I help, Dad?"

He shook his head. "We have a search party in progress. Just stay with your sister and mother. They need you now."

After her father left, Fianna knelt by Lizzie and took her sister's hands in hers. "Something might have happened. I'm sure there's an explanation."

"We'd agreed on a plan," Lizzie said softly. "We were going to tell everyone after the ceremony." Her large eyes loomed in her face, and in them Fianna saw the infinite sadness of lost love.

What could she say? Fianna was furious. She thought of all the things she'd say to him for leaving her sister at the altar.

How dare he do this to sweet Lizzie?

Five minutes passed, then ten, then twenty. Fianna paced the room while Lizzie sat with her eyes closed and her head bowed. Her mother and Davina clutched each other's hand. At forty minutes past the appointed hour, Fianna couldn't stand it any longer. She was just about to leave to find her father when he tapped on the door.

He was red-faced and out of breath. "Shane's back. The wedding is on."

"Well, the nerve of that guy!" Fianna exclaimed. "He doesn't deserve—"

"Fianna, it's okay," Lizzie said, looking relieved and serene. "He's back."

"Girls, it's time." Mary Margaret kissed Lizzie and then Fianna. The eldest brother came to collect his mother. "It's going to be a beautiful wedding after all."

Fianna hugged her sister and left Lizzie and her father.

She made her way down the aisle to the sound of organ music reverberating through the walls of the old stone church, which had stood for three hundred years on this land. The aroma of gardenias and lilies filled the sanctuary.

Fianna took her place across from Doyle, who was Shane's best man. She saw Brona sitting a couple of pews back, narrowing her eyes at her. Fianna gazed past her.

And here we are. The O'Donnell and Fitzgerald clans finally united after centuries of feuding. Fianna suppressed a smile. Their ancestors must be turning in their graves.

Shane took his place by Doyle, and Fianna shot him a

glance. She wanted to be angry with him for keeping Lizzie waiting, but he had such an expression of love on his face that her anger dissipated. She didn't know what had kept him, but it was clear he wanted nothing more than to be standing right there waiting for her sister.

Fianna blinked back tears. Her sister and her father started down the aisle. Lizzie was a vision in the gown that Fianna had redesigned. The wide neckline framed her face and shoulders, showcasing the Edwardian diamond necklace Davina had brought for her to wear. Shane beamed. Would a man ever look at her the way Shane looked at Lizzie?

She was proud of Lizzie and Shane. They'd been honest with each other and worked out their plan between them. Fianna couldn't wait to hear it.

Ryan Fitzgerald stepped aside, and Lizzie transferred her hand to Shane's.

Fianna swallowed against a lump in her throat and dabbed her eyes. Lizzie took her place, while Fianna arranged the modest antique lace and satin train she'd fashioned behind her. The organ music stopped. Fianna drew in a breath, ready for the ceremony to begin.

Instead, the sound of a soulful instrumental guitar filled the silence. Fianna's neck bristled. There was something vaguely familiar about it.

Within a few moments, a man's deep, gravelly voice accompanied the music, and Fianna's knees buckled. *How could this be?*

She craned her neck to see past the floral arrangement.

It *had* to be Niall.

Lizzie turned her glowing face up to Shane's. Fianna heard her whisper, *Niall Finley*. A murmur of recognition swept across the church.

Fianna blinked in shock. She peered around the flowers, nearly tripping in her heels as she did. It *was* Niall. Her heart thudded, and she nearly dropped the bouquet she carried. What was he doing *here*?

Shane was wreathed in smiles with the gift of this moment. Fianna quickly deduced his absence. He must have gone to fetch Niall and surprise Lizzie.

The sweet ballad wove its magical spell as Niall sang, entrancing everyone in the church. As Fianna listened, her throat tightened. It was the most beautiful love song she'd ever heard. Her eyes welled. The lyrics and music touched her deeply. She closed her eyes and listened, remembering how she and Niall had met in Malibu, the kiss in the ocean they'd shared, and how natural it had felt to wake up curled in his embrace. Her misunderstanding slid from her memory, and all she wanted was to feel his arms around her again.

Fianna snapped herself back to the present. Why was she acting like some lovelorn teenager? She hardly knew this man. Was she longing for him, or was it the thought of someone *like* him?

Her gaze traveled to Lizzie and Shane, and her heart warmed for them. Shane's eyes glistened with tears of adoration, and Lizzie was flushed with love for him. They'd been honest with each other about their deepest desires.

Either one of them could have called off the wedding, but they'd rededicated themselves to each other and were moving forward with their lives. That was love.

Her view of love was changing. It wasn't roses and wine and starry nights, although those were beautiful elements of life. No, it was sharing your deepest, most intense passions for your life experience on earth with another person. It was having their acceptance and support and doing the same for them. It was building a life together, as her parents had done, and taking care of each other when one faltered. Lizzie and Shane clearly had that.

Would she ever experience such an ideal love?

Niall's song drew her back in. He might not be the one, but if his music and lyrics were any indication of the type of man he was, then he had earned her admiration not only for his art, but also for the type of person he was. No wonder his fans adored him and clamored to hear him again. He helped them feel the ideal of love deep in their souls.

After Niall finished singing, all tension over the delay had eased in the church. Many people were already pressing a finger or handkerchief to their eyes, clearly affected by the beauty of Niall's music and the love that emanated from Lizzie and Shane, two very special people.

As Fianna listened to the ceremony, her emotion caught in her chest. She glanced in Niall's direction. He had shifted his chair, and she had a clear view of him now. She couldn't help but smile and saw his eyes light up when she did.

17

NIALL LISTENED TO the exchange of wedding vows and couldn't help but think of Laila. They'd known each other for so long, and she was his wife, his friend, his lover. He was the type of man who needed only one woman. He missed her, and knew he always would.

But something had shifted in him in Kauai. He'd felt Laila's presence there when he first arrived, but after the evening he and Kaitlin had spent with Eli, her spirit seemed to have vanished. Had she left him for good? He missed talking and singing to her, though maybe she had to continue on her journey and he on his.

Shane and Lizzie were exchanging their marriage vows. Shane was a good guy, and Lizzie was a lovely young woman, who looked stunning today in a magnificent dress of antique lace. Niall had been noticing women's fashions more since Kaitlin had started modeling.

Shane had called him and told him he wanted to do something special and meaningful as a surprise. He knew Finley Green was Lizzie's favorite group, but he'd never told her he knew Niall. Shane didn't wave his friendship with

Niall like a banner, like some people did. He was a good man, so Niall was happy to oblige.

Niall could tell Lizzie was moved. That stirred his soul, and made him feel good about what he had to contribute to the world. He was glad he'd agreed to sing, just for the appreciation in a young bride's smile.

He caught a glimpse of a willowy woman standing next to Lizzie. She wore a soft green dress that draped her superb figure and set off her flaming red hair. He peered closer. There was something familiar about the shape of her head, the elegant length of her neck, the long legs that seemed to go on forever. He felt drawn to her and leaned to one side to get a look at her face. Nearly slipping from his chair, he bobbled his acoustic guitar and gripped the neck to keep it from crashing from his lap onto the stone floor.

Composing himself, he sat back, utterly astonished at the coincidence. There was no doubt about it. *It's Fianna.* A warm sensation gathered in his chest.

She must be a friend, or relative, to Lizzie. He saw the resemblance in the angle of their cheekbones, the arch of their eyebrows, and the curve of their lips, although Lizzie was a fair blond. Family, probably sisters. What were the chances he'd see her here?

Niall clutched his guitar and scooted his chair so he could see past a floral arrangement that had blocked his view of her. As he did, her luminous mismatched eyes flicked toward him, drawn by his movement. With one slow smile from her, his exterior walls crashed down, just like the first time they'd met.

He felt compelled to know this woman better. That was all he wanted, just a chance, and it was all he could reasonably expect. From having been married, he knew it took time to know a woman to the depths of her soul, and vice versa.

Fianna was watching Shane and Lizzie. Niall suppressed a smile. She had no idea she'd inspired the love song he'd just sang.

He'd only met her once, but he had used his imagination, conjuring the woman of his dreams. As he sat here now, seeing her again in person, he wondered if any part of his fantasy was true. And yet, he detected nearly palpable waves of emotion flowing from her.

Niall shook his head to clear the velvety fog that clouded his mind with soft persuasion. At heart, he was a poet. Fianna was a real woman, not a mirage, not a spirit.

After the ceremony, Shane and Lizzie walked down the aisle amidst greetings and well wishes. Following them, Fianna slid her hand onto the arm of Shane's handsome best man. Niall watched, his heart yearning for her. He was feeling too much, too soon, but he knew that. He had to check his feelings.

Niall waited to the side while the wedding party posed for photos. After they had departed, several guests and family members made their way to the front to compliment him on his song.

"I've never heard that song," one woman said. "It was so touching. Did you write it for them?"

"I finished it just in time for their wedding." Kaitlin waved at him, and Niall motioned to her to join him. "Excuse me, my sister is here."

Kaitlin cut through the crowd surrounding him. "That was amazing," she said, giving him a hug. "Your best one yet, I think."

Niall beamed. "I'm glad you liked it."

She leaned toward him and whispered into his ear. "Can you believe Fianna Fitzgerald was the maid of honor?"

"I had no idea she'd be here. Or in Ireland, for that matter."

Kaitlin nudged him with her elbow. "Fancy that. Feel like cake?"

They followed the guests from the church, and the woman who'd complimented him on his song gave them a ride to the O'Donnell House.

As soon as Niall stepped inside the marquee, the large white tent that had been erected on the back lawn, he started looking for Fianna, though he tried not to be too obvious about it. After the receiving line was finished and Shane and Lizzie mingled with the guests, Niall tapped Shane on the shoulder. He held two small glasses of Irish whiskey. "To you and Lizzie, may you enjoy every day of your journey together."

"Thanks, Niall." Shane took a glass and clinked Niall's. He sipped the dark amber-colored whiskey. "Sure appreciate your singing to Lizzie. Even if she throws me over some day, she'll never forget that you sang to her on our wedding day."

Niall slapped him on the back. "Happy to do it, and thanks for the chauffeur service."

Shane laughed. "Everyone thought I'd skipped out on the bride."

"Speaking of your bride, I know her maid of honor."

"Do you now? Fianna is her older sister. She's a fashion designer."

"I met her in Malibu a few weeks ago. My sister Kaitlin modeled in her runway show, so I went along." He saw Fianna across the room and tried to catch her eye.

"She's a great girl. In fact, my cousin Doyle just asked her to marry him. That's him over there, walking toward Fianna."

Niall stared as disappointment surged through his veins. It was Shane's best man. He figured the two families must be close. The cozy picture unfolded for him, and he felt like an interloper. The world seemed to dim, as if the color had drained out of it. He talked with Shane a little longer, until other guests interrupted them.

He had to find Kaitlin. There was no reason for him to stay any longer. He turned to leave.

"Hello, Niall."

Niall caught his breath, dazzled by Fianna's appearance. She was even more enchanting than he'd recalled. Her eyes sparkled, her lips were full and moist, and her lightly freckled skin glowed with life. She was simply radiant.

And engaged.

"Fianna, what a surprise." He tried to conceal his shock.

Engaged.

She touched his arm, sending a quiver through him. "You sounded wonderful. That song you sang... you were humming it the night we met."

He couldn't help himself; he reached out to touch a strand of her hair, and lifted it from her ravishing face. Her glossy, burnished hair seemed to glow in his fingers. "That's the night it came to me," he said softly.

As a blaze of color rose in Fianna's cheeks, she lowered her eyes. "It was a beautiful song, like nothing I've ever heard before."

I wrote it for you, he wanted to say, but he bit back the words, too devastated to utter them. He couldn't have her, but couldn't leave her, either. His pain was palpable. *Kaitlin.* Where was she? He had to get away. But where were his manners? Fianna was staring at him. He cleared his throat. "Shane tells me congratulations are in order."

Fianna tilted her head. "Congratulations for what?"

He nodded toward Doyle. "Your engagement," he choked out. *Where was Kaitlin?*

"My *what?*" Her eyes widened and she followed his gaze. "Oh no, not Doyle. We are *not* engaged. Who told you that?"

Niall sucked fresh oxygen into his lungs and the world regained its brilliance. "The groom. He said Doyle proposed to you."

"Indeed he did, in a cocktail bar with fifty of his closest friends around." Fianna shook her head. "But that didn't change my answer. It was still no, and it's not likely to change. Besides, he has another girl chasing him." She caught Shane's eye and glared at him, but the groom was having such a good time he didn't notice.

Niall felt like bursting into song. Instead, he decided to stay longer. A server passed by with a tray of drinks.

"Champagne, or Irish whiskey?"

Fianna lifted a flute, and Niall did the same. The day had definitely turned into a cause for celebration. He raised his glass to her. "To the woman who saved my life."

She clinked his glass. "And to the man who saved mine."

Fianna rested her forearms on the table, drinking coffee and stealing glances at Niall. She was seated with her family at a large table under the marquee, and she'd felt the heat of his gaze throughout dinner.

"We have an announcement to make." Shane stood and clinked his champagne flute with a spoon, and Lizzie stood beside him at the table.

Fianna helped quiet the other family members.

Shane and Lizzie clasped hands. "We want you all to know that our plans have changed. Instead of living here, we've decided to go to university to continue our studies. We'll be moving soon."

Fianna was seated between Davina and her mother. She gripped Mary Margaret's hand, worried about how she might react to the news.

Lizzie cleared her throat. "Shane is going to medical school, and I'll study for my master's degree. We've decided to dedicate our lives to helping the underprivileged in the poorest parts of the world."

"That means going overseas," Shane added. "India, China, Africa… places like that."

A hush spread around the table. Fianna felt her mother's hand tighten in hers.

Shane's father spoke up first. "Son, let's speak about this," he said with a sharp edge in his voice. "There are better ways to provide for your wife."

Fianna's mother and father exchanged a look. Her father said, "Is this what you two really want to do?"

Lizzie's eyes glowed with happiness, and Shane hugged her to his. "Yes, it is," they said together.

"Then you have our blessing," Mary Margaret said, her voice quiet and steady. "I think you're both well suited to that type of work, but you'll be terribly missed here."

Fianna hugged her mother, relieved that Lizzie's secret was out now. It might not be what any of them would have chosen, but her parents respected the decision Lizzie and Shane had made.

The questions began to fly, and Fianna shot a grin at Lizzie. Shane's parents were still shocked and Fianna was sure the discussion would continue, but Lizzie and Shane had set the course of their lives and made their intentions known. Fianna was happy for them. Earlier, Lizzie had pulled her aside and told her how excited she was about their new path. Most important, they had come to the decision together.

After the wedding dinner, the band began playing and

Niall appeared by her side. "Care to dance? I don't often have the chance."

"I'd love to," Fianna said. She took his hand and quickly fell into rhythm with him. She thought she'd never danced with a man who had such finesse on the dance floor. His rhythm was impeccable, as if he felt the music in his bones, and she supposed he did. He swept her around the floor, and she felt herself blossom in his close embrace.

The night wore on, and they danced until the moon rose in the sky.

Though the band had left, the Fitzgerald and O'Donnell families and friends gathered at the large round tables under the tent, laughing and drinking and telling stories.

Fianna and Niall joined Lizzie and Shane at the table. She watched Niall and Shane bantering together, chuckling like old friends do.

Niall told the story of how he'd met Shane in Dublin at a pub when Shane was cutting classes at the university, and Niall was hiding from other members of the band. The two became fast friends before Niall let on what he did.

Shane cut in. "We'd known each other a month before he took his sunglasses off. I was beginning to think he had some sort of condition, or he was interminably vain."

Niall gave Shane a punch in the arm, and Shane slapped him on the back.

Doyle blurted out, "Why didn't you tell us about your famous friend, Shane?"

"I did, but you all laughed it off and accused me of

telling tall tales."

Niall laughed. "Your loss, Doyle." He winked at Fianna.

Fianna saw Doyle scowl, and felt the heat of his eyes on her. He'd been acting strange all day. He'd been overly attentive and had asked if she'd reconsidered his proposal. She moved closer to Niall.

Niall draped his arm easily across her shoulders. "More champagne?" he asked.

"I've definitely had enough." The wedding party was winding down.

Lizzie and Shane retired to a nearby country hotel, one of the most romantic in Ireland, to spend their wedding night. Niall had called a car service to take him and Kaitlin back to Howth, and Fianna had planned to stay with Davina in the little girl's room.

As they were leaving, Kaitlin spoke up. "You should see what Niall has done with the castle, Fianna. It's amazing."

Niall slipped his hand into Fianna's. "I'd like to show it to you sometime."

"Hmm, I'd like that, too." His hand was warm and sure in hers, and the memory of their night in Malibu came rushing back.

The front door was open and the O'Donnell family was saying good-bye to the last of their guests. When Fianna, Niall, and Kaitlin stepped outside, Fianna glanced around. She vaguely remembered telling her family to leave without her. "Could you give me a ride home?"

Before Niall could answer, Doyle sidled up beside her.

"You can stay here tonight, Fianna. I have a guest room for you." He bent close to her ear and slid his hand up her bare arm. "Or you can share my room."

The smell of whiskey was strong on his breath, and his hooded eyes bore into hers. Fianna took a step back. "No thank you, Doyle."

Niall said, "The car service is here. We'd be happy to take you home."

Doyle put his arm around Fianna and turned her away from Niall. "Stay with me, Fianna. You know how I feel about you." He pulled a slim jewelry box from his jacket pocket. "Please take the ring." He wavered on his feet.

Fianna pushed away from him. "Doyle, I've said no, and I mean it."

Niall hooked his hand through Doyle's arm. "The lady is coming with us."

Doyle's face grew red and he tried to jerk away, but Niall stood several inches taller and had the muscular advantage. Doyle reared back to throw a punch.

Niall caught his arm in mid-air. "You can't be serious." He let him go.

Doyle stumbled back against the red brick wall by the entryway. "You don't know who you're messing with."

"Keep your distance from her." Niall walked away. He encircled Fianna's waist protectively with his arm and started for the sleek black car parked nearby. A driver opened the rear door for them.

Kaitlin fell in step beside them. "We have plenty of room

at the castle. Why don't you come back with us tonight, Fianna? We have a guest suite with a giant bed and whirlpool tub. You'd love it."

Niall held up a hand and laughed. "I swear I didn't put my sister up to this."

"Let me think… Tiny twin bed in my niece's bedroom, or a sumptuous suite?" Fianna lifted her shoulder and peered up at him through her lashes. "Well, do I have an invitation or not?"

"Of course you do," Niall said, kissing her forehead. "I'd love to know you're sleeping under the same roof. And as before, anything you need I'm sure Kaitlin has."

Kaitlin giggled and winked at her. "Actually, I think anything you need my brother has."

Fianna sat next to Niall at a round oak table in the spacious, renovated family kitchen. She and Kaitlin had kicked off their shoes, and Fianna had gathered her silk maid of honor's dress around her legs, her manicured toes dangling on a chair. Hand-painted tiles, sparkling Irish crystal, and bright marine colors in hues of blue and green created a comfortable, welcoming ambiance.

Kaitlin howled with laughter. "Tell Fianna about the time you were all stuck at immigration and sang to the entire waiting line."

Niall was telling hilarious stories about his group during their first tour of America, and she and Kaitlin were laughing at the antics of four young Irish boys who'd become an overnight success with their first rock 'n roll hit.

Fianna hadn't realized he'd been such a star. *Is such a star,* she corrected herself, remembering the photos she'd seen. She'd been vaguely aware of Finley Green music, although she hadn't listened to pop and rock much. But she'd never really been aware of him. If she had been, she might have seen him as a star, rather than the real man under the façade of stardom.

Not that Niall has a façade, she thought. *Unlike Doyle.* She shook her head. Why did that pop into her mind? Ever since she'd turned down his proposal, his behavior had bordered on threatening. She would definitely keep her distance. She pulled her attention back to Niall and Kaitlin.

"We were four crazy young lads," Niall said, chuckling. "We were young and brash, and thought we could get away with anything. For the most part, we did."

"Please tell me you didn't trash hotel rooms or destroy musical instruments," Fianna said, wrinkling her nose.

"Nothing like that, happy to report. Our mams and dads would've had a fit. We were awfully young when we started. A couple of us were only seventeen." Niall's eyes danced as he recounted another funny story.

"When you were growing up, who was your musical idol?" Fianna rested her chin in her hand, enjoying the melodic timbre of his voice. His laughter lit his face, crinkling his eyes and relaxing his forehead.

"We grew up listening to U2 and the Beatles with our parents," Niall said. "There were a lot of others, like Pearl

Jam, Red Hot Chili Peppers, and Train. The early Beatles songs were easy for us to play when we were just learning how to play our instruments. And Bono was a big vocal influence. He reaches deep into his soul for his voice."

As Niall spoke, he circled his fingers on Fianna's arm, and warmth spread through her body. His charisma was undeniable. She couldn't remember ever having felt such attraction to a man so quickly. That feeling was intriguing, but for someone as independent as she'd had to be, it was also a little frightening.

Niall stood up. "How about a bottle of Bordeaux? I have some good vintages in the cellar."

"You should definitely see the cellar, Fianna." Kaitlin's eyes widened. "If you like wine, it's like going to Disneyland."

"It's one of my favorite parts of the castle," Niall said. "You can see some of the original walls of the castle down there." He offered his hand to Fianna.

She slipped on her shoes and clasped his outstretched hand. His grip was solid and his hand firm in hers. Calluses at the tips of his fingers from playing the guitar were evidence of his profession. They weren't rough, just built up over the skin.

He led her to a staircase off the kitchen, and she followed him down old stone steps. The walls and overhead arches were made of dappled gray, hand-hewn stone. As they wound downstairs, the air became cooler. The stone walls changed color and grew rougher, reflecting their older vintage. Fianna smelled the musty odor of earth and aging wine.

When they reached the bottom, Niall flicked on a light that illuminated the stone-lined cellar. Cedarwood racks cradling neatly organized wine bottles ran from floor to ceiling and wove throughout the cave. In the middle of the room, a pair of tasting tables were anchored on an intricate Persian rug, surrounded by Thai silk sofas and jeweled pillows of turquoise, pink, and purple. Tiffany lamps cast rainbows of color across antique Irish crystal glassware. Candelabras sat on low Moroccan inlaid tables. Irish antiques and artwork were placed throughout. She loved the sumptuous fabrics and jewel tones and could just imagine having intimate gatherings here.

"Really impressive," Fianna said, craning her neck. "Disneyland for wine... Kaitlin was right."

"Working on the cave brought me a lot of joy during a dark period. I wanted it to look like an Arabian Nights fantasy meets old Celtic lore. Come this way."

Niall led her farther into the wine cave and stopped beside a rack of older wines. He pulled out a dark glass bottle and blew a fine layer of dust from the label. "These have been here for years. They were included in the sale of the castle. These are quite special. I'd love for you to try this one with me. It's a rare vintage." He lifted a wayward strand of hair from her face. "You're a rare one, too, Fianna. I've never met anyone quite like you."

Fianna felt her face grow warm, and she was glad the light was dim. She inspected the label. It was a fine, twenty-year old Bordeaux. "I'd love to try this with you."

Niall placed the bottle on a tasting table and perched on a stool. Fianna stepped toward him. He slid his arms along her shoulders, and her heartbeat quickened.

"I have a confession to make, Fianna."

"What?" She braced herself. In her world, confessions were seldom good. Her mother, Doyle...

Niall took her hand in his. "Ever since the day we met when we barely survived the high tide, you've been on my mind like no other."

A nervous laugh slipped from her and heat rushed up her neck, flushing her face. "Really Niall, do you know how many times I've heard that line?" As soon as the words were out of her mouth, Fianna regretted them. She'd ruined the sweet moment. Her mam's words reverberated in her ears. *Fianna, hold your tongue. Think before you speak.* Niall's gaze dropped to the floor. Had she became so jaded living in L.A.? "I didn't mean it like that."

He raised his eyes to her again. "I know the power of words, Fianna. I don't fling them around like most men."

Should she tell him her heart hammered every time she thought of him? She hardly knew him. Yet here she was in his home and having tidal waves of feelings she'd never known before.

She brushed another strand of hair from her face. As she did, her hand shook slightly and gave her away. Niall caught her hand and brought it his lips, kissing her fingers. His eyes seemed to bore into her soul. She felt like she could bare her deepest thoughts to this man, and it scared her. *Why? Was it the possibility of ultimate rejection?* Over the years, she'd built a strong fortress around herself, choosing to focus her energy on her work. She exhaled to steady her nerves. "My mam often called me a smart mouth."

"You say what you feel. Do you know how hard it is to find people to tell you the truth?"

"I don't know... in my line of work, everyone's a critic."

"Mine, too. But you have to bare your soul to create your best work. And, if you're lucky enough to make a little money, everyone becomes your friend. Not that I don't like to help those in need, I do, but some people can take advantage." He paused a beat. "I don't think you're like that at all."

She started to say something, but he brushed his lips against hers in a feathery kiss. She wanted more, but a smile shadowed his mouth. He picked up a cork screw.

While he opened the bottle, Fianna moistened her lips. She glanced around the cave, and her eyes settled on the silk sofas and pillows. How many women had he entertained down here?

Niall eased the cork from the bottle. "This will need to air." Grinning, he took her hand. "Kaitlin's waiting for us."

Fianna started up the steps with him, but cast a longing glance back at the intimate setting. She squeezed his hand. Perhaps they both needed to understand each other first.

18

FIANNA DREAMED THAT rose petals were falling from the sky, the velvety petals caressing her face, their sweet scent swirling around her. In her half-sleep, a smile played on her lips. Niall was sauntering through the rose petal shower, a guitar slung over one shoulder with his thumbs hooked in the belt loop of his blue jeans. Pink petals dotted his longish hair, and mounds of red and yellow petals were strewn about his feet like autumn leaves. This dream had a soundtrack, too. Niall's rich, sensual voice drew her in. She gathered her arms around his neck and...

The sensation of silky petals on her cheek grew so real that she fluttered her eyes. A burst of salmon pink petals caught her eye. The touch on her skin was real. She drew in a breath of the flower's fragrant scent. Niall's mossy, marble green eyes—reflecting the vivid shades of Ireland's emerald slopes—gazed at her. He stroked a rose along her cheek, softly singing the song he'd sang yesterday at the wedding. "In your eyes..."

He knelt beside her bed. He wore a white cotton poet's shirt with full sleeves—similar to the one he'd been wearing when she'd first met him. His dark blond hair was brushed back from his forehead and swept the top of his shoulders. His face was tanned, and a smile danced about his lips.

"Good morning, my beautiful, crazy-eyed lady," he said, softly kissing her forehead.

"Hmm." She stretched luxuriously in the wide bed. A silky Egyptian cotton ivory duvet covered her; only a bare shoulder peeked from beneath the covers. Niall trailed the rose along her neck to her shoulder, and the sensation filled her with joy. She recalled the whisper of a kiss they'd shared last night and instantly yearned for more.

"Strong Irish tea or American coffee?" he asked.

"I should say tea, since I'm here, but coffee sounds marvelous." She wiggled her toes under the down comforter and looked around the room. A white brocade sofa was studded with marine blue pillows, and seascape paintings graced the walls. Through a stone flanked wooden window wafted the fresh, salty scent of the sea. Niall's acoustic guitar leaned against an antique nightstand next to her bed.

"Cream and sugar?"

"Just cream." She loved the thick cream of Ireland. He turned to leave and she watched him walk toward the door, appreciating his broad muscular shoulders and his narrow jean-clad hips. Height clearly ran in the family, and she'd have no problem wearing her favorite high heels with him. Not that it would have mattered, she reminded herself, but she had to admit it was a nice bonus.

After the wedding, she and Niall and Kaitlin had

returned to the castle on Howth. Niall had taken pleasure in showing her around the magnificent structure, which he'd been renovating for several years. It had been quite an undertaking.

Then they had stayed up half the night talking and laughing with Kaitlin over the fine vintage Bordeaux they'd found in the cellar. Listening to Kaitlin's stories, she'd learned a lot about Niall. He and his sister clearly loved each other and were good friends as well.

She smiled to herself, thinking about the touch of his hand in hers, his lips brushing hers, his fascinated gaze. She was falling fast.

Shorebirds squawked outside the windows, drawing her from her reverie. Her pragmatic side asked, *what's the point? He's here in Ireland, and you're in Los Angeles. Where could this possibly go?* She blinked against the truth.

"Here you are, one steaming cup." Niall placed the coffee on the nightstand and handed her a white terry cloth spa-style robe that he'd slung over his shoulder. "Thought you might want this." He grinned and turned around. "Kaitlin has some things for you to wear. We could go shopping, too. There are boutiques and pubs nearby, and I have a couple of bicycles."

She slipped into the robe. Her free-spirited side quickly won her over. The sun was shining and the thought of seizing a few days of pleasure with a handsome, talented, intriguing man was too much to pass by. "That sounds like fun."

Niall left and Kaitlin bounced in with an armload of

jeans and T-shirts and tennis shoes. "It's lucky that we're about the same size. I tower over my cousins. Both our parents were the tallest in their families, so we came out like giraffes."

Fianna chuckled, remembering her own adolescence. "I was the skinny, gangly one in the back of all the class photos."

"Me, too. I grew out of clothes faster than we could buy them." Kaitlin waggled her arms like an ape.

"But look at you now. You're using your natural talents."

Kaitlin sat on the bed and hugged her long legs to her chest. "I don't know if I want to do it forever, but the money is good right now. My brother would be happy to support me, but I like to make my own way."

"That's always wise. My aunt Davina taught me that."

Kaitlin rocked back and forth while Fianna sipped her coffee. "It's so cool that Davina is your aunt. And I heard about your show in Dublin from some of the other models. I'm really sorry."

"Thanks. The police are investigating. It looked like the shoes had been tampered with."

"Who would do that?" Kaitlin flung up her hands. "My agent tells me to ignore the tabloids, but it's hard, isn't it?"

"It is." Fianna sighed. She hadn't looked at the trade papers after the initial articles she'd read had skewered her. But evidentially the tabloids were continuing the story, writing about everything from the models to the shoemakers. Back in L.A., her assistant Evangeline had sent several messages about reporters who were trying to reach her. Fortunately, Evangeline shielded her, and no one had her mobile phone number.

"Did you know they've put you and Niall together as a hot item?"

"What?" Fianna spilled her coffee on the robe. "Where in the world would they get that?"

"I saw a photo of you and Niall in Malibu, drenching wet and hugging each other. It was kind of grainy, but there was no mistaking you two. Supposedly you're having a torrid affair."

"We'd nearly drowned!" Fianna sank her face into her hands. "I'm so embarrassed."

Kaitlin put her arm around Fianna. "Don't be. It happens all the time. Niall is accustomed to it. The press used to follow him around like terriers, but they haven't had much to write about since Laila died."

Fianna wondered how Laila had died, but she didn't want to ask. "Does he know about this?"

Kaitlin shook her head. "He ignores them. So they make up things. He was said to be dating a princess and an heiress last year. At the same time. It's amazing what they can do with Photoshop."

"None of it was true, I guess."

"Not a shred. Don't believe anything you read about him, especially on the Internet. We know who we are, and that's all that matters. Just ignore the tabloids." Kaitlin got up to leave. She paused by the door and glanced over her shoulder. "You know, I can tell my brother really likes you." She grinned and shut the door.

Niall was pumping air into the bike tires when Fianna stepped outside. He let out a low whistle. He'd changed into a T-shirt and hoodie, and he wore dark sunglasses. "Nice outfit. Kaitlin really dressed you up." He reached out to her.

"Jeans and a T-shirt?"

"I like you in casual clothes. But I like you dressed up, too." He removed his sunglasses and hung them on the neck of his shirt. He took her hands and kissed her lightly on the lips.

Fianna couldn't think of when she'd had a more perfect day. They cycled along the ocean, listening to the incessant roar of pounding waves. They climbed high rugged cliffs and gazed out to the wild, white-capped sea below. Niall pointed out different landmarks and shared ancient history and stories that had been passed down through the ages.

After they pedaled into the village, Niall took her to a local boutique run by his caretaker's sister. Fianna chose some casual jeans and sweaters that were more Lizzie's style than hers, but they were perfect for the Irish countryside. Niall watched her try on clothes, giving her a thumbs up approval for almost everything she tried on.

They cycled down the pier, surrounded by ocean. Inquisitive spotted seals surfaced, shaking their whiskered noses at them.

Fianna's stomach rumbled.

"Hungry?" Niall asked.

"Famished." Fianna laughed. "Either you read my mind or you heard my stomach." She nodded toward the seals. "I think they want carry-out."

"They can get their own," Niall said, grinning. "They're a friendly bunch of beggars." He nodded to a restaurant in back of them. "We can eat at Octopussy." He indicated a small stone-faced restaurant that fronted the ocean.

They parked their bikes and sat at a wooden picnic table in front of the small restaurant. "Their specialty is seafood tapas." Niall put his arm around her, and Fianna moved closer until their hips and shoulders touched. Just being near him sent chills of excitements through her.

They ordered oysters, crab claws, prawns, mussels, and monkfish with chorizo. They ate hunks of crusty brown bread slathered with butter, a crunchy salad, and washed it all down with a chilled white wine.

As Niall poured the last of the wine into Fianna's glass, her phone buzzed with a text.

"Do you need to get that?"

"Is there nowhere I can hide for an afternoon?" Groaning, she flicked open her text messages. It was from Scarlett. *Call me ASAP.* It was early morning in California. Fianna frowned and rubbed her forehead.

Niall touched her arm. "What's wrong?"

"It's my friend Scarlett. You met her in Malibu at my show. She's also my attorney." Fianna made a face.

He kissed her forehead. "Make the call. I have some

friends inside I'll say hello to."

He walked away and she tapped Scarlett's number.

Scarlett's voice echoed over the Atlantic Ocean. "Fianna, I'm so glad you called. Listen, I received a call from another attorney today about you."

"Me? Why?" Fianna could hear Scarlett draw a deep breath, but before she could say anything, the phone line clicked several times, and then disconnected. "Hello? Hello?"

She tried over and over to call her back, but the line only buzzed, and then her phone battery went dead. Frustrated, Fianna shoved the phone into her pocket. Why had another attorney contacted Scarlett? Perhaps it was one of the new licensing deals they'd hoped for. Excitement rose within her.

Or was it related to the disastrous Dublin show?

Niall was walking toward her, limping slightly. Her gaze travelled up to his tanned face and windblown hair. He was the kind of man women wanted to be with and men wanted to befriend.

"You look like you need a good massage, and later, a starlit Jacuzzi. At least, I do." He made a face. "I haven't ridden a bicycle that far in a long, long time." He rubbed his thighs through his jeans.

Fianna rolled her shoulders, feeling the ache of muscles she didn't normally use. "I couldn't agree more."

They pedaled through the village back to the castle. The marine wind blew fresh on Fianna's face, but she couldn't seem to shake Scarlett's call. It could be cause for celebration, but something in her gut warned her otherwise.

She'd call later. Now, a massage awaited her, and she planned to take full advantage of it.

19

NIALL HELD A thick, carved oak door open for Fianna. "I think you'll like this section of the castle." He'd built the spa for Laila. After she was gone, it had been a long time before he'd been strong enough to enter and appreciate it again.

When he'd finally managed to return, the exercise and relaxation had helped restore his well-being, though he'd often felt Laila's presence here. He glanced around. Today he felt nothing, just the joy of being here with Fianna. Had Laila really left him for good?

Fianna's face lit with pleasure, and he was deeply pleased he could share this with her. He'd asked his houseman to prepare the spa and arrange a masseuse for when they returned. Sure enough, the lights were dimmed and the Jacuzzi was swirling. Aromatherapy oils of eucalyptus and lavender permeated the old stone walls, and palm trees rustled under lazy ceiling fans. A waterfall trickled into the Olympic-sized pool at one end, which led to a private stone grotto.

"It's absolutely gorgeous," Fianna said, her voice edged with awe. "I've never seen anything like this." Her eyes traveled up to the glittering mosaic tile ceiling arching overhead. An arched glass-paned atrium opened the entire spa to the gardens and ocean beyond. Another pool stretched outside, too.

Niall rested his hand in the curve of Fianna's back and followed her gaze. "It was perfect for unwinding after the long concert tours I used to do, and far from the lenses of the paparazzi."

He motioned to one side. "Over there are massage rooms, a steam sauna, and a cedar-lined dry sauna. Beyond that is an exercise room, a basketball court, and a yoga-and-dance room."

"This is amazing," Fianna said. "I might never leave."

His heart swelled with joy at her words. "Stay as long as you'd like." He realized he truly meant it. "You'll find robes and a shower in the ladies locker area. Swimsuits, too, if you'd like a swim. Relax and do whatever you want, or join me in the Jacuzzi."

"With or without a swimsuit?" Fianna wiggled her eyebrows and laughed.

Niall grinned. "I'll let you be the judge of that, Miss Crazy Eyes." The sound of her laughter tinkled like a bell in his ears and he loved it. She turned to him and he encircled her waist, drawing her closer. He brushed his lips against hers in question, and she answered without hesitation. The connection between them was undeniable.

He lost himself in the softness of her lips, which quickly aroused him. After a while, he drew back and cradled her face in his hands. He adored this woman—her freckled nose, her cornflower blue and hazel eyes, and the determined tilt of her chin. He removed the elastic band that held her hair and threaded his supple fingers through her fiery red hair. "Simply gorgeous," he murmured, finding her lips again.

When she pressed the length of her slender body against him, it was all he could do to restrain himself. The masseuse would be here any minute, though if he closed a door they'd have their privacy.

He checked his desire; he wanted her to come to him when she was truly ready, not just in the passionate heat of the moment. He slid his hand down to the curve of her slim hips. He wanted no regrets or missteps in this relationship. Fianna deserved the best a man had to offer.

He crushed her against him and then quickly released her, his breath labored with lust.

Fianna flicked her tongue over her lips. "I hope there's more where that came from."

"Even more than you imagine. I've been dreaming of this."

She tossed her tousled hair and inclined her head, teasing him. "Have you now?"

Niall gazed at her lovely face, thinking. He knew what real love was, and what it wasn't. It was trust and companionship, and yes, passionate lovemaking. It wasn't neediness or jealousy. The love he longed for again would withstand the tests of life.

"I think we both need a cold shower before that hot

Jacuzzi." He feathered a kiss on her lips, and then he watched her walk away. She glanced back before she closed the door to the women's changing room behind her.

He went into the men's locker room. As he stripped off his clothes, he thought of Laila. He and his wife had been soul mates. All the passing relationships he'd had earlier with women meant nothing to him after they'd met. While they'd had their occasional disagreements, they'd always resolved their differences. They had been lovers and best friends, dreaming of their future and family they'd have when tragedy had struck.

He'd found Laila's journal after she died. She'd recorded her thoughts, goals, and dreams. She'd always had a certain prescience, which she laughed about, saying it was just women's intuition. But he knew it was more than that.

Laila sometimes felt, or saw, what the future held. He'd memorized one passage she'd written just before her death: *Niall is a man of such passionate expression, that if I were to die, I'd want him to find another woman with whom he could share his soul. If he can't express his deepest passions, he too, would wither and die. That's how much I love him, and always will.*

He blinked hard against the moisture that clouded his eyes. Had Laila sensed she had only a fortnight to live?

Laila's writings proved true. He'd withered personally and musically. His wife had known everything about him and still loved him. Without her, on starless nights he'd found himself yearning for the cloak of death to relieve his unbearable loss.

And yet, he'd survived.

His deepest passions... Passion meant many things to him, from the creativity that coursed through his veins to the expression of life he infused in his music. Passion was the brilliant dawn of morning, the incessant roar of the sea, the silence of knowing one's truth. It was the strength of his convictions.

Niall stepped into the shower and turned it to cold, letting the water prickle his skin. He closed his eyes and put his head under the shower head, letting his thoughts wander.

He saw this evidence of passion in Fianna's eyes. It was her obsession for her art and for life itself. He'd felt it in her determination to free him from the rocks and the sea in Malibu.

Fianna lived with passion; could that include him someday? Once he'd experienced real love, nothing less would be good enough for him. Not a sizzling tumble on a shivering night, not an arm trophy girlfriend to dazzle the eye. No, only the genuine article could satisfy him now.

He stepped from the shower and toweled dry. He opened a locker and pondered a thought. Swimwear, or not? He made a choice and then put on a robe.

Most of his mates wouldn't dare admit to such deep, raw thoughts. They saw yearnings as weaknesses that needed to be concealed lest their hearts be trampled and left to bleed in the harsh light of day. With his poet's heart it was up to him to give voice to these feelings, to set them to music and share them with the world.

If he had a secret to his success, it was this.

Fianna made him want to create again. Ever since he'd met her, life seemed fresher and finer. Music and lyrics had been bubbling from his soul-scape like a wellspring, where once it had been dry and barren.

His passion had finally returned.

Could he spend his life with Fianna? He wasn't sure yet. If only he could ask his best friend, the person he trusted most in the world. Where was Laila when he needed her? Had she finally left him? He stroked his chin. If she had, maybe that was her answer.

Fianna wrapped her hair in a terry cloth turban she'd found in the changing area. Everything she might have needed was there. Robes, slippers, and swimsuits in every size that looked like new, fresh makeup and skincare, and all the hair styling tools she could imagine. A woman had definitely equipped this area.

She didn't see Niall around, so she opened the glass door to the steam sauna. A wave of eucalyptus-scented steam billowed toward her, surrounding her with heavenly warmth. She placed a towel on a shimmering azure blue tile ledge and eased onto it, stretching her sore limbs. The bike ride had been fun, but her muscles had gotten a work out. She leaned back with thoughts of Niall dancing in her mind. The taste of his lips, the rapid beat of his heart…the firmness of his arousal against her.

She smiled as another wave of steam rose around her. Niall sure knew how to move on the dance floor, and she'd melted into his magnetic kisses. She wasn't the type to fall into bed with men she hardly knew, but there was something distinctly different about Niall. She enjoyed every moment with him. He made her laugh, he loved to share stories, and she could see compassion in his soul.

Shielding her eyes with her forearm against the steam, she thought about their blossoming relationship. How long could she stay here? Not long, really. She had to return to Los Angeles. Her business wouldn't run without her. Niall had just sold his home in Malibu. How could they continue a relationship?

Or maybe he didn't want one. The steam became too much for her, and she stepped out. Cool air blasted her face. Was this just a holiday romance to him?

His kisses certainly didn't feel that way.

She walked into the pool area and sucked in her breath. The sun was setting in a magnificent show. The impressionist sky was painted with smudged strokes of rose and lavender. A storm of brilliant color splashed around her. She paused, rooted to the spot, appreciating nature's incredible display framed in the atrium windows that soared high above.

After enjoying a moment of creative rejuvenation, she strolled toward the bubbling Jacuzzi and glanced around. Maybe Niall was having a massage. She slipped out of her robe and eased into the warm water. She closed her eyes, shifting underwater until she found just the right jet to massage her sore shoulder muscles. *Ahh…*

"Well, look at you." Niall stood gazing at her, slowly unwrapping his robe. "How's the water?"

"Um, it feels great." Surprised, Fianna blinked up at him, and then she looked away out of modesty. But she *had* to sneak a glance. She darted her eyes to the side.

Fianna covered her mouth and started laughing. "You're wearing a *Speedo?*"

Niall held out his muscular arms. "What's the matter? I thought it looked pretty good. I mean, I'm no Michael Phelps, but I didn't think it looked *that* bad." He turned around. "I've been told it looks good from behind." He wiggled his back end.

Unable to contain her giggles, Fianna slid under the water, and then sputtered to the surface.

"So, what did *you* wear?"

"Oh, no you don't." Fianna wrapped her arms around herself and leaned over.

Niall put his hands on his hips. "Come on, which swimsuit did you choose? Bikini or one piece?"

She shook her head vehemently, smothering another laugh.

At once it dawned on him. "Why, you little wench. Come closer, lass." He stepped into the Jacuzzi after her, but quickly halted, unable to continue. "Wow, that's hot. Ouch, oh, ouch." He backed out, grasping for the edge.

While he was turned, Fianna shrieked and lunged from the Jacuzzi for her robe. She quickly draped it around her nude body.

"Hey, that's not fair," he said.

"Who's ready for a massage?" A fair-haired, Nordic-looking couple appeared in the doorway to the spa.

"Saved by the masseuse," Niall muttered. "I'll remember this, I will."

"Maybe you'll get your chance later. Or maybe not." She shrugged and winked at him over her shoulder. She'd never had so much fun with a man.

He caught her wrist and planted a kiss firmly on her mouth. "Next time I won't bother to change." He waggled his eyebrows.

"Promises, promises." She laughed and headed toward the massage rooms to have a quick shower before her massage.

When Fianna entered the massage room, the masseuse introduced herself and asked what type of massage oils she'd like. "Relaxing, invigorating, or sensual?"

Fianna hesitated, weighing her option. "I'm not sure."

The woman rested a hand on her shoulder. "I think this is an evening for sensual oils," she said with a knowing smile.

After her incredible massage, Fianna padded back to the pool area. Niall was already in the Jacuzzi. The sun had set while they were having their massages, and now the moon shone through the atrium glass, casting a slanting glow around his shoulders. His wet hair was brushed back, and his well-defined shoulders glistened with oil.

"Care to join me?" His eyes twinkled with mischief. "I

have more of that Bordeaux you liked."

"Tempt me more," she said.

"I could if you'd let me."

Fianna twirled her fingers in a circle to indicate that he turn around. With a sigh, Niall turned to pour a glass a wine for her, and she slipped off her robe. The water was warm, but not as hot as it had been. She slid in, feeling completely pampered and restored.

Niall handed a glass of red wine to her and held her gaze. "To a perfect day, and to you, Fianna. You shine as bright as the stars above."

She grazed his lips and clinked his glass. "And to you, Niall. You've brought music to my life."

He ran a hand along her back, sending shivers through her. She hesitated only slightly before moved into his embrace, resting her head against his broad chest. His heart was hammering against her cheek. He trailed his fingers reverently over her skin, awakening every cell within her. She nestled in the curve of his body.

They languished in the hot tub, becoming comfortable with each other. Fianna ran her hands along his strong cheekbones, down his neck, and onto his smooth, well-defined chest. She shifted her leg underwater, feeling nothing but bare skin. "No Speedo?"

He shook his head. "I want you to know me as I am. Whenever you're ready, that is." He brushed her lips with his, and then he poured another splash of wine in her glass. He tilted his head back. "Look up."

She leaned her head back, and the sky was ablaze with a shower of stars above them. "Utterly amazing."

"It is, isn't it?" He waved his hand. "I've been so blessed, Fianna."

"You're very talented."

"Many people are talented. I had a lucky day, that's all. One day led to another, and then another…"

She heard a catch in his voice. "And then your luck ran out, didn't it?"

With his eyes fixed on the sky, he spoke. "One day I had everything, and the next day everything that was important to me was gone."

Fianna drew her hand across his jawline. She asked softly, "How did your wife die?"

He turned into her hand and kissed her palm, and then raised his eyes to hers. "Laila died of a brain aneurism. She was driving to meet me when it ruptured. The doctors say she died before the accident occurred."

"You must have been devastated." She saw traces of pain in his eyes.

He nodded. "She was also two months pregnant."

Fianna slid her arms around him. "I'm so sorry you went through that. You must have loved her very much."

"I did, and I still do. Love doesn't die when a person leaves this world."

"No, it wouldn't."

Niall sipped his wine. "After she died, I had to sort through her papers, and I found a journal she kept. She had a premonition, I believe. She wrote that if she died, she wanted me to find another to share my life with."

Fianna blinked back tears, wishing that she'd known Laila, too. "She sounds like a generous woman who loved you."

"She was." Niall held his wine glass to the sky above them. "Here's to you, Laila. Meet Fianna."

Tears flowed from Fianna's eyes as she raised her glass. She silently thanked Laila for sharing such a fine love with Niall. At that moment, she sensed a loving presence and felt as if Laila was surrounding them, giving her approval.

Niall turned to her, his eyes glistening. "Did you feel that?"

Fianna nodded in amazement. Something she couldn't explain *had* touched her. "I did."

"It felt like she gave us her blessing." He kissed the top of her head. "Fianna, you've turned my whole world around."

She smiled up at him. "And you've shown me your beautiful heart." She was glad they'd talked about Laila. It might seem odd to some, she thought, to discuss his deceased wife while relaxing in a whirlpool and drinking wine, but she'd definitely felt a presence here. And it was good and pure.

Is this the man I'm destined to love? She usually didn't believe in destiny—she thought people made their own fate, but here in Ireland, with a starry sky above, and the most incredible man she'd ever met beside her, destiny seemed quite plausible.

"Would you like to have a swim? The water is warm, and there's a private grotto at the end of the pool."

Fianna touched his face. "I'd like that very much."

He eased out of the Jacuzzi and helped her out. Though they were nude, it seemed like the most natural thing in the world. Something had shifted between them; they'd already bared themselves to each other in a hundred little ways since they'd met.

They dipped into the warm saltwater, which felt silky on her skin, and pushed off from the edge, feeling the freedom of gliding through the water. They swam together, and when they reached the end of the pool, Niall led her through a mountain of rocks. A hidden lagoon opened before her.

"How romantic." She laced her arms around Niall's neck, and he bent to kiss her. He tasted of Bordeaux wine and saltwater and smelled of spicy wooded oils. Together they swirled in the lagoon, exploring and appreciating each other.

When they neared steps on the edge, Niall lifted her easily from the water and placed her on a wide lounging bed. He draped a cushy soft blanket around them. Holding himself above her, he caressed her face.

"Is this what you want, Fianna?"

She said not a word, but encircled his neck and brought him to her in answer. Soon they moved together as one, and Fianna felt a bliss like she had never known before.

All her worries—attorneys, mangled shoes, buyers—

shrank and burst like champagne bubbles. In the end, what did any of it matter as long as you loved and were loved?

Fianna closed her eyes, and the world around them ceased to exist.

20

FIANNA WOKE IN Niall's rumpled bed, which was still warm from their lovemaking. His arms were wrapped around her, and joy filled her like sunshine. She stroked his powerful, sinewy arm.

"Good morning, my love." Niall shifted against her.

"I feel like I'm waking up from the most wonderful dream."

"That was no dream. But with you, life is like a dream."

She laughed softly. "Isn't that a song?"

"You got me." He raised himself on an elbow. "You know the first song I sang at Shane and Lizzie's wedding?" He hummed and sang a few words.

"I love that song."

His lips curved. "I wrote it for you."

Fianna gazed into his sparkling green eyes. From any other man, that would've sounded like a line, but Niall was a genuine man. All night they'd made love, laughed, and shared feelings.

He rolled out of bed and sauntered to the baby grand piano in his bedroom. He perched on the stool and ran his fingers over the keys, singing to her. "I was drowning in the dark, thirsting for your love..."

Fianna loved it. She framed this moment in her mind: A beautiful nude man playing a song he'd written just for her on the piano. *How did I get so lucky?*

He finished the song, the final notes reverberating through her body like waves of pure love. Niall stood and offered his hand to her. "Mademoiselle, may I have this dance?"

"Why, of course." Fianna swung her long legs over the bed and fell into his arms. He swung her around and executed a perfect dip. She threw her head back, laughing, and loving his romantic, playful nature.

"How about a special shower?" He spun her around, and then tangoed into the ivory marbled bathroom. He dipped her again and turned on a showerhead, and then he spun her around, turning on another spigot on the opposite wall. Soon they were surrounded by warm, gently pulsating water flowing from several showerheads lining the marble walls of the cavernous shower. He hugged her to him. "And now, for the *pièce de résistance.*" He pulled a chain and a waterfall flowed from the ceiling, showering them with oxygenated water filled with airy bubbles.

Fianna turned her face up, loving his enthusiasm. "I feel like I'm showering in Perrier water."

"Even better." Niall motioned to an array of fragrant shampoos and body washes on the wall. "Verbena, lavender, or ginger? What's your pleasure?"

"Besides you?" She teased her leg around his. "How about verbena and ginger together?"

"As the lady wishes." Niall squirted each body wash into the palm of his hand, rubbed them together, and then, with a mischievous glint in his eye, he lathered her with foamy soap.

Fianna followed his lead, and soon they were lathered and making love under the warm pulsating jets. They clung to each other as water dappled their skin, rinsing them clean.

I'm in heaven, she thought, arching her neck back under his touch and luxuriating in the moment.

A little while later, Niall brought out a stack of fluffy white towels and dried her from head to toe, and she did the same for him. He shook his hair and brushed it back, while she fluffed her curly hair with her fingers.

"I love your gorgeous mane. You look like an Irish Rapunzel," he said, kissing the tip of her nose. "If you're hungry, I have a breakfast specialty that Johnny and Lance taught me how to make." He helped her with a robe, and then he took her hand.

"You can cook, too?" She followed him from the bedroom. "Can you be any more perfect, Niall Finley?"

Fianna sat on a stool in the kitchen as he explained the recipe.

"First, you slice the croissants," he said, drawing a stainless blade through three flaky half-moons. "Add strawberries and cream," he continued, slicing fresh strawberries. "Or chocolate, like *pain au chocolate.*" He looked up in question.

"Chocolate sounds delicious." She rested her chin in her hand, enjoying watching him.

"Good choice, my favorite, too." He placed sliced strawberries onto the open croissants, and then shaved chocolate on top. He put the croissants back together and dipped them in egg batter. "Now we add chopped macadamias, Hawaiian-style." He quickly sautéed his creations in a skillet. Then he drizzled maple syrup over the croissants and sprinkled powdered sugar on top.

"Here it is. French toast, my way." He placed the plates on the counter with a flourish.

Fianna took a bite. "Mmm, I think I could live on this alone." She'd never tasted French toast made this way, and it was delicious. A man who could cook, even a little? *Very sexy.*

Kaitlin wandered in wearing yoga gear. "I thought I smelled something fabulous." She hugged Fianna. "It's so nice to see you here in the morning." She raised her brows and jerked her head toward her brother.

Fianna understood her meaning and nodded, feeling herself flush.

Kaitlin clapped her hands with glee, and Niall turned around. "You sure get excited over my French toast croissants."

"Indeed I do," Kaitlin said, giggling.

"Good thing I made one for you, too." Niall put another plate on the counter and sat on a stool next to Fianna.

"Life just doesn't get any better than this," Fianna said,

giving him a kiss. "Thank you, chef."

"Don't get any grand ideas. I'm pretty handy with a barbeque, too, but I'm also a devoted patron of our local restaurants."

"I'm not too bad with corned beef and potatoes any way you like them, but in L.A., I'm more of a granola and organic veggies kind of girl."

"There's a happy balance there somewhere," Niall said, grinning. He took a bite, clearly enjoying his cooking.

Somewhere a phone rang. "Whose phone is that?" Kaitlin asked.

"Sounds like mine." Niall had plugged in her phone the night before.

Kaitlin sprang up. "I'll get it for you." A moment later she returned with Fianna's phone.

Fianna checked; it was Scarlett again. She hated to let the outside world back into their private abode. Still, Scarlett was her friend. "Hello?"

Scarlett's voice crackled through the line. "Thank goodness I reached you."

"What is it, Scarlett?" Fianna sat up, suddenly concerned.

"I'm sorry to tell you, but the model who fell from the runway in Dublin is suing you."

Fianna had half-expected this, but this was like an Arctic blast of air into their warm cocoon. "Of course, I understand. I feel so responsible."

"Don't say that, you're not. You didn't rig the shoes.

Someone else is responsible for this. Have the police found any leads?"

"Not that I know of." Fianna clutched the phone. "Scarlett, I'll pay for her injuries. How much does she need?"

"Brace yourself." Scarlett paused for a long beat. "Ten million dollars."

"Wh-what?" Did they have a bad connection? She thought she'd heard—

"She's suing for loss of wages, injuries, and damage to her career."

Fianna's stomach dropped. She stared out the kitchen window to the sea, dumbfounded. That amount of money was absolutely unattainable.

She shot a look at Niall. He and Kaitlin were watching her, their brows creased in concern.

"Fianna? Are you there?"

"Yes," she murmured. She blinked back hot tears of shock. This would mean the end of her business and her career. She tried to remember if she'd seen anyone near the shoes—anyone who might have tampered with them.

She closed her eyes in thought. She wished she could remember something, but she'd been so focused on the event and making sure everything was perfect, she hadn't thought of anything else. Had the other models or stylists seen anything?

Or was it simply too late?

"I can't raise that, Scarlett. That's way beyond my ability." She swallowed. "That would put me out of business." Regardless of what Scarlett said, she still felt responsible and wanted to make amends, but ten million dollars? It seemed excessive, even for a model. "I spoke to her the next day, and she sounded okay. How badly was she really hurt?"

"She fractured her ankle and had to have a pin put in. But she should recover well, certainly well enough to walk the runway. The amount she wants is really excessive. I think a greedy attorney got hold of her."

Niall slid his arm around her, and Fianna was grateful for his support. "Scarlett, what should I do?"

"First, don't give up. I've been talking to your insurance carrier."

Fianna grasped at her words. "Will they cover it?"

"It's complicated. It was out of the country, the police are involved, and it has a lot of hair around it. But I'm working on it."

They spoke a few more minutes, and then Fianna hung up. She was thunderstruck and still baffled how someone could have done this to her and the models. She pressed a hand to her chest. Her heart was pounding, and blood rushed through her ears.

"What's wrong, Fianna, love?"

She shook her head with sorrow. "I wish I could stay longer, but I'm afraid I have to return to Los Angeles right away."

Niall wrapped his arms around her. "Whatever I can do to help, please let me know."

Some women might have immediately asked for assistance, but Fianna wasn't one of them. She wouldn't do anything that might damage this relationship that now meant so much to her. Besides, she really hadn't known Niall but what, a handful of days? Did he care for her as much as she did for him? She swallowed against a lump in her throat and looked into his eyes.

"There's nothing I can think of," she said, taking his hand in hers.

21

NIALL SAT ON an overstuffed sofa in the sitting room connected to the kitchen, picking out a new tune on his guitar. Fianna occupied his thoughts and dreams, and he could still smell her perfume that reminded him of sweet morning jasmine. She'd truly inspired him, awakening his creativity.

His thoughts were increasingly shifting from Laila to Fianna. Laila would always occupy a special place in his heart, yet he no longer felt her presence.

The song he was writing today was a personal tribute to the first woman he'd ever loved, the woman who had showed him what true love really was. "Good-bye Laila" was his farewell ode to her. He sang softly, "*Slán leat*, Laila, *au revoir*, good-bye. Until we meet again…" *Slán leat* was Gaelic for goodbye.

He'd finally adjusted to Laila's absence and was at peace for her.

Fianna was alive and radiant and filled with love. And on the other side of the planet from him. Now that he'd experienced the magic of love once more, he felt more alone than ever before.

Kaitlin hurried in, holding her airline tickets and rolling a small Louis Vuitton suitcase behind her. "The car is here. I'm ready to go." She wore an oversized Pucci print blouse, black leggings that emphasized her long, lean legs, and tall boots that rose above her knees.

Niall put his guitar aside and got up. "I'll miss you. It's going to be awfully lonely here without you." She was leaving for a series of modeling jobs from London to Paris to New York.

A smile played on Kaitlin's lips. "What you really mean is that you're lonely since Fianna left. You've been rambling around here with sad puppy dog eyes."

"How did you get so smart?" He wrapped his arms around his sister. "But I swear I'll miss you, too." He picked up her suitcase. "Is this all you have?"

"I'm traveling light this time. There are plenty of clothes where I'm going. But you know me, I'll probably end up buying another suitcase for the trip home."

Niall walked outside with her along the gravelly drive in front of the castle. A driver took the bag from him and opened the rear door of a large black sedan for her.

Kaitlin paused with her hand on the car door, staring at him with her vivid green eyes. "Have you spoken to her since she left?"

"Several times." Niall pushed a hand through his hair. "But it's no replacement for being together."

"Too bad you sold the house in Malibu."

He kicked a few pebbles with the toe of his shoe. "Yeah, lousy timing."

"So, book a room. Get a bungalow at the Beverly Hills Hotel."

He glanced back at the castle that rose behind them. He'd been a recluse here for a long time. Visiting Fianna was tempting. But how long could he live in a hotel room? He loved his privacy on Howth. Dealing with the paparazzi trailing his every move in Los Angeles was mentally exhausting. "You know how I feel about L.A."

"So, what do you really want? Get your priorities straight, Niall. That's what you always told me when I was partying too much."

Niall hooked a thumb in the belt loop of his faded jeans. She had a point, but was he ready to venture out again?

Kaitlin pecked him on the cheek and slid into the backseat, arranging her gangly frame on the smooth leather seat. "I love you, brother. Think about what I said." She smiled, though her brow was creased with concern for him.

"Love you, too, sis. Be safe, and buckle up." He waited until she'd put on her seatbelt and then closed her door. He bumped the young driver's fist. "Take care driving."

Niall stood and watched the car until it had disappeared from view. He strolled back into the house, thinking about Fianna. As he did, another tune crept into his consciousness.

Once inside the main parlor, he sat on the bench at the shiny black, baby grand piano where he'd written some of his best music. His fingers slid over the keys, and he hummed along as the tune emerged from his creative soul.

"Hello Fianna, hello, my lady of the midnight moon…" If he couldn't visit her, he could at least sing to her over the phone.

A few minutes later, the piano fell silent, his hands hovering over the keyboard. He heaved a sigh. How were they going to manage this?

Scarlett waved to her from a table inside the bay window at La Conversation on North Doheny Drive in West Hollywood, just opposite the Beverly Hills flats, as the bordering neighborhood was known. The quaint little French restaurant and bakery was one of their favorite places to meet for brunch or lunch, besides Bow-Tie. Scarlett had suggested they come here so they wouldn't be disturbed by well-meaning friends at Johnny and Lance's restaurant.

Fianna always felt like she was entering a café in France when she stepped inside the little corner jewel box decorated with lipstick-red-and-white-striped wallpaper, pictures of France, and a profusion of flowers. A glass case of French pastries at the front tempted her. The chocolate éclairs were to die for.

"Look at us, we almost match," Fianna said. They were both wearing turquoise blouses, though Scarlett wore blue jeans and Fianna had slim white jeans with turquoise heels and wrist bangles. Scarlett hugged her and they sat down.

"So good to see you again, Fianna. How's it going at the shop?" Scarlett brushed her dark blond hair over her shoulder.

Fianna pressed her fingers to her lips and shook her head. "I had no idea the press could be so brutal. They've blasted the Fitzgerald Flop around the world. Someone videotaped part of the show on a mobile phone and posted it to YouTube. Views have skyrocketed."

"Sometimes negative press is good. Have sales increased?"

"Not really, but the line of tourists outside the shop posing for photos sure has. And photographers have been following me, waiting for me to make a misstep. Literally. I stumbled at the farmer's market and the next day Evangeline showed me the photo in a tabloid newspaper. She keeps shooing people away from the shop, but they just come back."

Scarlett eyes her closely. "You look good, though. How was Ireland? And how did you leave things with Niall?"

Fianna had confided in her. "He's half a world away. My shop is here, his place is there. I don't know what to do."

Scarlett touched her hand. "You deserve the best, Fianna. He seems really nice, despite the fact that he's a hot rock star."

"I really don't see him like that." Heat rose in her face. "As a famous rock star, I mean. He's definitely hot."

"Good for you." Scarlett motioned to a waiter. "Let's order, and then get down to business." They ordered poached eggs with smoked salmon on croissants and fruit on the side. "Now, about this case. Can you get a police report?"

"It's under investigation now, but I haven't heard anything. We all had to give statements—me, the models, the stylists. As far as I know, nothing has been discovered."

"Find out as much as you can for me." Scarlett sipped her tea. "You're essentially a small business, and it's odd that they'd go after this much money. Your insurance doesn't cover this kind of event, certainly not to ten million dollars' worth. It makes me wonder if there's more to this than meets the eye. A plaintiff's attorney will always go after the deep pockets. Can you think of anyone who might have been involved who has a lot of money, or insurance?"

Fianna thought for a moment. "Maybe the hotel?"

Scarlett flipped open a small notebook. "I'll need your contact there. Did they set up the runway?"

"No, it was a different company, a small independent contractor."

Scarlett scribbled a note. "And who obtained the shoes?"

"I did. The designers sent them directly to me. The failures spanned Jimmy Choo, Manolo Blahnik, and Prada shoes, so it couldn't have originated at the factories. Besides, I unpacked everything and set it up in order. I would have noticed."

Scarlett arched a brow. "Who had access between the time you set up and the show began?"

"The door was locked. I opened it with an assistant I'd engaged. The stylists began arriving early." She ticked off her fingers as she spoke. "Catering came in, the models arrived later, a photographer stopped by. I don't think any of them could have done it. There were too many people around."

"How much time was there between the time you set up and when you opened the door for the show?"

"Overnight. If anyone got into the room, it must have been during the night. It would have been recorded on the security camera. The police confiscated the digital files, as well as the shoes."

Scarlett made another note. "I'd like to see those images. I'll have to find an attorney in Ireland to help me get access. Do you know anyone?"

"I can ask my dad." Fianna shifted in her seat. "I hate to involve them, though. My mam's having some medical tests done soon."

Scarlett raised her eyes, concerned. "I hope she's all right."

"I saw them before I left, and she seems like she's handling it well. I think it's been caught early enough. With dietary changes and exercise, and maybe some medication to help manage her health, I think she'll be fine. I did a lot of research on her potential condition."

"Good, I'm happy to hear that. Now, who else could you ask for help?"

Lizzie and Shane knew a lot of people from school, maybe even some young lawyers. She could ask her dad, though she hated to add to his worries over her mother. "I'll find someone."

Scarlett continued asking questions, and Fianna answered honestly and to the best of her ability. Her head began to ache and she pressed her fingers to her temples to alleviate the pressure. "I have to admit, this is really overwhelming, Scarlett. I have client fittings, next season's line to create, and buyers to call. Meanwhile, I'm being ridiculed in the media and stalked by paparazzi, and now, sued for more money than I'll probably ever earn."

Whenever Fianna needed a moment to relax from the stress, she let her thoughts wander to Niall and the time they'd spent together at his home in Howth. She conjured the sparkle of his green eyes, the sensation of his chest against her cheek, and the richness of his voice in the night. But even this mental fantasy offered only a brief respite from her troubles.

Scarlett took her hand in hers. "Fianna, I know this is difficult for you. I'm here for you. Dahlia, Verena, and Penelope are, too. Whatever we can do for you, just ask. You're always the first to help us when we need it."

"As outspoken as I am, I find it hard to ask for help when I need it." Another failing she'd have to work on. Since she'd left Ireland, her world had been on a downward spiral. How could she have worked so diligently for so many years, only to see her business crumble with the twist of a shoe? The Fitzgerald Flop was aptly named. "Tell me honestly, Scarlett. Will I lose the business?"

Scarlett drummed her fingers on the table. "Anything could happen. But if I were you, I'd be considering every alternative. I won't lie to you, Fianna. It's not good. Unless we can find out who did this and clear you, eventually I'll have to bring in a defense lawyer, and they won't be cheap. Even if we manage a partial settlement."

Fianna sank her face into her hands.

Scarlett whispered to her. "Don't turn around, there's a paparazzi outside. Do you want to leave?" Their food hadn't arrived yet. "We could get our lunch to go."

How dare they follow me here? She'd had all she could take. She could give up and slink out, or she could stand and defend herself.

Fianna raised her head and threw her fiery red hair back. "No, not this time. I've had enough of this. I have every right to be here. In fact, remember what you said about negative publicity? I'm going to make them start working for me. If people want a piece of the Fitzgerald Flop, then that's what I'll give them."

Scarlett lifted a corner of her mouth. "That's the Fianna we all know and love."

After lunch, Fianna charged back to her boutique on Robertson Boulevard. Evangeline was in the front, shooing away gawkers.

She stopped, planted her hands on her hips and struck a pose in her turquoise heels for the photographers. "Hello everyone. I'm Fianna Fitzgerald of the Fitzgerald Flop. Come back tomorrow at 2:00 pm, and I'll have a surprise. You won't want to miss it," she added with a wink.

Evangeline hurried toward her, gesturing in frustration. "What're you doing? These people hate us. They're making fun of us."

"Taking control, that's what. We need money to find the truth behind this sabotage, Evangeline. Here's what we're going to do." She quickly outlined a plan and gave Evangeline a list of tasks.

"Lock the doors. We're closing down, going to work, and we'll reopen tomorrow with a brand new attitude." She picked up one of her design notebooks. "I'm going next door to see Elena."

Fianna marched out and locked the door behind her. The jeweler next door was Elena Eaton, a good friend and one of the most creative women she knew.

And later, once the sun rose in Ireland, she'd call Niall.

Hours later, after an exhausting day, Fianna tapped a number on her phone at the stroke of midnight.

Within moments, Niall's sleepy, husky voice shot around the globe. "Fianna, love. How I wish you were here beside me."

"I'd love nothing more." They spoke for a few minutes, and then Fianna told him what Scarlett needed.

"I used to perform at a ball the police force threw for charity. I know a couple of lads there fairly well. I'll see what I can find out for you."

They spoke a little longer, and then Fianna hung up. As much as she would have loved to talk all night, she still had work to do. By tomorrow afternoon, she had to be ready.

22

NIALL EASED INTO a chair at the police station in Dublin nearest the hotel. The station was so crowded, few people took notice of him. He wore black jeans and a gray untucked shirt with dark sunglasses and a charcoal-colored fedora hat.

Detective Malloy, as identified by his plastic name plate, tapped on his computer keyboard. "Name?" he asked in a raspy, cigarette-laced voice.

"Niall Finley."

"Sure and I'm Santy Claus. Tell you what, try again." He coughed loudly.

Niall removed his sunglasses. "Niall Finley."

The detective looked over the tortoise shell rim of his glasses. "Why it *is* you. Well why didn't you say so?" His tone changed from one of disinterest to one of friendly animation. "Now what can I do for you?"

Niall was used to this. He began in a gracious manner. "I've been given a power of attorney for Fianna Fitzgerald. Here's a fax from her attorney in Los Angeles." He slid a piece of paper across the worn desk. "We need information about the investigation of Fitzgerald's runway show where several models were injured."

"Ah yes, the case of the sabotaged shoes." Detective Malloy guffawed.

"With all due respect, it's no laughing matter. Several young women were seriously injured as a result. One had multiple fractures and had to have a pin inserted into her leg. She's out of work and is facing a long, painful recovery." His eyes were drawn to a family photo behind the detective's desk "What if that were one of your lovely daughters?"

"Right you are." The detective tapped the keyboard and pulled up a file. "Actually, we have a suspect. He had motive and opportunity. And we have him on film."

Niall leaned forward, narrowing his eyes. "Why hasn't he been arrested?"

The detective tossed his glasses on the desk. "He's in custody now. Just came in."

Niall sat back, rubbing his hands on his jeans. "Can you tell me his name?"

"Sure I can." He put his glasses back on and spun the computer screen around. Recognize him?"

Niall was shocked. He sure hadn't seen that coming.

"Anything else I can help you with?"

"Not today." His attorney would handle the rest with Scarlett. Niall's eyes roved back to the family photo. "I sure appreciate your help. How about I sign something for your girls?"

Detective Malloy broke into a wide smile. "That would be grand. Are you sure you don't mind troubling yourself?"

"Put the velvet rope on this side." Fianna turned to Evangeline. "We'll bring the line through the front and out the side. I'll be inside signing shirts, hats, and photos."

Evangeline consulted her clipboard. "Tiffany's classmates will arrive soon. Some will set up with lights and cameras outside, and there will be another film crew inside. The website with T-shirt sales is set up, and all the press has been alerted. Finally, a food truck with a new sandwich called the Fitzgerald Flop will be outside."

"Well done." Evangeline was so experienced and organized; she often ran the boutique while Fianna was designing. "Now let's check on those shirts and hats." Elena had sketched a Fitzgerald Flop logo and design for her, and she'd found a T-shirt printer in the garment district who opened his shop and printed overnight for her. Tiffany was busy ripping and embellishing the shirts as Fianna had instructed. "These will be couture rags. Think Eurotrash meets runway," she'd told her intern.

"How's it going?" Fianna glanced around, impressed with the speed at which Tiffany and her team worked. Her classmates at FIDM were excited at the chance to work for Fianna and be involved in the launch of the new Flop line, a casual Euro street look. Several had volunteered to messenger T-shirts and hats to Los Angeles television studios and radio stations. Another batch was being sent overnight to New York. Her publicist was working overtime for her.

Tiffany held up a shirt she was working on. They were

ripping necklines and attaching remnants of lace, chiffon, and other fabrics. "I love these! They're so hot." Tiffany's black kohl-rimmed eyes glittered with excitement.

"Excellent, just as I envisioned." Fianna had scoured her workroom, digging through all her short lengths of leftover fabric and embellishments. Her friends in the garment industry had given her more of their leftover end pieces.

Fianna turned toward the music player. Niall's voice was low, but she recognized it at once. "Turn that up, please," she said. She snapped her fingers and swayed to the music. "I want Finley Green blasting all day."

The interns looked at each other and burst out laughing. Tiffany said, "We saw the gossip online. Is it true? You're dating Niall Finley?"

As long as it was out in the open, she might as well admit to it. "That's right," she said, her heart aching for him. She wished he could see all this and watch her creativity at work. How would they ever manage this long-distance relationship?

"I'll sketch up a couple of other designs. Let's mix it up." She hurried to her sketch table.

More than anything, she wanted to take care of the models who'd been injured. Scarlett had talked about a settlement offer. Fianna picked up a pencil and chewed her lip in thought. If only she could raise the money to do that *and* stay in business.

She quickly sketched a simple line drawing. One thing she'd discovered in Los Angeles was that if there was a velvet rope and a film crew, people would quickly line up, clamoring to be a part of whatever it was. Insist on numbered slots, and they'd even buy them to get in line. It was crazy, but scarcity sold. Soon more of Tiffany's fashionable friends would line up, act excited, and the public would follow. Other friends would manage the line.

Fianna gathered her thoughts. Her publicist was busy promoting through social media, and she had created a special hashtag. A couple of celebrity models had volunteered to wear her shirts in support of models on national talk shows they'd been booked on. Many models suffered from anorexia, bulimia, and depression, and they often didn't have health insurance. The industry often pressured models to become even thinner than they were. Size zero was difficult to maintain. This was an opportunity to make a statement for her industry. A percentage of the proceeds would go to support models who were having health issues and financial difficulties.

Fianna was slender, but by model standards, she'd be too large for runway work. She fully supported a healthier model look, and in her shows she had cast models that looked healthy and normal. She completed another sketch and raced to deliver it to the T-shirt team. There was no time to waste.

If she could shift the paparazzi lens to a worthwhile project, then she'd done the best she could. And if she lost everything, at least she could be proud of her efforts.

"Fianna!" Dahlia was rushing toward her, shopping bags in her arms. "I've got the Runway perfume samples. My graphic designer took Elena's logo and created a mock-up bottle. You can start taking pre-orders today."

"Thanks, Dahlia, this is magnificent." She opened a sample vial. "I really love this, the jasmine is so sensual. How did you get Camille to agree to this?" She applied the sample to her wrists and neck.

Dahlia arched a brow. "She didn't agree."

"Then how did you manage this?"

"I've decided to create my own indie line. It's time for me to make my mark in this industry. I want to show people what I can really do, outside of my family's business."

Fianna hugged her. "That's what you've always wanted."

"If it flops, then we flop together." Dahlia laughed, though Fianna could tell she was nervous, too. They both had to step onto the stage and take a chance that people would like what they'd created. Fashion and fragrance were highly subjective, and timing was everything.

Fianna hoped she had the timing right for this. Or the media would soon be touting her as the Queen of Flops.

While Dahlia set up, Fianna went to change. She put on one of her new over-sized T-shirts. The neckline was frayed, vintage lace angled down one side, and chiffon peered from beneath the torn hem. On the front was emblazoned "Flop by Fianna Fitzgerald," with a line drawing of a trio of models, and a broken heel. The T-shirt colors were vivid. She wore lime green to set off her hair, while Tiffany had chosen deep purple, and Evangeline wore fluorescent pink. *Young, haute, hip.* That was the message.

It was almost time.

Fianna slipped on an ivory pair of Dolce & Gabbana booties made of lace and suede, knotted the T-shirt over slim cream-colored jeans, and fluffed her wild mane to maximum volume. Today was no time for half-measures. She added an armload of bangles.

She glanced at the time again, gulping breaths to calm her nerves.

"Ready?" Evangeline tapped on her door.

"Come in." Fianna adjusted the zipper on the back of her shoe. She would not have any footwear mishaps today.

"The line stretches down the block now." Evangeline's eyes were bright with excitement. "Fianna, this was genius."

"Hold that thought. Let's see how Flop is accepted." She'd been in this position before. She'd triple checked everything at the hotel, and yet the worst had occurred. Anything could happen. What if Flop flopped?

Fianna straightened to her full height and then strode into the boutique. Dahlia had changed into an orange Flop top and her perfume counter was organized and ready. The publicist stood by the door, ready to funnel media her way. Fianna gave a thumbs-up sign. "Open the door, and let's rock."

At once, pandemonium broke out. The crowd outside surged and people were shoved through the door. Two young women tumbled onto the floor. Fianna's heart pounded as she raced to aid them, recalling the disaster at the fashion show. "Let me give you a hand," she said, helping them to their feet and hoping they were okay.

The two women stood and brushed off their jeans. "We're not hurt, but can we have your autograph?"

Fianna had never been asked for her autograph. Thankfully, Evangeline came to her assistance and quickly formed a line. Her publicist rushed over with several media crews, who began to set up equipment to film Fianna's statement.

Tiffany and her team helped manage the line and get T-shirts, hats, and perfume samples for people, while Evangeline rang up sales. Dahlia was busy sharing the perfume tester with people.

Fianna scrawled her name on hats and T-shirts with a gold permanent marker made for fabric. Once the film crews were ready, she rose to speak.

"Welcome to the debut of Flop, a new casual line inspired by street fashion in Europe and my native Ireland. As most of you know, I recently had quite a flop in Dublin. Some of the shoes were rigged to give way when the models walked the elevated runway. I was devastated, so I had to figure out how to make lemonade from the proverbial lemons. I've embraced my professional flop, and I hope you will, too."

She went on to explain her new Flop concept, and how a percentage of funds raised would benefit the injured models and others with health issues. "Modeling is considered a glamorous profession, but there's a darker lining to the industry." She finished her presentation, and then she took questions from the reporters.

A man's hand shot up. "Do you have a comment about Doyle O'Donnell?"

Fianna was bewildered. Why would he be asking about Doyle? "He's been an old family friend for years."

"What was his motive?"

"I beg your pardon, but I have no idea what you're talking about."

"Doyle O'Donnell was just arrested and charged for the shoe sabotage." The reporter shoved a handful of photos toward her. "These are shots from the security surveillance film. Evidently he bribed a housekeeper to let him in the dressing room the night before. Now do you have a comment?"

"Since I knew nothing about it until now, I can't comment." It was all she could do to keep her composure. She flipped through the photos. Doyle, arrested? *Impossible.* And yet, there he was in the photo she held. And in another, with a female housekeeper. She studied the photos in disbelief.

Finally, she lowered the photos. Doyle was a jerk, but this action was utterly despicable. She wouldn't have thought him capable of such a devious plot to injure others. Did he do this because she'd spurned him? *How horrible.* But here was the evidence. She'd have to call Scarlett later. She dragged her attention back to the next question.

After fifteen minutes of questions on topics ranging from bulimia, to her new line, to her relationship with Niall, she wrapped it up. The reporter who'd asked the first question had already gone, but she still had the photos he'd given her. She placed them under the counter before sitting at a table to sign shirts and hats for customers who'd been waiting in line.

They were nearly at the end when they ran out of the merchandise they'd made, so they switched to pre-orders for the next batch.

Fianna and her team worked as long as there were people in line. When they finally closed the doors after dark, she kicked off her shoes. Dahlia, Evangeline, Tiffany, and the other interns did the same.

Fianna raised a hand to get everyone's attention. "You all know what I've been through, and I can't thank you enough. Wonderful job, everyone. Now it's time to celebrate!" Everyone started clapping, and she raised a bottle. "Who wants champagne?"

She popped the cork and everyone cheered. As Evangeline poured champagne, Fianna thought about Niall, wishing again that he could have been here. She had no idea about how they would handle a distance relationship, or even if they could. She'd left in such haste. Now that she was home, her time with Niall seemed like a dream. Is that all it would ever be?

And yet, she was thankful to have known him. She was also grateful that her hasty line had been well-received today. No telling what might be printed in the tabloids, but Scarlett had been right about negative press. Sometimes it could be used to an advantage. They'd done well today.

Despite feeling bone-tired, Fianna smiled as she watched

her team laugh and enjoy their camaraderie.

A photo dropped to the floor, and she bent to pick it up. It was one of Doyle the reporter had given her. He was coming out of the dressing area with a housekeeper, and he was holding her arm around her bicep. Something clicked in her memory. She squinted, held it to the light, and sucked in a breath.

This isn't correct. Not at all.

She had to call Scarlett right away.

23

IT WAS SUNDAY afternoon and Fianna was hurrying to meet Scarlett at Bow-Tie before everyone else arrived. As usual, the restaurant was closed to patrons on Sunday, but this was the day they gathered and brought friends and family. Fianna put on one of her new pink Flop T-shirts with narrow white pants and left her apartment.

She'd tried to call Niall late last night and again this morning, but he hadn't answered. He hadn't returned her messages either. Maybe he'd decided the distance was insurmountable. She had to admit it probably was, but she still longed to hear his voice.

When she arrived at Bow-Tie, Scarlett was already there with a plate of her mother's empanadas hot from the kitchen.

Fianna greeted Scarlett and sat down across from her. "Those smell delicious."

"The next course is paella. And wait until you see the desserts."

Fianna reached into her purse and pulled out a small cloisonné magnifying glass and the photographs the reporter had left behind. "Scarlett, look at these photos. They were taken from the security film."

Scarlett's eyes widened. "This is evidence. How did you get these?"

Fianna told her about the reporter. "They must have been leaked to the media." She handed her the magnifying glass. "Now look. Tell me what you see."

Scarlett tucked her coppery blond hair behind her ear and inspected the images. "It looks like nighttime. A man in slacks and a nice shirt, a female housekeeper, they're leaving a room... and he's holding her arm around her bicep muscle in her upper arm. That's a little odd."

"Why would a man hold a woman's arm like that?

Scarlett put the magnifier down. "To support her, or guide her. Or make sure she doesn't get away."

"Go on, keep looking." Fianna bit into an empanada while Scarlett leaned over the photos.

"This is weird. She has a dark skirt hanging beneath her white housekeeper's uniform."

"And what else?" The woman's head was bent forward, so her face couldn't be seen, though the man's face was clearly depicted. There was no doubt it was Doyle. But who was the woman?

"The shoes don't look quite right. Most housekeepers wear comfortable rubber-soled shoes. Those look like thin leather."

Fianna clasped her hands. "The police assumed Doyle bribed this housekeeper to let him into the dressing room so he could sabotage the shoes." She'd already filled Scarlett in on Doyle, the ancient family feud, and his proposal. "But look at those shoes and the little grosgrain bows on the toe cap. I've stayed in a lot of nice hotels, but I've never seen a housekeeper working in five-hundred dollar Ferragamo Varina flats. I bet if these are blown up, the logo would be visible on the brass plate."

"Ay-yi-yi," Scarlett exclaimed. "But why do you care, as long as this proves you had nothing to do with it? Which is *fantastic*, by the way. The lawsuit will probably be dropped. And Doyle's family has deep pockets, so the plaintiff would go after the O'Donnells."

"Because Doyle is my sister's cousin by marriage. He's a jerk, but I don't think he's capable of planning to harm people. He might even be salvageable someday." She smirked. "Just not by me."

"Then who is this woman?"

"I have a theory." Fianna pointed to tiny time stamps at the bottom of the photos. "If you look at when he went in, and when he came out, he didn't have time to inflict all the damage on those shoes that I saw."

"Is there a photo of her entering the room?"

"If there is, I don't have it. But he looks angry, doesn't he?"

Scarlett looked closer. "He sure does."

"What if she called him and told him what she was doing. He might have been furious. He came to get her and took her from the room."

"Or they might have planned it together."

Fianna thought about that, though she preferred her explanation. "It's possible, I suppose."

Scarlett picked up an empanada and broke it open. "You have to tell the police."

"I will. I have the detective's email. And I think I know who the woman is." She remembered the day Doyle had proposed. The clicking of a woman's shoes across the floor as she was leaving. Sensible Ferragamo flats with a tweed skirt. Limp, mousy brown hair, like the woman in the photo. "Her name is Brona. She follows Doyle around like a lovesick puppy. What I don't understand is why she did it." She shrugged a shoulder. "Maybe she was avenging me for jilting him, with the hope that he'd fall into her arms in gratitude."

"People have crazy ideas we can't understand."

Fianna opened her email on her phone and tapped out a message. "It will be Monday morning there in a few hours." She hit send.

Scarlett picked up another empanada. "Look, here's Verena and Dahlia."

Dahlia sat beside them, and Fianna detected the scent of their new fragrance. "That perfume is so beautiful and sexy. Thank you, Dahlia, for mocking it up and filling the samples so quickly."

"The pre-orders were fantastic. It was a risky concept, but you sure carried it off with aplomb, Fianna. You're a star." Dahlia applauded her friend.

Johnny greeted Scarlett with a kiss. "Mimosas, ladies?" He passed out flutes with champagne and orange juice.

"Fianna, we're celebrating you, today. Have you seen the buzz on social media? You're hot. The Flop tops are a huge hit."

Fianna reached for a glass. "What a relief." Everyone would have an opinion, but this was good news. Now she'd have to step up production. She thought about Davina and wondered if she'd like to help organize new Fitzgerald Flop runway shows. Without the actual flops.

"I wish I could have been there," Verena said. "But we were filming a new infomercial segment for a new product, and we were working overtime to get it done." She reached for an empanada and took a bite. "Hmm, mushrooms. Oh, this is delicious."

Fianna took another one, too. "Can you imagine I threw this concept together in a day? My intern, Tiffany, brought in her fashion design classmates. It was incredible." Fianna knew Scarlett had been with another client, too.

Dahlia wound her dark hair into a messy bun as she spoke. "Fianna really needed this break after the Dublin disaster. But she made her own luck. The paparazzi were hunting her, looking for a juicy story. And our Fianna sure gave them one." She secured her hair and then raised her flute. "Here's to you, Fianna, and to all of us, for always making our own luck."

Each one of the friends agreed and clinked glasses.

Lance sent steaming bowls of paella from the kitchen. He and Scarlett's mother, Isabel, retired from the kitchen to join them. Minutes later, Verena's grandmother Mia arrived.

Fianna thought the three elders looked fabulous. Soon they were all talking and laughing and having a wonderful time.

Fianna watched the interplay between Scarlett and Johnny, and Verena and Lance. These couples had been through hardships, but they'd overcome their challenges together. They had been truly lucky to find each other.

She couldn't get Niall out of her mind. Fianna propped her elbow on the table and rested her chin on the palm of her hand. Why wasn't he returning her calls? They'd had such a deep connection. How could he let her go so easily? She blinked back tears that pooled in her eyes. Or was he unable to overcome the loss of his wife after all?

Brushing the corners of her eyes, Fianna tried to listen to her friends, but the memory of Niall tugged on her mind. The days she'd spent with him in Ireland had been ideal. It wasn't the wine, or the massage, or the castle—it was Niall. They had fun together, they laughed, and they cared for each other. She hadn't held back with him.

Love hurts. She sipped her champagne, swallowing against the lump in her throat.

She adored her friends, but she needed a moment alone. Leaving the table, she wandered through the restaurant and stopped by a carved marble fireplace, a relic from when this cottage had been a private home, before businesses were built around it, encroaching on its character. It was a courageous holdout, and the owners had reinvented it as a restaurant.

Isn't that exactly what she had done? She'd reinvented the way she did business. She'd been thinking of creating a less expensive line, but she'd been forced into it. Now she was glad. She needed something to keep her mind off Niall. She shuddered. She'd have to be content just listening to his music on the radio.

She paused by the fireplace and sipped her champagne. She was here with friends she loved, the lawsuit would be dropped, and business was looking up. Wasn't that enough?

Fianna had always been the little girl who grabbed life with both hands. She hadn't changed much. She still wanted it all. And most of all, she wanted a man she could share it with. She knew that now. Tears slipped from her eyes. She longed for Niall.

Johnny must have turned on the music, because she heard the low strumming of an acoustic guitar. She closed her eyes and leaned against the mantle, remembering how she'd listened to Niall playing the guitar and the piano. She loved the music in his soul.

More than anything, she simply loved Niall.

The music grew louder and humming soon accompanied the piece.

Will everything remind me of Niall?

Slow, measured footsteps sounded on the wooden floor. She squeezed her eyes tighter, unwilling to share this moment with any of her well-meaning friends.

A rich voice rose with the melody. "Hello Fianna, hello, my lady of the midnight moon…"

How can it be? That voice—*his voice*—sounded so real, so sensual and rich and gravelly. Full of experience. *And that song...* She opened her eyes and found herself gazing at Niall, who stood in the doorway, strumming his guitar.

"I wrote that one for you, too." Swiftly he swung his guitar on its strap around to his back and stepped toward her.

"Niall!" She raced to him. He caught her in his arms and whirled her around, peppering her face with kisses. "I called and called. I thought you'd forgotten about me."

"Never. I was on an airplane." He cradled her face in his hands and hungrily kissed her.

She responded to him in an instant. Her heartbeat strengthened, her neck flushed, and her skin thrilled to his touch. They drank in each other as though they'd been lost in an arid desert.

He pressed her to his chest, swaying gently, his chest reverberating with a deep throaty hum. It was the song he'd been singing. A song he'd written just for her.

She melted in his taut, muscular arms. This was where she was meant to be. Forever.

Niall threaded his fingers through her hair. "After you left, my home was emptier than it had ever been. I couldn't imagine being there without you."

"You came here for me? How long will you stay?"

Niall kissed her forehead. "As long as it takes, Miss Crazy Eyes. I've booked a bungalow at the Beverly Hills Hotel, but I have a feeling I should look for something more permanent. I'm going to start an indie music label."

"Here?" When he nodded, Fianna flung her arms around him, ecstatic.

"Think you can get away to Ireland from time to time?"

She brushed his lips with hers. "I can design anywhere, and Evangeline is really running the shop."

His eyes sparkled with passion. "I called Johnny to make sure you'd be here. He told me you had a big, breakthrough hit yesterday with the media and buyers alike."

"That's true." She ran a hand down her shirt. "I figured I'd make it memorable. This is part of my new line, the Flop."

"You're joking about that name, right?" Niall looked to see if she was teasing him. When she shook her head, he threw his head back and laughed. "That's what I love about you, Fianna. You've got guts—and a whole lot more."

"So do you, Niall." Fianna lifted her face to his, and their lips met. This man was her destiny. She just knew it.

Niall nuzzled her neck. His day-old beard was slightly scratchy, but she loved it.

"You've turned my world around, Fianna. I feel like I've known you forever. I never thought I could love again, but Fianna, my love, you saved me from drowning and brought me back to the world of the living." He encircled her waist, pressing gently against her lower back.

She smiled. "We saved each other, remember?"

The End

Read on for an excerpt from *Runway*, the next novel in the *Love, California* series by Jan Moran.

Essence

"I KNOW IT was sudden, but I wanted to attend the film festival." Dahlia sat at an outdoor table at a café overlooking yachts in the Vieux Port harbor of Cannes, hoping her grandmother wouldn't detect her studied nonchalance over the phone—or the undercurrent of nervousness she felt. "Several actresses are wearing Fianna's gowns," she added, proud of her friend's work.

"And I hope they're wearing our perfume." Camille's imperious voice crackled across the Atlantic. "Just as important, while you're there you should meet our Formula 1 driver. Alain Delamare has a home in Cannes and he's quite charming. He just won the Grand Prix in Spain. He's from a fine family originally from Normandy, though they live in California now." She paused to take a breath. "You should have dinner together, *ma chére.* I've known his family since before you were born. His aunts was a friend of your—"

Camille broke off and Dahlia knew she'd started to say

"your mother," but caught herself. Still, she recognized the conspiratorial pitch of Camille's voice. "I appreciate the thought, but I don't need your matchmaking."

At that, a man at the table near hers glanced up with interest, and Dahlia found herself staring into his blazing blue eyes, which crinkled at the corners in a bemused expression. She couldn't help but smile. With the Cannes Film Festival underway, the area was teaming with filmmakers, actors, and press. She wondered who he was.

Camille continued. "I think you do need my help, as evidenced by Kevin." She sniffed in disdain. "Alain has such lovely manners. We had dinner together in New York."

"I don't want to hear any more about Alain Delamare." Dahlia glanced away from the man, breaking his captivating gaze.

Another pause. "Kevin is with you, isn't he?" Camille's tone was flat. "Tell him it's business, which technically it is. What's one evening?"

"That would be awfully rude. Besides, I'm no longer part of your company. I have my own business now."

Her grandmother was relentless, but Camille's inexorable drive was how she'd made her fortune and continued to expand it. Today, Parfums Dubois ranked in the lofty upper echelons of luxury perfume beside Guerlain and Chanel. The purchase of the Formula 1 team and the rebranding of it to Team Dubois had catapulted the company to front pages and magazine covers around the globe, increasing sales and the value of the company even more.

"My offer still stands, dear. Both offers, but we can start with Alain."

Camille had been angling for Dahlia to return to work for the family business, but Dahlia had plans of her own. "And I appreciate it, but the answer is still no. On both counts, Grand-mère." She was pleasant but firm. Nothing was going to spoil this special trip.

A fragrant *café au lait* steamed before her, chasing away the fresh morning chill. The early sun warmed her bare shoulders and clear skies formed a canopy over the turquoise water of the Mediterranean Sea. Chirping birds flitted through gracefully arched palm fronds and bracelets of vivid magenta bougainvillea tumbled across ancient stone walls. Lovers strolled hand in hand, pausing to admire sleek harbor boats and artful boutique windows.

Dahlia glanced at the time on her phone. Kevin should have been here more than half an hour ago.

The man at the nearby table had returned to reading his book, but she wondered if he were still eavesdropping. Her interest piqued, she studied him surreptitiously through half-lidded eyes. He was undeniably attractive; he wore a dark blue T-shirt that was stretched across his trim muscular frame, along with white cotton pants and deck shoes. Slight morning stubble matched his short, sun-bleached chestnut hair. Probably belongs to one of the boats, she surmised.

Her grandmother continued talking about the success of the Parfums Dubois Formula 1 team. Camille had been a fan of the sport since she'd been a child in France and her father had raced a Bugatti in an early French Grand Prix. Parfums Dubois had long been a sponsor next to Red Bull and Rolex, Chandon and CNN, but ownership now elevated the brand to a rarified level. Team Dubois was the newest owner in a sport in which few in the world could compete.

Camille read part of an article to her over the phone from *Fashion News Daily*, the industry trade paper, which hailed the new ownership as "'a bold move timed with the launch of a new masculine fragrance line from Parfums Dubois,'" Camille said. "The editor included photos of Alain and the racing team, too. Alain is quite handsome. He'll be an excellent spokesman for the new line."

As Camille spoke, Dahlia let out a breath of relief. Her grandmother had no idea of the real reason of her trip. After hanging up, Dahlia lifted her coffee to her lips. Once again, she met the steady gaze of her neighbor.

"I couldn't help but overhear your conversation." He sounded American and his baritone voice had a gravelly quality that was intriguing. "Matchmaking? I haven't heard that term in a long time."

She laughed. "That was my grandmother."

"Ah, I see. I hear that from mine, too." A friendly grin creased his tanned face. "Are you here for the film festival?"

"We've seen a few films." Kevin fancied himself a producer, but he had yet to make a film.

"I heard you say you have a business. What do you do?"

"I'm a perfumer." She drained her coffee cup, half-wishing she could stay and talk with him. Kevin should have been here by now. He was probably still on his business call in the hotel room. He'd told her he had a quick call to make, but then, he usually ran late.

"Sounds interesting." The man inclined his head. "I'd like to hear more about your work. Perfume is a new passion of mine."

Unlike most men, he truly sounded interested in what she did.

The man shifted toward her in his chair, his movements demonstrating quiet confidence. "Would you like to join me for a walk on the Croisette? I'd really like to learn more about what you do."

His magnetic gaze drew her in, and she caught herself imagining strolling the wide boardwalk promenade by the sea with him. Everything about him stirred her emotions, and she grew uncomfortable by her fascination with him. "I can't today. But thank you."

"Tomorrow, perhaps?" He held his hand out to her in a gesture of hope.

"Actually, I'm here with someone. And I really must go." As she got up to leave, the strange tug on her emotions was almost palpable, but she swiftly swept her feelings away. She was nearly a married woman. She hoped to have a family of her own soon, and she would never, ever leave her children as her mother had done.

Dahlia hurried along the Boulevard de la Croisette, a light breeze cooling her heated chest and rippling the long skirt of her azure print sundress. As she walked, she breathed in the fresh sea air and the sweet scent of dewy morning jasmine to clear her mind of the man she'd met. With her senses on overload, an idea for a romantic perfume emerged and danced in her mind.

Soon she neared the grand Hôtel Martinez, where Kevin had booked a palatial suite that resembled a film set from Downton Abbey. Inside the hotel lobby, she threaded her way through guests in fashionable summer resort attire on her way to the elevator.

"Dahlia, I was just on my way to meet you." A robust, barrel-chested man strode toward her. "Had a long business call that kept me in the room." Kevin's breathing was labored. He brushed her cheek with a hurried kiss.

"Relax. I had a long call with Camille." She leaned in, detecting a familiar fragrance that clung to his clothing. Bulgarian rose, to be precise. With a touch of bergamot. Was it on his thin windbreaker jacket?

"And how is the dragon lady?"

At his curt tone, she shot him a reprimanding look. "Kevin, that's my grandmother."

"Hey, I'm only kidding," he said, laughing a little too loud.

She shrugged off his comment, though it was partly true. Camille was known to be demanding, but she was also highly creative and fiercely protective of those she loved. Still, she wished he'd show more respect toward Camille, even if they didn't get along. "What was so important that your client called from Los Angeles after midnight?"

Kevin coughed and cleared his throat. "Well, he's not really in L.A."

"Where is he?"

Kevin ran a hand over his hair, which looked windblown. "He has homes all over the world." He sounded stressed, too.

"So where is he?" she repeated. Kevin had been acting odd ever since they'd arrived in France. He had booked the trip months ago for the festival. When he had invited her and proposed, it had been wildly romantic to imagine eloping. Now that they were here, she had to admit she was tense, too, but she imagined that was how every bride felt.

"Where is he? Oh, somewhere in Asia, I imagine. Hong Kong, I believe." He removed his jacket and swept his arm around her. "I'm hungry. Let's have breakfast in the café here. After that, we can go shopping." He winked. "There's a wedding dress in your future."

There it is again, that scent. Dahlia wrinkled her nose. It wasn't on the jacket; it was on his skin. "Where'd you get that fragrance you're wearing?"

"Fragrance? I'm not wearing anything."

She tapped his neck. "Yes, you are. I have an excellent nose."

Kevin sniffed his shirt collar. "Oh yeah, some cheap cologne I picked up somewhere. It was in my bag. Forgot all about it."

"Doesn't smell cheap to me. In fact, that's one of ours."

"Our what?"

He sounded like a parrot, repeating everything she said.

"Parfums Dubois."

"How can you tell?" He sniffed again. "Maybe it was something you wore that didn't wash out from the fabric."

She'd never worn that perfume. "You must have been fairly close to someone who had it on."

He shrugged with exasperation. "Who knows? Maybe the maid had it on, Dahlia."

She arched an eyebrow. Unless he'd been hugging the maid, he shouldn't be reeking of perfume. "I have a sensitive nose, that's all." She'd been trained since childhood to identify scents. Still, she let it go. She didn't want to argue with him, not on the romantic trip that would be the beginning of their new life together. Turning to one side, she inhaled to clear her nose. Maybe he'd stood close to a woman in the elevator. *Very close.* "Let's get a table by the window."

Dahlia tossed her dark hair over her shoulder. They were both having a case of nerves, but wasn't that normal for a couple who were about to exchange vows?

To continue reading *Essence*, visit your favorite retailer.

About the Author

JAN MORAN IS a writer living in sunny southern California. She writes contemporary and historical fiction. Keep up with her latest blog posts at JanMoran.com.

A few of Jan's favorite things include a fine cup of coffee, dark chocolate, fresh flowers, and music that touches her soul. She loves to travel just about anywhere, though her favorite places for inspiration are those rich with history and mystery and set against snowy mountains, palm-treed beaches, or sparkly city lights. Jan is originally from Austin, Texas, and a trace of a drawl still survives to this day, although she has lived in California for years.

Her books are available as audiobooks, and her historical fiction has been widely translated into German, Italian, Polish, Turkish, Russian, and Lithuanian, among other languages.

Jan has been featured in and written for many prestigious media outlets, including *CNN, Wall Street Journal, Women's Wear Daily, Allure, InStyle, O Magazine, Cosmopolitan, Elle,* and *Costco Connection,* and has spoken before numerous groups about writing and entrepreneurship, such as San Diego State University, Fashion Group International, The Fragrance Foundation, and The American Society of Perfumers.

She is a graduate of the Harvard Business School, the University of Texas at Austin, and the UCLA Writers Program.

To hear about Jan's new books first and get special offers, join Jan's VIP Readers Club at www.JanMoran.com and get a free download. If you enjoyed this book, please consider leaving a brief review online for your fellow readers.

Made in the USA
Coppell, TX
11 March 2020

16743762R00166